FORGET ME KNOT

THE LOST SERIES
BOOK ONE

HALLIE GRACE

CRAWFISH PUBLISHING

CONTENTS

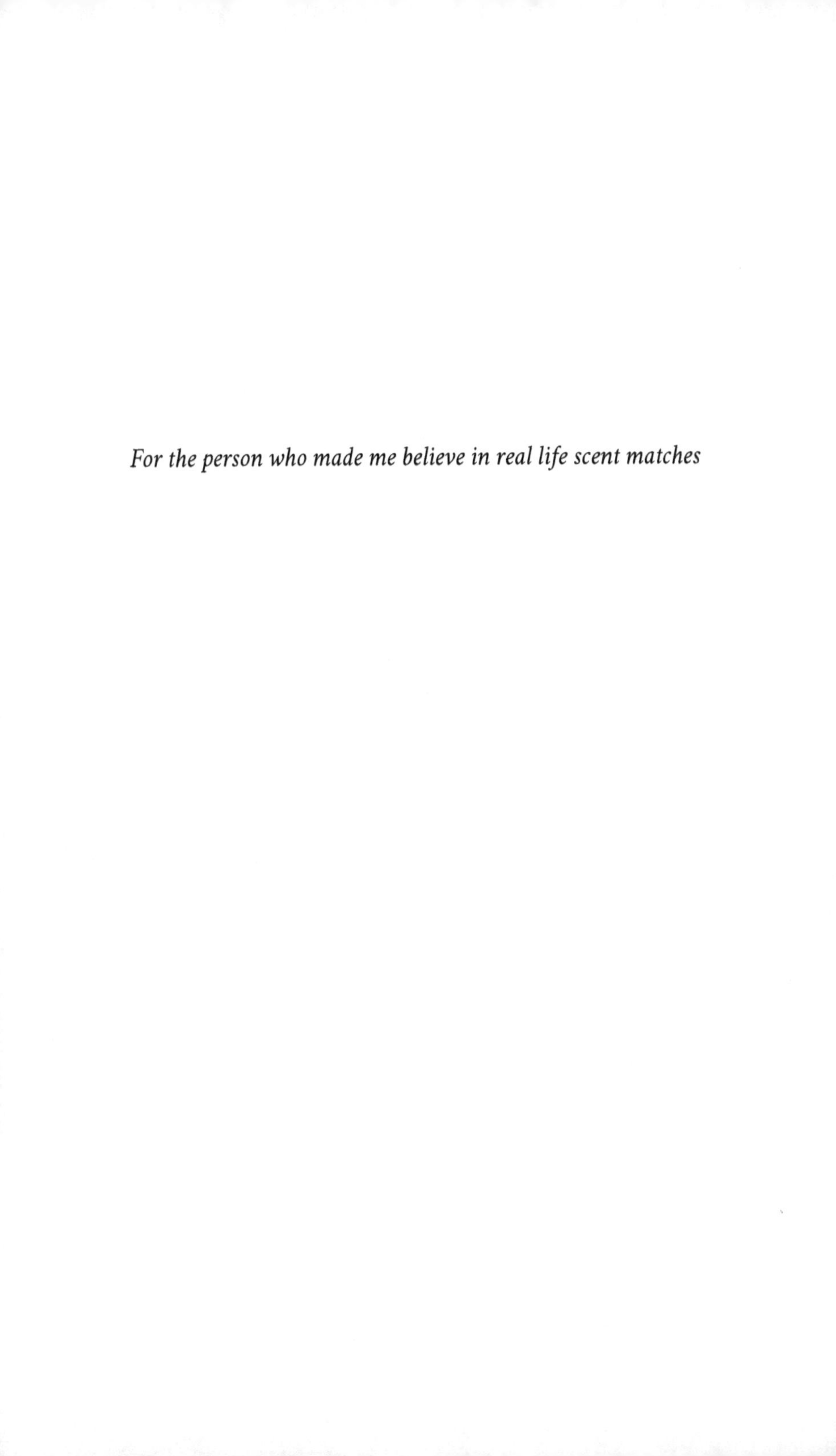

For the person who made me believe in real life scent matches

TRIGGER WARNINGS

Though this is not a dark book, it does tackle some darker themes. Triggers include, but are not limited to:

Child abuse (both on page and referenced as past events), abuse, drugging, attempted SA, panic attacks, somnophilia, c*ck warming, snowballing, stalking, kidnapping, short-term imprisonment, long-term imprisonment (very briefly shown on page and in flashbacks), mentions of sex trafficking (though none is shown on page), primal play, mild breath play, light domme scene, Daddy kink.

No book is worth your mental health. If you feel that one or more of these triggers could be a problem, this may not be the book for you. And that's okay! There will be other books without these triggers. You, as the reader, are my priority and, as much as I would love for you to read my book, your mental health is more important. Take care of yourself, Shortcake. 🩶

PROLOGUE

Hades
Age Thirteen

I'm getting really tired of moving and seeing all of my clothes and hand-me-down skates in "foster kid luggage" (or if you're new here; black trash bags) once again. It's honestly pretty depressing. I've been in this new foster home for a week now and even though the social worker promised me it would be different this time, it's not. Shocker, I know.

I don't really know how to explain why I'm not used to all the moving yet. I've been doing it every few months since my egg donor left me in a grocery store parking lot five years ago, to the delight of her latest sleazy Alpha boyfriend… Russ? Rob? Whatever his name was, I called him "The Turd" because he always smelled like he'd taken a long bath in a dumpster full of poop.

My mom is a drug addicted Beta so the boyfriends never stuck around long once they realized she was just using them for her next high or so she could say she had an Alpha boyfriend. Turd, though, had been hanging around for close to six months when he finally convinced her she'd have more money if she "dumped the freeloading brat", and that was that. I spent my 8th birthday on a bench outside our local Handi-Mart until someone called the police and they placed me into foster care. Which leads us to today, with me sitting on the window seat in this dirty, sardine can of a room I share with three other kids, listening to my foster parents argue *again*.

Jamie, one of the other foster kids here, comes sprinting into the room. He's panting with his hands on his grass-stained knees when he wheezes out, "D, will you come check out the new kid they just dropped off? She won't talk to any of us, and Phil is being weird again." He rolls his eyes as he stands up after finally catching his breath.

I whip my head around to glare at him and hiss, "Weird how? And what do you mean, new kid? I thought they weren't allowed to place any more kids here after they removed Katie?"

Katie is an eleven-year-old girl who was removed two days after they placed me here because she told her teacher that Phil, our foster father, had been touching her inappropriately for months. They were threatening to remove the rest of us, too, but because Katie had a history of acting out, they didn't really believe her. It's honestly amazing the shit you overhear when the adults around you forget you can actually hear and understand them.

Just as Jamie is about to answer me, we hear Phil tell his wife, Dianne, "Don't worry, I'll get the girl settled just fine on my own. I don't need a nitpicky nagging bitch watching my every damn move." That just sets Dianne off screaming again. If there's one thing I learned in the last week, it's that these people can't go one sentence without screaming awful things at each other.

Jamie quickly shuffles closer and mumbles under his

breath, "I guess it was an emergency or somethin'. The social worker was telling Phil and Dianne she was bruised up real bad and couldn't go back home from the hospital, so they brought her here. They said she's ten, but dude, she's so small there's no way."

Just then, Phil comes around the corner with his arm around the skinniest girl I've ever seen. His hand is gripping her shoulder so hard I can see her wince, even through the mess of bright red hair covering her tiny face. "Boys," Phil says loudly, "Meet your new roommate, Blair."

As soon as Phil says her name, her head whips up and the most insane green eyes I've ever seen lock onto my face. She scowls, looks up at Phil, lifts her chin the tiniest amount, and quietly says, "My name is Blake. Not Blair."

I'm blown away by this tiny girl correcting my foster father with no fear on her face. I'm sure she can smell Phil's light scent exposing him as a Beta since he's so close to her, so maybe that's why she's not as scared of him as she should be. I've seen him get mad over almost anything in the last week. This time, he just glares at her for a second before turning to face me. Phil sneers at me while saying, "Hell boy, get Blair here some sheets and make sure she knows the house rules. I'd hate to have to punish her."

The way he says it makes the hairs on my arms stand on end, and if I didn't already believe Katie, I sure as hell do now. "Yes sir. I'll make sure she knows the rules," I quietly say back while staring at the floor.

I learned real quick around here that it's best to avoid eye contact and treat Phil like an Alpha. He's so bitter that he doesn't have the dominant designation. Especially when my file states that I'm showing signs of an Alpha presentation already; even though my designation won't actually come in for at least another three years. He turned his anger on me pretty quick after that little fact came out during my placement last week.

He finally leaves the room and Blake turns back to me and quietly asks, "Which bed can I use?"

I don't really know why I point at the bed right next to mine, but I do, and she walks over to drop her small backpack on the bed. She takes off her sweatshirt so she's just in a too-big top that looks like something you'd find at a hospital. Which, if what Jamie heard is true, definitely makes sense.

She balls her sweatshirt up to put in her bag and I suck in a breath and let out my first ever growl when I see that her entire upper body, from her chin down to her fingers, is covered in bruises and cuts. My mouth is gaping open in shock that *that* sound came out of *me*. I snap my jaw closed as she whips her head to stare up at me, trembling as she sits down on the edge of the bed and twisting her fingers. I clear my throat and mumble an apology as I think about what she needs to know, all while I try not to stare at her bruises.

Clearing my throat again, I look at her and say, "Sorry 'bout the growling, and about Phil. I'm D, and this is Jamie. We should probably tell you the rules if you're gonna stay here." She nods her head fast, still trembling slightly. I watch her for a second before I continue, "So, there's really only three rules they give us all, and the most important one is to be quiet at all times. Children are to be seen, not heard. That one is from Dianne, Phil's wife. She works the night shift, so unless she's at work, we have to be silent in the house, okay?" She nods again, frowning hard.

"Rule number two, we're not allowed in the kitchen. We eat when they tell us to, otherwise we stay in our rooms or outside." Blake's eyes widen in shock at that, and she looks like she might cry. But then she looks at Jamie standing at the end of her bed, and I can see her pulling herself together. It's honestly impressive. I definitely couldn't stop my tears at her age. Then again, my mom had just abandoned me, so maybe that wasn't my fault.

I tune back into reality when Jamie speaks, not realizing I had zoned out. "And the last rule from the fosters is don't be a snitch. Whatever happens in this house stays in this house, and if they find out you tattled, they'll know, and it will be bad for you. You got it?" Again, Blake nods without saying anything. Something about her is making me feel something I've never felt before; almost like I want to keep her with me all the time so nothing can hurt her. It's making me nervous.

Blake looks between us nervously now. "I'm really tired, so I'm gonna lie down now... Is that okay?" she asks, looking at me.

"Of course it is," I say. She crawls into the bed without waiting for the sheets. Blake covers everything except one of her light green eyes with the small blanket on the end of the bed as I continue talking. "I'll wake you if there's an emergency. And Blake?" I ask. She raises her one visible eyebrow, and dang it, that might be the cutest thing I've ever seen. "Please wake me up if you need anything at all. I'm gonna lay down too, but my bed is right here." I point at the bed she's facing.

She looks like she might cry again, instead she whispers, "Thanks D. You're being really nice." As she rolls over, I get angry, barely stopping myself from growling out loud and scaring her again.

Who the hell hurt this tiny, sweet girl?

I've barely talked to her at all, but I decide right then I'm going to protect her as long as I can. As long as she'll let me. I don't know how long we'll be in the same foster home, but I'll find a way to protect her even if one of us gets moved. She's too small and there are too many monsters in the world, like Phil. If I have my way, what happened to Katie will NEVER happen to Blake.

A little while later, I'm finishing up some Algebra home-work for class tomorrow when I hear a tiny whimpering sound. At first, I can't figure out where it's coming from, but when I look over at Blake, I see her thrashing in her bed. As soon as I go to stand up, her whimpering gets louder before turning into crying. I get out of bed and quietly crouch down next to her, touching her shoulder as carefully as I can, but I'm not prepared for her to wake up swinging and shouting, "*NO!* Don't touch me!"

Glancing behind me to the closed bedroom door, I quickly give her shoulder a little shake. "Blake, *Blake!* Stop! It's D, you're safe." I try to stay as quiet as possible while I wake her, because I know if Phil hears us, it won't be good. Her eyes pop open and she sits up so fast she slams into my nose, making us both groan. I get a whiff of her sweet strawberry scent that honestly makes me a little dizzy. Or maybe it's a concussion? "*Ouch!* Damn, Blake. Who knew such a tiny girl could pack such a vicious head-butt?" I say, smirking and trying to make her smile.

She's sitting here white as a ghost, shaking so hard I'm afraid she's going to break a tooth with the way her teeth are knocking together. I'll try anything to help her feel better. She gives me the smallest smile before her whole face falls, and she starts to cry. These huge tears are just rolling down her cheeks as she frantically wipes them away and looks at me with the saddest eyes I've ever seen while mumbling, "I'm sorry. I'm so sorry. I won't do it again. Please don't hurt me; I'll stop crying," over and over again.

I have to try really hard not to let out the growl that wants to rip out of my throat at her begging me not to hurt her. Instead, I lean over and gently grab her face, tilting her head up to look in her shockingly green eyes. They're the lightest color green I've ever seen, and not only is the girl's face covered in freckles, her eyes are too. The pale green is somehow so bright, even in the dark, and has little light brown freckles in it that lead to a dark green ring around the outside. I'm speechless for a second before remembering she needs my help right now, not me staring into her eyes and making her uncomfortable.

I lean just a little closer and whisper, "Blake, I know you have no reason to trust me, but will you come with me for a minute? I want to show you something that might help you not feel so scared. It's the same thing I do every time I get scared in a new place."

She still looks scared, but she nods, so I take her hand and lead her out the window to the flat part of the roof above the porch. The one place I feel like I can breathe, hoping the stars and warm night air will help her feel it too.

SINCE THAT FIRST night that Blake came to live with us, she and I have gone up to the roof together no less than three times a week. We used to go a lot more those first few weeks she was with us, but after a while she didn't need it as often. It's been almost a year now, and we've had a routine since that first week. We go to different schools since she's in the sixth grade and I just started ninth, but we get out at almost the same time. So, every day on my way home from school, I walk the mile down the road to pick her up and we walk back to the house while she chats excitedly about her day.

You would think with her being three years younger than me, we wouldn't have anything to talk about. Apparently, being verbally (and sometimes physically) abused by your foster parents really bonds you to a person, no matter how old they are. I can honestly say Blake is the best friend I've ever had, especially since Jamie was adopted earlier this year. So far, I've kept my silent promise to always keep her safe, keeping her from Phil and Dianne's wrath. Lately, though, I've noticed Phil paying extra attention to Blake, and it's making both of us uncomfortable. I keep her away from him as much as possible by never leaving her there alone, and even bringing her along with me to the rink when I go for free skate.

Tonight is another roof night. Blake and I are laying side by side on the same blanket we've been using for the last year. I'm pointing out constellations I've learned and have been trying to teach her. Tonight, I'm trying to point out the Orion constellation, but she's just staring at me, so I look over at her and ask, "Whatcha thinkin' about, Shortcake?"

She smiles at the nickname I gave her the first night I brought her out to the roof. From day one I've always just told her it's because her red hair and freckles remind me of the cartoon character. But really, it's because she smells exactly like strawberry shortcake. Not only is it my favorite food, but it's also a smell that now feels like home. Strawberries will always remind me of my best friend in the world.

"Honestly, D? I'm wondering what my life would be like without you."

I shoot up to my knees, staring at her in shock, as I choke out, "*What?*"

She looks at me like I'm crazy before rolling her eyes. "Hades Blaze Abbott, you *know* that's not how I meant it. I just mean, I'm wonderin' what my life would look like if you weren't here to calm me down that first night. I don't know if you know this, D, but you're my best friend. My only real family. Every time I wake up crying from another nightmare, I can look over at your bed and know that I'm safe. I don't know what I would do without you..." she trails off, getting choked up.

I lay back down and straighten my legs before pulling her

to lean back against the roof with me, linking our pinkies together in the way that's become our thing.

"Shortcake, I promise you'll never have to find out what life without me is like. I will always be here for you, as long as you want me to be. And when I finally turn eighteen, we can run off and live our lives without anybody else to worry about. You know I'll take care of both of us, even if it means getting three jobs so we can find a place as far away from here as possible." She still looks unsure, so I go to reassure her again when my phone rings.

Surprised since it's after nine p.m., I look at the caller ID to see my friend Rook calling. I wince and look over at Blake, who's already closed her eyes and turned to face the sky. "Do you mind if I take this? It's one of the guys from the rink."

She just shakes her head with her eyes closed. "Go ahead. I'm not going anywhere," she mumbles.

I haven't told her much about these guys, just that I met them when they were in town for a hockey tournament a few months ago. The truth is, though, they're my best friends outside of Blake, and we've decided to form a pack together when I turn eighteen and can get the hell out of this place. Normally they don't call unless they're in town and even then, they'd just send a text to our group chat. It's giving me a gut feeling something is really wrong.

I quickly hit the button on my ancient flip phone to answer. "Hey man, what's up?"

I can hear yelling on the other end of the phone, and the pit in my stomach grows. Rook says, "Hey D, listen we're in town at the rink for another tourney and these assholes from the other team just picked a fight with the twins. It's bad, and we could really use your help before somebody calls the cops. Can you get over here?" Rook, Achilles, and the twins Kaspian and Kairo, are all from one of the wealthiest towns in the country, Lockwood.

It's basically nothing but mansions and castles and giant houses on the beach. Think old southern millions and then multiply it by a hundred and you've got Rook's family. They've got more money than God. Not that you'd ever know it looking at them. The Beaumonts are some of the kindest, most down-to-earth people I've ever met. The last time they were in town, they drove me home from the rink every night. They waited until I was safely inside to go back to their hotel downtown, which was twenty minutes in the opposite direction.

It's because I owe these guys so much, I immediately respond, "Of course dude, I'll be there in ten minutes. Can you guys hang in that long?"

He responds with a quick, "Yup, hurry," before hanging up.

I turn to Blake to see she fell asleep while I was on the phone, so I carry her inside and tuck her in before whispering that I'll see her later. She cracks one eye open just long enough to grab my hand and squeeze it.

Her voice is raspy with sleep when she says, "Love you, D. Be careful. Wake me up when you get back, okay?"

I squeeze back before kissing her forehead. "Sure thing, Shortcake. See you in a bit."

Blake

Age Eleven

I wake up to sunlight streaming in through the still open window, way too bright for this early in the morning. D hasn't woken me up yet, so I must have at least a little while before we have to get started on chores. I'm just falling back asleep when suddenly my blanket is ripped off of me, exposing my gangly limbs to the cool morning air where D's tee I stole last month doesn't cover them and my usual sleep shorts.

The shirt is huge on me, so it almost looks like I'm not

wearing shorts, a fact I can tell my foster father appreciates as he leers down at me. His lingering looks are happening more often and they make me feel gross, like I need a really hot shower to wash off the ick. He grabs my elbow hard enough to bruise and huffs, "Your little devil friend ain't around to help you anymore, slut. God only knows what you were offering him to keep you away from me all year, but I can take a guess. " His nasal voice as he runs his eyes up and down my exposed legs hurts my ears.

I snatch my blanket off the floor and wrap it around me as I ask, "What are you talking about, Phil? D was here last night. I need to get ready or we're going to be late for school."

I go to side step him to head to the bathroom when he grabs my shoulder and throws me back onto my bed. My hip hits the footboard, making me yelp as I go down.

He sneers down at me, but I can see what looks like sick delight shining in his dishwater-colored eyes. "That's where you're wrong, my little Jezebel, that little punk you liked to hang out with so much? He's gone. Not coming back. Some rich pricks adopted him this mornin' and he wanted me to tell you he ain't comin' back for your scrawny ass. So, get used to seeing my face, sweet pea. You and I are hittin' the road tonight. Dianne's kickin' me out, and you're comin' with me."

CHAPTER 1

KAIRO

If I have to hear one more goddamn negative word out of my brother's mouth, I'm going to deck him.

He's been complaining about the cold for the last hour while we sit outside of Hades' childhood foster home. Today is Blake's eighteenth birthday and my brother and I are checking the house one last time to see if she came back here. She hasn't been here any other time over the years, but I don't know. I just have this feeling in my gut that says we missed something when we were questioning Dianne earlier. D has been a wreck all day, and we're starting to really worry about what will happen to him if we never find her.

Earlier that day

"Rook, I don't want to fucking talk about it right now! Y'all have been helping me search for a girl you've never even met for *seven years*, when I have no idea if she even presented as an Omega. It feels like we're never going to find her. I'm so damn tired of being heartbroken every time we search a new city with nothing to show for it," D says miserably. He collapses onto the couch in our rental home as the apple in his scent goes sour. "I miss her so much. I know I need to keep looking, but *fuck.* Knowing she could be auctioned off to some criminal right now is making me sick, man."

Rook looks around the room at the rest of us to try to get a read on our feelings through the pack bond. We all know what he'll find, though. Hades has been talking about Blake since we were kids, absolutely adamant she belonged in our pack, and when he was taken from their foster home with no notice, it devastated him.

The night of that fight seven years ago, after we were all arrested, Rook's parents took Hades home with them, and that's when he officially started going by "D". He didn't want the constant reminder of his crappy birth mother.

They eventually adopted him, and because of that, he never got to say goodbye to Blake. We had been looking for her passively during our teen years. The minute we were all finally eighteen, we solidified our pack bond and used every resource available to try to find her again. And considering Rook is a billionaire, there were a *lot* of resources.

The problem is, she vanished into thin air. There's no record of her anywhere. No school, no doctor, no police reports, absolutely nothing. There's no death certificate anywhere, either, and I think that might be the only thing that's kept our hope alive all these years we've been searching.

Rook realizes we're all in and crouches down in front of Hades. "Look, I know it's been hard not finding her, but today is her eighteenth birthday. What if she's out there looking for you now that she's legally aged out of the system? Do you really want to miss our chance at finding her because you're too busy whining about how we haven't found her *yet*? And trust me, D. It is *yet,* because we *will* find her. Have a little faith in your pack, brother."

He stands up and holds his hands out to help him up. As Hades rises off the couch, he heaves a deep sigh. "Okay... Okay, you're right. But somebody else needs to go to that house. If I see Phil or Dianne, I can't promise I'll be able to keep my cool, and I don't feel like spending the night in jail, again." He cracks a small smirk at that as he looks over at me. "Kai? Will you and Kas go check out the old house? Maybe try to talk to Dianne again and turn on the charm if you have to?" he asks.

I'm already nodding my head before he even finishes speaking, glancing over at my twin to see he is, too. "Of course we will, bro. We've got your back, although I can't promise I won't *accidentally* run my fist into your old foster father's face if I see him there." I shrug, putting both my hands out in a "what're you gonna do" gesture.

Kaspian looks over at me and smirks, saying "Yeah, I mean we all know how clumsy Kai and I are. One of our fists might just *accidentally* land on his nose. You never know."

Our youngest pack mate, Achilles, has been sitting in the corner silently as we debate. He finally stands up while stretching his tattooed arms high above his head and yawns. "I don't know 'bout y'all, but I'm starving, and I want to hit up that incredible taco truck by the fosters on Fifth." He smirks over at the guys. "One of y'all wanna come with me? Or am I on babysitting duty for Sad Sal over there?" he asks, pointing over at a still sulking Hades.

Glaring over at Achilles, Hades snarls at him. "Do you think I *want* to be sad? Do you think I want to spend every waking hour of the day wondering if I left my best friend in the world to be hurt or worse by those awful people? I was so happy to be adopted, but losing her broke my heart, Lee. So yeah, sorry for being fucking *sad*."

Achilles walks over to Hades, looking like somebody kicked his puppy, and wraps him in a huge bear hug. Achilles may be the smallest and youngest of us, but he's still over six feet tall, and seeing him being so gentle with our pack mate is always cute.

"I'm so sorry, D. You know I want to find her too; I truly didn't mean anything by it. I was just trying to lighten the mood a little. I promise I'm taking this as seriously as all of you," he mumbles, still holding on tight to our friend. Hades finally releases an enormous sigh and hugs him back even harder. It causes Achilles to choke out, "Alright there, big guy, you're gonna crack a rib, and my chest is too pretty for bruises." This gets a laugh out of all of us while he looks indignant. "Hey! Don't laugh at me, it's true." He's dangerously close to pouting, so with one last chuckle, I grab Kaspian's arm and we make our way towards the door.

As we're walking, I turn my head to face the guys and yell, "We'll be back tonight! Kas will keep you updated while we're gone."

As Kas and I settle into our rental for the week, an unassuming silver minivan, he buckles up and turns to face me. Quietly, he asks, "Do you really think we'll find her, Kai? I know we haven't met her but after hearing D talk about her so much since the day we met him, I feel like she's my best friend too. I'm scared we won't find her, and if we don't, nobody else will ever be enough."

I understand where he's coming from. I don't know what it is about tonight specifically after searching for seven long years, but I just have a gut feeling we're going to find *something*.

Canting my head to the side to show I'm listening to him, I grab his hand and quietly say, "Kas, I know it's been hard. Staking our teen years and our entire adult lives so far on someone we've never met is crazy. But we love D, and he loves Blake. I don't really know how to explain the feeling in my gut, but I know we're going to find her. And even if the other guys give up after tonight, I won't. I need to find out what happened to her, because even if they pretend otherwise, I know the guys will never move on from this."

My brother would never admit it because of the two of us, he's always been the dark and broody twin. But the man has a gooey marshmallow center with a heavy dose of anxious thoughts. He looks back at me, and I'm pretty sure his eyes are misty.

"Kaspian Jack Sparrow! Do my eyes deceive me, or are you tearing up? I mean, I know my speeches are moving, but I definitely wasn't expecting such an emotional audience tonight," I tease him as he scoffs and not so discreetly wipes his eyes.

Reaching over to punch me on the arm, he says, "Shut the fuck up, you dick. I thought we agreed not to say my middle name out loud ever again. Or do you enjoy being named after a *pirate movie*, Kairo *Johnny* Sparrow?" He smirks as he says my full name, reminding me exactly why we don't say them out loud.

You see, our mom is obsessed with Johnny Depp. According to our fathers, Kas and I were conceived during a "pre-heat" Pirates of the Caribbean marathon. We try our best to absolutely *never* think about our parents having sex, but unfortunately, we're reminded every time we hear, say, or write our full names. Our last name being Sparrow is a complete coincidence, to the delight of our mother.

"Okay, okay, I give. Please, for the love of God, do not remind me," I say, cringing and fighting a gag.

Soon enough, we're pulling up outside the dilapidated old house where Hades met Blake. My brother and I take a minute to double check that this is the right house before we look at each other with wide eyes. I know Hades said the house was old when they lived here, and yeah, that was seven years ago, but I wasn't expecting *this*.

The once blue house is leaning precariously to the right. The moldy, rotten siding falling off into piles in the over-grown landscape. The roof where I assume he and Blake did their stargazing is bowed dangerously over the rickety-looking porch, looking like it's going to cave in at any moment.

Kas leans toward the windshield to get a closer look, and I hear him suck in a breath. "Kai… is this really where they lived? What if she's still here? There's no way this place is safe, and what if it's even worse on the inside?" he says, sounding panicked.

I grab his hand again, squeezing it to get his attention. "Kas, breathe. If she's here, we'll get her out and bring her home with us. I promise you; it's going to be okay. Whatever we find here, we'll handle it as a pack. Okay?"

He takes a deep breath, grabs the door handle, and says, "Let's go. I need to know one way or another if she's here."

"No, I'm afraid you can't come in. My son isn't home and even if he was, he wouldn't be interested in *hockey*," Dianne says with a sneer.

We've been standing on this crumbling porch for the last ten minutes, trying to get her to let us in so we can look around, but D wasn't kidding when he said she was a hag. When she opened the door, she was threatening to shoot us until we said we were with a youth hockey foundation offering free lessons to kids in the city. Even then, she only opened the door a crack to talk to us while adamantly explaining her son was into football, *not* hockey.

Our pack started a hockey program for underprivileged kids several years ago alongside the other work we do. I'm thankful for it now because it allows us access to places Blake might be.

"We completely understand, ma'am. We won't take up any more of your time tonight. Would you mind too terribly much if I used your restroom before we head out? It's a long drive back to our hotel," I tell her, giving her my most charming smile.

She looks me straight in the eyes and with a curl of her lip, gives me a curt "No," before slamming the door in our faces.

My brother starts to speak, so I quickly hold up my hand. "Let's wait until we're in the car. We don't need anybody overhearing us."

He nods in response, and we turn to walk down the stairs when he steps on a weak board and his foot falls through the bottom of the porch.

"MotherFUCK! That hurt!" he says, and I can't help but laugh. He throws me a dirty look before holding out his hand. "Help me out, would ya? Who knows what's underneath this cesspool of a house? As it is, I'm probably going to need a tetanus shot... or some antibi—" he trails off and lets out an awful high pitch squeal that has me doubling over with laughter.

"Dude, what the hell was that? You sounded like a preteen girl at a boy band concert," I say, wiping tears from my eyes.

He looks at me with huge eyes, panting like he's just run a marathon, "It's not *funny* Kairo! Something just ran over my foot. Get me the HELL out of here before I tell everybody I know about that time you peed your pants and passed out watching The Conjuring when we were sixteen."

"You. Wouldn't. *Dare*." I narrow my eyes at my twin.

He looks at me challengingly. "*Try me.*"

Knowing the asshole will absolutely follow through on his threat, I reach down and grab his arm, hauling him up and out of the hole. "C'mon you big baby, let's get out of here before Dianne realizes we left a hole in her porch."

We're walking back to the car when Kas pulls me to a stop and sniffs before putting his finger to his lips.

"Do you smell that?" he asks. "I swear I just got a whiff of strawberries."

Just then, we hear what sounds like glass breaking coming from the backyard, and I forget about his original question. I take a second to listen closely, and I can hear glass tinkling like it's falling on cement, and what sounds like someone crying. I look over at my brother and give him a small nod.

"Let's go check it out. It's probably just an animal or something."

Walking around the side of the house as fast as we can, we stop short when we see a small cottage out back, not much larger than a shed. What makes us stop, though, is the person trying to crawl out of the broken basement window, audibly crying and wriggling like they're stuck.

One of us must make a noise because suddenly her head whips up. When her eyes lock on us, she struggles harder, frantically whispering, "Please. *Please* help me. Get me out of here. I can't get my belt loop unstuck from the glass. *I'm begging you.* Please help me!"

Kas snaps out of his stupor before I do and runs over, easily unhooking her and pulling her out just as we hear a door slam somewhere in the cottage. He passes her to me while he reaches down to grab what looks like an overstuffed backpack she must have thrown out ahead of her. As soon as she falls into my chest, I get the strongest whiff of strawberry shortcake, making my eyes widen.

The girl seems even more frantic now. She looks up at me with the most incredible green eyes I've ever seen in my life, slurring out, "He drugged me. We have to get out of here, please," before passing out in my arms, making me scramble to catch her.

Kaspian looks over at me, and I can immediately tell we're thinking the same thing.

"We found her."

CHAPTER 2

BLAKE

Am I dead? Did Phil finally kill me? If so, why does it smell so dang good here? Do they have bakeries in the afterlife? I feel like that's probably a thing. I mean, you go through this miserable life and then when you die your reward is delicious, warm pastries? Honestly, it might be a fair trade.

I'm not dead though. My head is throbbing in time with my heartbeat, my mouth is dry, and my stomach is dangerously close to emptying its meager contents all over my…

Wait.

Where am I? My bed is definitely not this comfy. I feel like I'm lying on a cloud. I peek my eyes open and immediately slam them shut again and groan.

Why is it so freaking bright? I definitely don't get this much light in the basement at Phil's. Which brings me back to my original question. Where am I?

Taking a deep, steadying breath, I try to figure out the last thing I remember, and suddenly, it hits me.

"Honey, I'm hooome! Do you feel like a woman yet?"

Phil's voice grates against my eardrums like nails on a chalkboard. I've been simultaneously dreading and anticipating this day for seven years. Since that first day I was left alone with him as my only company, I've been counting down the days to my 18th birthday. Now, 2,557 days later, I'm ready to escape.

Hearing footsteps on the stairs leading to my basement room, I quickly hide the overfull backpack I have ready for tonight. Unfortunately, I use the term "room" loosely, since it's just a mattress on the floor and a clothesline with the few items of clothing I own.

The door to the basement is locked from the outside, as always, and Phil's voice drifts through, muffled by the steel reinforced wood. "I brought you some dinner for your birthday. Figured we should celebrate, with it being such a big deal n' all." He sounds... nice, and it immediately puts me on high alert.

Finally unlocking and opening the heavy door, he walks in with a bag of food from my favorite taco truck across town. Normally I would never trust food from him, but it's been days since I last ate and I'm so hungry I'm willing to deal with whatever the catch is for this meal.

My eyes are wide as I take in Phil's cleaned-up appearance. The last several years have not been kind to the middle-aged man. His usual look of choice is a dirty white undershirt, sagging sweatpants, and being many days un-showered, unshaved and half drunk. Today, though, he looks freshly showered and shaved. He's wearing a hole-free pair of jeans that are just a touch too big on his stout frame, and a cleaner than usual black tee.

"You... you brought me dinner?" I stammer out, looking from his face to the bag and back again.

"Course I did, you ungrateful little bitch. What? Do I not get a hug? Or even a 'Thank you, Daddy Phil?'" He sneers down at me from where he still stands on the bottom step. He stalks forward and, stopping mere inches from where I sit on the floor next to my small collection of books, slaps me across the face hard enough to make my ears ring. "You're going to learn one way or another to be grateful for the things I do for you. I didn't put up with your bratty ass for so many years just for you to turn into an uppity bitch who thinks

she's too good for me and this house. Got it?" he hisses at me, so close I can feel drops of spit hitting my face.

His breath forces me to swallow back a gag, whimpering out, "Yes Phil, I'm sorry, sir. It won't happen again. Thank you so much for my birthday dinner." My face is burning from the slap, and my lip stings, but I know better than to cry. He gets off on the tears.

Running his fingers over my cheek where I'm sure his handprint sits; he lowers his voice to a murmur he probably thinks is alluring and takes a deep inhale of my newly presented Omega scent. "Aww sweet pea, you know I love it when you obey me. Now be a good girl and eat your dinner so we can get started on all the birthday fun." He smirks lasciviously at me before tossing the food down, walking out, and relocking the door.

It's less than fifteen minutes later when I've finished my food that I notice something isn't right. My scent is stronger, my body hot and achy, and my head feels like it's stuffed full of cotton. I look down at the food with horror, suddenly understanding why he brought me food so willingly, rather than our usual battle.

I've been drugged.

Taking a steadying breath, I give myself a quiet pep talk. "Alright, B, you've got this. You were already going to escape tonight. This just moves up your timeline a bit. You have to get out before whatever he put in the food takes full effect."

I'm sure I sound crazy, but when you only have yourself to talk to for your formative years, you learn to take comfort where you can get it. Talking myself through things brings me comfort in scary situations, and I'm not ashamed of that.

I quickly take inventory of the small room before grabbing the hand trowel I stole out of the shed last month and quietly moving my books to the floor directly under the window. I'm only going to have one shot at this, and it needs to be now. I can hear the TV blaring upstairs and before I have a chance to chicken out, I slam the trowel into the small window near the ceiling of the basement, *shattering it. I thank every God I can name that Phil hasn't put bars on this window yet.*

I stop, listening for footsteps on the stairs. When I don't hear any, I toss my backpack out the window onto the damp grass before using the trowel to knock out the remaining glass.

Just as I'm attempting to lift myself up and out of the window, I hear the TV shut off upstairs, and know I'm out of time. My belt loop gets caught on a stubborn shard of glass and because my limbs are weak and clumsy from whatever drug is coursing through my veins, I can't get it free. When I'm ready to give up and drop back down, I see a man approaching from the side of the main house. At least, I think it's one man. There are currently two of him walking towards me, but I'm assuming it's double vision from how dizzy I am.

Reaching my arms out as far as I can, I frantically whisper to the man, "Please. Please help me. Get me out of here. I can't get my belt loop unstuck from the glass. I'm begging you. Please help me!"

Either I was wrong in my original assumption that I was seeing double, or there's a glitch in the matrix, because one of the men immediately runs to my side while the first man stands there looking stunned. The wide-eyed man finally snaps out of his stupor just as I hear the locks being undone on the basement door. The first man pulls me out before passing me to who I assume is his brother, just as I hear the door slamming open behind me.

"He drugged me. We have to get out of here, please." I can hear myself slurring the words before my whole world goes black.

AFTER RECOVERING that fun little memory, I have the *who*, so now I just need the *where*. Knowing I need to figure out where I am and where my backpack is, I open my eyes a fraction to try to let them adjust to the sunlight streaming in through what looks like a sliding glass door. I can see a pool outside the doors, which definitely explains why everything is so freaking bright and sparkly. Normally I'd love a view like this, but right now it makes me want to crawl under the bed with this wildly overstuffed comforter and not come out until the sun goes down.

A throat clears, making me flip over so fast I fall off the bed. "Owwww," I whine as the room spins wildly around me.

"Shit, sorry! Sorry, sorry, sorry. I didn't know how else to get your attention. We've been waiting for you to wake up. It's been so long, I was worried we would have to take you to a hospital." The masculine voice comes from directly in front of me, and I slowly lift my head, hoping to get some answers.

Dizziness receding, my eyes focus and land on one of the men from last night. I know I saw him already, but between the drugs and the darkness, I didn't get a good look. Only now, I'm wishing I had. This man is *beautiful*. He's tall, easily over six feet, forcing me to crane my neck uncomfortably far back to take in all of him. He's built like a swimmer, with big broad shoulders tapering into a trim waist and lean, tan legs, visible because of his athletic shorts that end above his knees. He has neatly styled blonde, sun-bleached hair, honey-colored eyes, and a friendly smile that showcases straight white teeth. The overall look gives him a wholesome, boy next door vibe.

Keeping his distance, he crouches down in front of me on the floor, holding his hands out to show he means no harm. The weird thing is, I'm not scared. He, or his brother, pulled me out of that hell and clearly kept me safe while I was unconscious. I'm still in my clothes I was wearing, there are bandages on my hand and hip, and the room smells like a freaking bakery.

Without consciously deciding to do so, I blurt out, "Is there a bakery nearby?"

The pretty stranger's eyes widen, and it looks like he's fighting a laugh. He clears his throat and smooths out his expression before answering. "No, sugar. There's no bakery nearby. We're only a few miles from where we found you. Do you remember anything about last night?"

There's no judgment in his tone, only gentle curiosity, which is why I feel comfortable answering him truthfully.

Nodding slowly, I murmur, "I remember everything... Please tell me you didn't call the police. I'm eighteen, I swear!"

I raise my eyes to look at him again. I struggle not to give into the panic threatening to hijack my body and turning the strawberry in my scent sour to the point of being rancid. I'm losing the battle quickly, my breaths coming in little pants now as my heart begins to race. Moving slowly so as not to startle me, he gently pulls my blanket wrapped body into his chest and squeezes tightly, stroking my hair and shushing me softly. A low purr builds in his chest, loosening the tightness in my chest a fraction.

"Shh, it's okay, sugar. You're safe. We didn't call the police or tell anyone where we found you. I swear you're safe here with us."

Trying desperately to calm my breaths, I'm realizing now that one scent I'm smelling is *him*. I almost moan when I get my first full hit of his strong Alpha scent. He smells like warm pumpkin pie with lots of cinnamon and whipped cream. Exactly how I like it. I don't realize I have my face buried in his neck until my cheek vibrates with his soft chuckle. I pull back, embarrassed to be caught sniffing an Alpha I just met on my first day of freedom. I feel strange, almost like my body isn't my own. I'm not the kind of person who just lets people touch her, especially not men I barely know.

Maybe it's a side effect of whatever Phil used to drug me? Whatever it was, couldn't have been good.

Seeing my blush, the Alpha smiles down at me and brushes a lock of sweaty hair off my cheek, still chuckling lightly.

"Please don't be embarrassed, Sugar. I'm the one who

picked you up and touched you not only without your consent, but without even introducing myself first. My mama would tan my hide if she was here right now. My name is Kairo, but you can call me Kai if you'd like. And hopefully you also remember my brother from last night. His name is Kaspian. I'm sure you have a lot of questions, but first, would you like to shower and change?"

My voice is croaky when I try to speak, so I clear my throat before I speak again. "Yes, please. Can I also have some water and maybe something for my headache? It's really bad and I don't feel very good."

His gaze sharpens, and he leans in to sniff near my neck, startling me enough that I rear my head back, nearly falling off the man's lap.

"Sorry, that was probably really weird, huh? I was just checking your scent. Can I ask you a few questions, Blake? I think I know what you were drugged with, but I'd like to know all of your symptoms, to be sure." He grips my arm gently above my elbow and guides me to sit in the desk chair when I wobble, trying to keep my balance after moving my head so suddenly.

Shocked, I turn to face Kairo, almost falling out of my chair as I do. "How do you know my name?"

Now it's the Alpha's turn to blush. "Uhh, can I explain that after the questions and the shower? I think once you meet my whole pack, things will make a lot more sense." He flashes a charming grin at me.

Eyeing him suspiciously, I realize I'm too tired to argue with him. So, I mutter, "Fine. Let's skip the get to know you and move straight to the medical questionnaire, then, shall we?"

Not expecting the booming laugh that showcases his gorgeous smile, I jump in my seat before catching myself.

Then I cross my arms, raising one eyebrow at him in question.

"God, I feel like all I've done this morning is apologize." He chuckles. "I'm sorry again, Sugar. I wasn't expecting you to have so much snark readily available after being out cold for almost a full day. I love it."

Sucking in a breath, I'm a little surprised to realize I *was* being my old, snarky self. Just for a second. And not once did I worry about the consequences of something that came out of my mouth or brace myself to be hit.

Who is this guy, and why am I so comfortable with him?

"Sorry. My foster parents always used to say I had a smart mouth. I guess I just can't kick the habit, no matter how many times I was punished for it," I whisper, my eyes trained down on my lap in case he doesn't want to be looked in the eyes like Phil.

"Blake… Darlin', look at me." He uses one finger to pull my face up gently so I can meet his eyes. "Please don't ever be afraid to be yourself with us. Stare us down, talk back, be snarky, tease us, call us out when we're wrong. I told you, you're *safe* here. We will *never* punish you for something you say or do, okay? I promise."

He holds out his pinky to promise me, and I suck in a sudden breath, suddenly reminded of another promise someone made me and he broke the very same night. Not wanting to upset this sweet man who's been so kind to me, I take his pinky and lock it with mine, looking into his amazing honey brown eyes and nod. Being this close to his face, I can see tiny gold flecks that I didn't notice earlier. The effect is stunning. Letting go of my pinky, he starts back in with his inquisition.

"Great, well, have you noticed any changes in your scent since last night? Even something minor?"

My eyes widen. "Actually, yeah. My scent has been super

strong. I know it only just came in fully when I turned eighteen yesterday, but last night just before you found me and today it's been noticeably stronger."

He nods. "Alright, and have you noticed any other physical changes? Dry mouth, dizziness, hot flashes or fever?"

Again, I nod at him, getting more concerned by the minute as his expression darkens and a low grumble builds in his chest.

"Okay, last question: how's your mental status? Are your inhibitions down? Do you feel more open to suggestion? Less guarded and maybe even a little aroused?"

My mouth drops open. "How do you know that? Do you know what he drugged me with?"

With a grimace, he pulls out his phone and turns it around to show me the screen. "This is a drug called Predatocin, but the street name is Heat Fleet, or HF. Blake, he gave you a drug to bring on a heat. I don't think it was a full dose, or maybe it was a faulty batch, because you're clearly not in heat, but you are showing symptoms of what's called pre-heat. Are you familiar with heats at all or how they work?"

I want to be surprised that the man who raised me would do such a horrible thing, but honestly? I'm not. I had an idea when I realized he had drugged me. Between how he looked, the dinner, and the way he spoke to me and touched me, I knew something bad was coming. But maybe I didn't realize it was *this* bad.

If I had been alone with Phil when the drugs fully kicked in...

My whole body begins to shake as terrifying scenarios play on a loop in my mind.

Me, face down, begging for a knot and angering Phil to the point where he beats me again.

Breaking out of the basement and asking the first Alpha I see in the street to knot, breed, and bite me.

Out of my mind, writhing in pain, crying for relief that won't come.

Phil, taking what he's always wanted and couldn't have until yesterday, me. A newly presented Omega.

It's that last vision in my head that has me snapping out of my panic attack long enough to tell the Alpha in front of me, "Kai, I'm gonna be sick."

He grabs the trash can from next to the bed and slides it under my face just in time for me to throw up last night's drugged dinner. Holding my hair back and whispering soothing words from above my head.

"It's alright Sugar, let it out. You're safe now. We've got you. Just breathe, Blake. That's it. Nice, deep breaths."

I tilt my head up, tears running down my face, as he grabs me a warm wet washcloth from next to the bed that he must have brought in with him earlier. Lightly grabbing my chin in his strong hand, he uses the cloth to wipe away my tears gently, before wiping over my mouth. Handing me a glass of water, he holds out his opposite hand and in it are four pills. Two that are plain white and oblong, one that is round and yellow, and another that's round and white.

He points at the while pills and says, "These are basic pain relievers for your headache, and they shouldn't react to the drugs already in your system. You can take these now." He hands them to me, waiting for me to swallow them before he points to the other white pill. "This one is for any nausea you might experience due to the drugs he gave you, but it might make you sleepy, so if you don't want to take this one, I understand."

"Actually, I would really like to not be so nauseous anymore, so I'll take it if that's okay. I hate throwing up more than almost anything. I'm terrified of it, actually." I give a humorless chuckle.

Sympathy shines in his eyes as he looks at me. "It's okay,

Sugar. Kas is that way, too. Take this now and then we'll talk about this last one."

Tossing the white pill back, I point to the last pill in his hand and tell him, "That one's pretty, so it can't be bad… right?" I gently tease Kai as he chuckles at me, flashing that grin again.

"Good guess, this one isn't anything *bad,* but it might not be very fun." He looks a little anxious as he begins to explain the innocuous looking yellow pill. "This one is a heat suppressant. You'll need to take one every day for about a week, to counteract the effects of the Predatocin and make sure you aren't thrown into a premature heat. There are a few side effects, like headaches, mood swings, cramping, and fatigue. Basically, it would be like having a nasty case of PMS. Are those symptoms something you can live with for the next week or so?"

I start giggling. I truly can't help it. It's such a *man* thing to ask. It's nice though. As long as I didn't bother him, Phil never mentioned my "overdramatic women's troubles". Soon I'm laughing so hard tears are forming in my eyes again.

He looks shocked for a minute before he laughs, too. "That was probably a dumb question, huh?" he asks, shaking his head. "I don't have any sisters, so forgive me if it takes me a minute to get used to having a girl around the house again. I haven't lived with an Omega since I left home at eighteen, and that was like six years ago now."

I smile at him. "It's okay. I grew up alone for my whole life but for one year, so I really only have myself for reference. I won't hold it against you."

He shakes his head before holding out his hand, drawing us back to the reason for the giggling. "Alright, Sugar. Let's get this first dose down now, then. It's best to do it as soon as possible."

With a small smirk, I grab it out of his hand and swallow it down with the last of the water in my glass.

Rolling his eyes playfully, he slaps his palms down on his legs. "Alright, let's get you to the shower, yeah? And then you can meet the guys. I'll show you to the bathroom real quick, and while you're showering, I'll take care of this," he says, pointing at the trash can.

I look at Kai with a grimace. "You really don't need to do it. I can take care of it myself. I'm sure this isn't how you imagined spending your weekend."

"Sugar, look at me," he says, wrapping his hand around the back of my head while his fingers burrow into my knotted hair. "There is *nowhere* I'd rather be than here with you right now. Let me, no, let *us* take care of you. It's the least you deserve. Plus, all five of us are caretakers, and none more than Rook, who you'll meet in a bit."

Slowly agreeing, I tilt my head. "Okay. I'll try."

He beams down at me and winks, leaning down to whisper, "Good girl. Now let's get your pretty behind in the shower before you meet the guys."

I shiver, sighing deeply. This guy managed to put a crack in the walls around my heart in less than an hour. I don't like it one bit.

"Alright, charmer. Let's go."

CHAPTER 3

ACHILLES

I'm standing outside Kairo's room, simultaneously hoping he'll need me and hoping he won't. Being the only Beta in a pack of Alphas who all have very strong personalities can be... interesting. To say the least. But man, seeing Kai come in carrying an unconscious Omega last night was a new one.

I'd love to be able to say I never gave up hope we would find D's childhood friend, but honestly, I had. I thought for sure everybody would come back last night disappointed once again, and I'd be left to pick up the pieces of my pack's broken hearts. I got the shock of my life when they came home with a girl the twins *insist* is Blake, which is another reason I'm standing out here in the hallway like a weirdo.

Finally ready to give up and head back to my room, I go to walk past. Only to have Kai's door crash open and get hit in the chest with a cloud of hair that looks and smells *exactly* like strawberries. I'm instantly thrown back to a memory of last night, while I was getting tacos.

Watching Kaspian and Kairo walk out the front door with hope shining bright in their eyes almost makes me roll my own. We've been searching for this girl for seven years, all over the damn country. If we haven't found her by now, we aren't going to.

As I turn to look over at Rook, I can see he's already giving me a disappointed stare. He lifts his chin toward the kitchen in a silent demand to follow him. He leans down and murmurs something to Hades, too low for me to hear, and walks into the kitchen while D walks toward the garage.

Walking into the kitchen, he immediately rounds on me, getting right in my face and growling.

"Lee, I don't give a fuck if you've given up hope. We're losing our pack mate to the guilt that's been eating at him every single day for the last seven years. If you want to give up hope, fine. But keep it to your damned self and don't make the rest of us feel bad for wanting something that could change our lives for the better in every way. We all agreed to look for Blake and we will continue to do so until Hades is ready to move on. Pack supports pack, and I love you, but you're being kind of selfish. If you don't want to help, stay home next time."

He walks to the door leading to the garage and turns back. "Think about how you would feel if it was your sister who went missing. Would you ever stop looking for her?" Shaking his head, he slams the door, leaving me with my spiraling thoughts and thoroughly chastised.

Less than fifteen minutes later, I'm standing on the porch of my assigned foster home for the night, but it's a bust. The foster mom is very sweet, but her oldest child is only four, so I politely thank her and soon enough I'm back on the road to get myself a metric fuck-ton of tacos.

Pulling up outside the taco truck, I hop out and practically skip to the ordering window, where there's only one guy. He's being a total asshole to the staff, though. If I had to guess, I'd say he's in his early to mid-forties. He's short, maybe 5'6" at most, with a pot belly that hangs over his too-big jeans, and a greasy comb over. I can't hear what he's saying, but based on the volume, the hand gestures, and the look on the cashier's face, it can't be good.

When the man finally gets his food and turns to leave, I notice he looks vaguely familiar, but I can't place why. I've been coming here for years, whenever we're in town, so maybe he's a regular too and I've seen him here before. He stalks past me, stomping like an angry toddler. As he does, I get a sudden whiff of strawberry, but with undertones of whipped cream and something else that's too faint to name.

Not thinking anything of it, I turn back around and greet the cashier and order my tacos, leaving an extra big tip to make up for the last guy. Then, I get back in the car to head for our temporary home.

I'M JOLTED back to reality when the Omega backs up and starts frantically apologizing.

"Oh god I'm sorry, I'm so, so sorry. It was an accident, I swear. I'm sorry!" She's practically trembling in my arms, and every single calming Beta instinct I have is screaming at me to reassure this tiny girl I won't hurt her.

I lean down just enough to look in her eyes and I'm momentarily stunned silent. She has the most breathtaking eyes I've ever seen. I shake my head to clear it and make sure she's looking at me before I speak.

"Please stop apologizing, ma jolie fraise. Not a single man in this pack is ever going to raise his voice at you, let alone lay a hand on you. I will personally kick their asses if they try. Okay?"

She looks up at me with those gorgeous eyes on the verge of tears. "Okay... I really am sorry," she whispers.

Brushing a lock of wild red hair away from her face, I lean

in and get a hit of her incredible scent. I'm assuming that's why the nickname rolled off my tongue without conscious thought. It's so much stronger than the small amount of it I was able to smell last night. Sweet strawberries and sugar, with undertones of vanilla whipped cream and sweet, fluffy angel food cake. She smells like a goddamn dessert, and I would give anything for a taste.

Bending down close to her ear, I whisper back, "None of that now, jolie fraise, let's start over. It's so nice to meet you, Blake. I've heard only the best things and I can't wait to get to know you myself. My name's Achilles, but most of the guys call me Lee. And listen, if ya ever need a break from the Alpha nonsense but don't wanna be alone, you come and find me, okay? The nice thing about Betas is that we're very cuddly." Giving her a wink, I step back, desperately fighting my body's reaction to her scent.

Her blush is just about the sexiest thing I've ever seen, and I can't help wondering just how far down her body it'll go when she's turned on. My dick jumps at that as the powdered sugar in my scent intensifies. Fighting a blush, I have to remind myself that she's younger than even me and coming out of a really traumatic situation, so he just needs to chill the fuck out for a bit. Turning slightly to the side so the tent in my jeans isn't so obvious, I hold my hand out in a gesture for her to pass me.

"I believe you were on your way to the shower when we collided?" I throw a little extra twang into my voice, hoping to get a small smile out of the beauty.

What I get is so much better. She beams at me, still blushing bright pink, and right there on her left cheek is a dimple.

Lord save me. I think I've died and gone to heaven. Is there any part of this girl that isn't perfect?

"I'm not— I mean yes, I was. Kai gave me some medicine and I'm ready to wash last night off of me if that's okay."

Be still my heart.

"Blake, you never need to ask to use anything of ours. I swear. What's ours is yours," I tell her gently.

She looks stunned. "But you barely know me. Why would you open your lives to me like that? Plus, the rest of your pack hasn't even met me yet. They could hate me or not want me here, or…" she trails off.

Christ, has this girl ever had any *freedom or kindness in her life?*

I can see her spiraling, so I decide to get a little more firm with her. "Blake. I need you to listen and listen good, okay? You may not know any of us yet, but we know you. We *want* to know you. We've been looking for you for a very long time and now that you're here, we're all in. Take as long as you need, get to know every member of this pack, but you need to know we want you, and nothing is going to change that. Now, go take a nice, hot shower, get some fresh clothes on, and come down when you're ready so we can all have lunch. Do you have any food preferences or allergies?"

She blanches. "Umm… just… no tacos please. I can't… That's what he used to drug me, and I don't think I could stomach them right now." Her stammered sentence ends in a whisper, and I'm ready to go tell the guys what I know so I can go kill this bastard. Making people sleep with the fish is still a thing, right? I'd love to toss her foster father into the ocean. Or a shark tank.

Instead of letting my anger show on my face, I let out a breath and run my thumb over her dimple. "You got it, no tacos. Are you hungry for anything specific? Anything at all. Name it and it's yours."

She looks unsure, so I smile to encourage her to be honest. This girl went seven years, maybe more, with nothing. We're damned well gonna make sure she has everything now, no matter the cost. Hell, if she told me she wanted Italian food, I'd be tempted to haul her cute butt on the jet to Italy.

Kai gives me a look over her head that's clearly meant to say, "Slow down before you scare her off, Frenchy". But I'd bet my sweet strawberry doesn't scare easily.

Looking up at me with a shy smile, she says, "I would love a Hawaiian pizza with black olives. I haven't had pizza since I was a kid, but it's one of my favorite foods."

She's going to make me cry. I dam the building tears back, so I don't upset her and instead, with a small smile, say, "That sounds great. Anything else? Anything to drink?"

The sweet girl thinks hard for a moment before asking, "Can I have a Dr. Pepper and maybe some ranch for my pizza, please?"

I'm nodding before she even finishes her question.

"You don't even have to ask, Pretty Girl. Who would ever eat pizza without ranch? It's a requirement in the Beaumont pack," I say with a wink. "And I will make absolutely sure we get your soda, too. Have a nice shower, okay? I think Kai is probably—" I look over to the man in question and he gives me a slight nod. "Yeah, so Kai is gonna hang out up here until you're done, so you aren't alone in a strange place. Just yell if you need him, okay?"

She gives me another nod and a big smile, her eyes sparkling more than they have since she came out of the bedroom. I lean in and give her a quick hug and lightly brush the top of her head with my lips and mumble, "Blake?"

"Yeah, Achilles?"

Hearing her use my full name gives me goosebumps and threatens to wake my dick up again, but I try to stay focused on the task at hand.

I hug her a little tighter, just for a moment, and say, "I'm really happy we found you. Welcome home."

HADES

I'm pacing in the living room like a caged animal when Achilles comes tripping down the stairs, narrowly avoiding face planting at the bottom. He's panting like he just ran a marathon, and I don't think I've ever seen him look so angry.

"He— that fucking— mother of—" He's panting so hard he can't get a full sentence out, so I walk up to him and shake his shoulders.

"Lee, shut the hell up for a second and *breathe* so you can tell us what happened." Normally I'm more patient than this, but my *best friend* is at the top of those stairs, and she has no freaking clue I'm here. That this is my pack. That I've been looking for her every single day since I left.

Sucking in a huge, gasping breath, he tells us about how last night when he went to get tacos; he ran into a man who was being a grade A douche-canoe to the employees. As the dude was leaving, he caught faint traces of strawberries coming off of him, not realizing until bumping into Blake just now that it was *her* scent.

Taking my own deep breath to subdue the rage coursing

through my veins, I'm shaking as I ask, "Lee… what did the man look like?"

He looks at me hesitantly and gives me an exact description of my god-awful foster father. It takes a second to sink in. Without a second thought, I turn around and throw my fist into the wall. Still breathing heavily, I whip my head around when I hear a soft gasp.

Holy. Shit.

Blake is everything I remember and an entirely different person all at once. Her gorgeous bright red hair is still long, easily to the middle of her back, and set in her natural soft waves. She hasn't grown much since she was eleven, and I hate not knowing if she's just naturally tiny or if the fosters started starving her again after I was taken away. The biggest difference in my girl is the look on her face when she realizes it's me.

"What. The. *Fuck.*" She looks absolutely devastated, tears already streaming down her face. Her hand flies up to cover her mouth as a ragged sob escapes, and she spears Kairo and Achilles with a look of betrayal.

I step forward, hoping to pull her into a hug I desperately need. "I've missed you so fucking much, Shortcake. I can't believe we—"

She interrupts me, shouting "*NO!*"

Holding her hand up to stop me in my tracks, she continues, "How are you here? *Why* are you here? Did you suddenly grow a conscience after abandoning me and leaving me with those monsters for seven years?! You LEFT ME without a goodbye. Just like my parents. Just like every other person has my entire life."

Her voice is growing progressively louder as I stand stunned silent. What does she mean leaving her with them? We were told she followed me the night I was arrested and never came home.

Seven years earlier

"FREEZE! Everybody stop and put your hands in the air where we can see them! If you have weapons, drop them now. I won't ask again!"

Bruised and bloody, all twelve of us do as the pissed-off looking cop says, turning around slowly with our hands in the air.

"Officer..." Rook, ever the calm and collected leader of our friend group, begins to speak, only to be cut off by a new cop.

"Save it, Beaumont. Your parents are already down at the station and demanding to see you and mister Abbott right away," the man says, rolling his eyes.

I startle at the mention of my name. "M-me? Why do they want to see me? I need to get home before my foster parents... get worried." I stumble over my words before trailing off, not wanting to reveal that I need to get home before they realize I snuck out and take it out on Blake.

"I don't get paid to know the answers, kid. Let's go, I'm not gonna cuff you as long as you cooperate, got it?"

Nodding, I step into the back of the police car for what isn't the first and probably won't be the last time, squished next to Rook with Achilles sliding in beside me. There wasn't any big fanfare arriving at the station since Rook's parents aren't exactly the reactive type. We're led to what looks like a small meeting room at the very back of the precinct, away from the other officers and people in the lobby.

As soon as the door closes behind us, Amy, his mom, wraps us both up in tight hugs, making me stiffen up immediately. Don't get me wrong, I love Amy, but I'm not used to physical contact unless it's from my Shortcake. I hope she's okay at the house.

Connor, one of Rook's three dads, clears his throat. "Boys, we need to talk to both of you. Will y'all sit down, please?"

Rook and I look at each other and I can tell he's as confused as I am, so I shrug. We both move to sit at the table across from his parents and some guy who looks like he might be a lawyer, and I straighten my shoulders, prepared for the worst.

Spencer, another of the dads, pats me on the back and says, "Hades, with your permission, Amy, myself, Connor, and Aaron would like to adopt you."

My jaw drops open as I stare at them, waiting for someone to start laughing and tell me this is a joke. But the room stays silent, and they all look at me, waiting for an answer I can't give them.

"You... want to adopt me? I mean... I can't. I can't leave. I'm sorry," I say, hanging my head in shame. These people have been nothing but kind to me and here I am, rejecting them. Just like my mom did to me. But I know I can't leave Blake alone in that house with those horrible people.

Aaron chuckles, shocking the heck out of me. I whip my head around to stare at him with wide eyes.

He smirks. "What? Did you really think we would adopt you and not figure out a way to get Blake out, too? D, we knew you wouldn't leave without her after hearing you talk about nothing else every time we saw you. Our best friends, the Underwoods, were never blessed with children of their own. When we told them our plans to adopt you and mentioned we wanted to find a way to bring Blake along, they offered to adopt her if she's open to that."

I can feel tears forming in my eyes and for the first time in six years, I let them fall. Amy immediately jumps out of her chair and crouches down in front of me to pull me into a hug, and this time, I sink into the comfort it brings.

Quiet enough that only Amy can hear, I whisper, "You really found a home for Blake too? You aren't going to make me leave her?"

Pulling back and cupping my cheek in one of her small hands, she smiles at me sadly. "Oh, sweet boy. No. If this girl means so much to you that you're willing to give up being adopted just to stay with her, she must be pretty darn special. That's the kind of girl we want to know, and the kind we want around our boys. Hades, if you love Blake, we do too because we love you. Will you let us adopt you and make you a Beaumont?"

Looking back at Rook to see how he feels, I see him with his hands held up in the prayer position, with the biggest smile I've ever seen him give on his face.

"Please, please be my brother. I have four older sisters, dude. I'm literally begging you to save me."

Looking around the room, I see everybody with huge smiles on their faces; the dads hiding laughs in their fists at Rook's begging. Even the lawyer is smiling as he pulls a thick stack of papers out of his briefcase.

Sucking in a deep breath and wiping the last few tears away, I smile back. "Okay."

We stayed at the Beaumonts' hotel suite across town last night because I legally couldn't be returned to Phil and Dianne's. Something about having the paperwork expedited and special permission to remove Blake and I from an unsafe environment. We couldn't go get her last night because the Underwoods didn't get in until this morning to sign the paperwork for legal guardianship.

Pulling up outside the house I'll never have to see again, I'm practically vibrating in my seat. Hopping out before we're even in park. Spencer puts his hand on my shoulder, pulling me back before I can run to the door.

"Let the police officer serve the papers first, okay? We don't know how they'll react to having their license suspended pending investigation, and I don't want you in the crossfire," he murmurs in my ear.

I know he's right, but I'm so eager to get to Blake I can barely stand still.

Dianne finally answers the door, and she looks awful. There's a huge bruise forming on her cheek and she's crying, and when the officer begins to speak with her, she cries harder. I look on warily as the officer calls the lawyer over, and then another two officers join them. I don't know what's going on, but I have an awful feeling in the pit of my stomach, and I think I might be sick.

One officer and the lawyer walk over to Amy, Aaron, and Connor. Connor looks back, nodding to Spencer to join them. He turns back around to face me, asking me to stay where I am, and walks over to join the others. Amy is crying, and I'm starting to panic, that sick feeling growing with every passing second. Deciding I can't wait any longer, I take off at a sprint into the house and up the stairs to our room, but Blake isn't here.

"Blake? BLAKE? Are you here?" I'm yelling at this point, my heart threatening to beat out of my chest.

The shirt I pretended not to notice she stole is hanging off the side of her bed, torn at the neck, and I bring it to my nose. Desperately hoping that if I inhale deeply enough, I can permanently embed her scent into my memory. Bringing the shirt with me, I stomp back downstairs and outside. Stopping in front of the growing group of worried-looking adults, I growl.

"Where. The hell. Is she? Somebody better tell me something before I lose it." I'm shaking hard, and my breakfast is threatening to escape my stomach.

Amy walks over slowly, hands up like she's approaching a cornered animal. Can't say I'm much calmer than one right now, anyway.

"Hades, will you come sit in the car with me for a few minutes so we can talk?" she asks in a soothing tone.

I can't bring myself to snap at her the way I could somebody else right now, so instead I grind out a "Fine."

She doesn't get on me about my tone as we walk to the car, so I know whatever she's about to tell me is going to hurt. Once we're settled in the back seat, she turns to me and says three words that tear my heart straight from my chest.

"Blake is missing."

I quickly lean out the car door and throw up everything I've eaten my entire life, probably. At least, that's what it feels like.

Everything hurts, and my vision goes fuzzy for a second before a gentle hand runs down my back and I hear Amy saying, "It's alright, honey. I know. Just let it out."

And I stop holding back the sobs that are fighting to break free.

Wiping my mouth with the wipes she pulls out of the console, she pulls me into her chest and rocks me like I'm a child. Normally I would hate this, but right now I feel like a child. My best friend in the whole world is missing and I don't know what to do.

She goes on to explain that according to Dianne, who was told by a neighbor that called her around midnight, Blake snuck out shortly after I did and never came home. When they woke up this morning to find both of us missing, they assumed we had run off together and were waiting the requisite twenty-four hours before reporting us as runaways to the police. Me showing up here alone means Blake was most likely kidnapped.

None of it makes any sense. I talked to her before she fell asleep, and she knew exactly where I was going. Even if I didn't come back, there's no way she would have followed me to the rink in the middle of the night after all the times I've lectured her about safety. The girl is as wild as they come. I mean, her middle name is Wilder, for God's sake, but she's not stupid and she's not naïve. Going out alone in this city after dark is both of those things, and Blake knows that. So, what really happened?

I'm going to find Blake, no matter what it takes.

I'm jolted out of the memory when Rook elbows me in the side, nodding towards a very angry Shortcake.

"*Blake,* that's not—I'm *so* sorry," I whisper, my eyes pleading with her for a chance to explain.

She looks like she's ready to rip me a new one when suddenly she cries out, doubling over and clutching her abdomen. Kai catches her before anyone else can get to her, and he scoops her up with an arm around her back and one under her knees. He's murmuring questions to her, too quietly for me to hear, and she nods in response.

Turning to me, her face is a mask of pain while she croaks out, "I can't do this right now. I need you to give me some space and let me process… all of this." She gestures around the room at me and my packmates.

Feeling my heart slowly breaking, I nod slowly. "Okay... I can... I can do that. Will you please consider hearing me out at some point? I'll get down on my knees and beg if I have to. I missed you so much, Short—*Blake*. I want to explain what happened the day I left. It's not at all what you think."

She looks wary, and rightfully so, if she thinks I abandoned her, but she finally gives me the tiniest nod before Kai carries her upstairs and away from me.

∼

LESS THAN TEN MINUTES LATER, Kai comes back down alone and calls for a pack meeting.

He gives us all a serious look I'm not used to seeing on his perpetually happy face. "This needs to be done while she can't hear us. Y'all need to hear this and I don't want your reactions scaring her."

I already feel sick, and I just know I'm not going to like whatever he's about to say.

He takes a deep breath before starting. "So, we all know Blake was drugged." Growls sound out around the room at that, and Kai cuts a glare at all of us, waiting until it's silent before speaking again.

"After speaking with her about her symptoms, it's clear she was experiencing the beginning stages of pre-heat,"

My jaw drops open in shock, as do several of the others.

"When we brought her here last night, we had a concierge nurse come by and draw blood and send it off to a private lab to get 24-hour results. I already had a pretty good idea of what she was drugged with, but I just got the email confirming it."

He pauses, and we're all surprised when it's Rook who snaps, "Get on with it already, I'm gonna lose it, man."

Clearing his throat, he murmurs, "It was Predatocin, or

more likely the half-assed street version, Heat Fleet. Y'all... her foster father was trying to induce an early heat."

The room explodes into chaos.

I cup my hand over my mouth and fight the urge to be sick as tears form in my eyes. Rook punches the wall. Kaspian strips naked and goes out to swim, which he only does when he's really stressed or anxious. Even Achilles has his head dropped into his hands, pulling at his hair roughly.

Turning towards us, breathing heavily and looking half feral, Rook growls. "I can't be here right now. I'm going to go check on Blake. Yell if you need me."

He stalks off, stomping up the stairs. I would be worried, but the guy is a marshmallow, and I have zero doubt Blake is going to plant herself firmly in his heart in no time at all. The urge to be sick is passing enough that I can look up and over at Kai, who looks absolutely devastated.

"Is she okay? Will she go into heat? What can we do to help? Does she need anything? Oh, god. If she goes into heat, she won't want me anywhere near her! We haven't even talked yet, let alone even began building a friendship again. What if—"

"Jesus, D, shut UP and let me talk for a damned second," he barks out at me, urging his Alpha influence into his voice.

Stunned, I close my mouth and stare at him with wide eyes. I can count on one hand the number of times he's used his Alpha bark on someone, and he has *never* used it on anyone in this pack.

He looks sheepish. "I'm sorry, man, but you were working up to an anxiety attack. Just take a deep breath and listen to me. Do you really think I didn't consider every single one of those things and get *very* detailed instructions from the nurse, *and* call a doctor to verify? I explained everything to Blake when she woke up this morning and gave her the first dose of heat suppressants this morning. She's going to be moody, have cramps like she did earlier, headaches, and be exhausted for the next week as she takes the suppressants. Followed by another week once she stops and they leave her system."

I take several deep breaths and realize he's right. There's nobody I trust more with my Shortcake than my pack, and if she doesn't want me with her, I'm happy she wants them.

Blowing out a breath I say, "Okay... so the best thing to do is just... pay attention, right? If she's not going to be feeling well, we need to have the things she'll need and want, which means I need to go to the store and stock up on supplies. Maybe y'all could give things to her, though? I'm worried she won't take them knowing they're from me."

There's sadness and a bit of exasperation in his expression when he looks at me. "Good god, D. You're the most melodramatic little shit I've ever known. She's going to come around, especially once you explain how she was lied to and how we never stopped looking for her. Give it time. She's going to come around. I feel it in my gut. I mean, she's our scent match. Do you really think she won't recognize that when the drugs wear off?"

"I...*I don't know.* She didn't recognize it when we were younger. I'm not even sure she knows what it means to be scent matched. I mean, for god's sake. I haven't even had a chance to explain everything to her. She hates me right now."

He rolls his eyes at me. "Are you really that dense? That girl still loves you so much, and it's written all over her face when she looks at you. You see her anger and resentment, but I see a girl who needs love and desperately wants to feel like she has a *home* again."

I gape at him, mind racing with all the times I was on the verge of an anxiety attack or woke up crying and being near Blake fixed it all. How I still sleep with her favorite stuffed animal she gave me after a particularly bad nightmare just weeks before she went missing. How, since the day I met her,

I've associated the scent of strawberries with *home.* Hell, the only candles I've ever let the pack burn are strawberry shortcake scented.

Was she feeling it too, even after all these years? Does she associate my scent with home?

Smirking at me, he leans back in the chair, holding his hands out palm up before clapping them together in the prayer position. "*Now* you're getting it. Thank the good lord." He chuckles.

It's my turn to roll my eyes at him, used to his theatrics. "Yeah, yeah. I'm a little slow on the uptake. Sue me. Do you think she knows?" I ask, simultaneously hoping she does and doesn't, struggling with wanting her to know so we can try to move on from the past and work on making her *our* Omega.

He looks pensive for a minute as he thinks. "Honestly? I think she might suspect but doesn't know for sure. And I'm fairly sure the meds are messing with that natural, primal feeling that screams 'mate' when your scent matches are near."

I nod, feeling relieved rather than nervous, like I was expecting. "Good. Okay, well, where do we go from here? You seem like you have a plan."

He raises his eyebrows incredulously. "Seriously?"

I roll my eyes once again. "I'm clueless here, Kai. Can you stop looking at me like I'm a moron and just help? I'm terrified I'm going to push her away."

His eyes soften and he nods. "Here's what we do…"

CHAPTER 5

BLAKE

I've been in the bathtub for close to a half an hour, but I haven't calmed down. After Kai brought me up here, he left me in the bathroom with more pain medicine for the cramps, a bright pink bath bomb he found under the sink, and an apology for not being honest about how he knew me. I forgave him pretty quickly for the last one, especially knowing I likely would never have come out of his room if he had told me who was waiting for me downstairs. I think it helped that I got a hit of his pumpkin pie scent during his "mandatory apology hug".

How can one pack smell *this* good? Kai smells like warm pumpkin pie, Achilles smells like lemon bars that have been *drenched* in powdered sugar, and I know I got a whiff of gingerbread and something fruity when I was downstairs with the other guys, too. Not to mention Hades' caramel apple scent that felt like coming home. It doesn't help that they're all stupidly good looking. But really… am I that upset about it all? I'm not sure.

I was eleven when Phil took me, and I'm starting to wonder why I trusted him when he told me D abandoned me.

It's not like he could have found me in the abandoned warehouse Phil kept me chained in while he tried to get Dianne to let him move back home. I do believe they adopted him because three weeks later, when we moved into the cottage out back, I never saw Hades through the basement window. That doesn't mean I'm ready to forgive him, though. I need to know what happened, and why he never came back.

With that thought on repeat in my brain and the pain meds in full effect, I drain the tub and get dressed. As I'm pulling my sweatshirt over my head, there's a knock at the door. I open it, expecting to find Kai or even Achilles. Instead, it's the one man I haven't met yet, even in passing.

He's shockingly tall, easily six and a half feet, and huge. The guy looks like a solid wall of muscle. I drag my eyes up off of his chest, and up, and up. Until I meet a pair of pale blue eyes that remind me of ice chips. They're so startling I almost don't notice how intimidating he looks. He has black, chin length hair, a broad nose with a black ring through it and thick eyebrows, one of which is also pierced with a black stud. Then if you take in the tattoos that cover both arms and his throat, he's someone I would be terrified to meet under any other circumstances.

This close, I can smell his thick orange creamsicle scent and I'm instantly relaxed, knowing this was the fruity scent I picked up downstairs. I don't think I've ever smelled anything so good in my life. Before I can lean in and beg to use him as my personal teddy bear, I remember I quite literally have never met this man before. Snapping my eyes to his, I catch his tiny grin before he smooths his face into a mask of stoicism. Not necessarily cold, but definitely not warm and fuzzy, either.

I clear my throat. "I'm so sorry. That was probably super weird. I'm Blake." I smile up at him, hoping to soften him up a little.

It works for a second, and I see his lips curl up before the mask is back. The deepest voice I've ever heard reaches my ears when he says, "I know. My name is Rook, I'm Hades' brother."

My eyebrows shoot up, surprised, and he nods.

"My parents adopted him seven years ago," he says, giving me a pointed look. "Listen, I'm not here to tell you what to do, but I think you should give him a real chance to explain. Things went down a lot differently than you think they did, and it's not fair—"

I quickly cut him off. "I know," I say, raising one brow.

He gives me a clear look of confusion. "You… know?"

I pat his chest so he'll step back, and I can get through the door. "Yeah, big guy. I know. And I will absolutely hear him out eventually, but I need food before I even consider having that conversation. So, if you're done being all mountain-like, can we please go eat?"

Releasing a tiny chuckle, he asks, "Mountain-like?"

Rolling my eyes and walking backwards, I sass back, "Yeah. You know, tall and immovable?"

I'm completely caught off guard by the full bellied laugh he lets out, and I trip on the top step. I brace myself for the familiar pain of falling down the stairs when two giant hands wrap around my waist and lift me to safety.

He chuckles again. "Woah there, Angel. That ain't the stairway to heaven. Why are you in such a rush to get down it?"

I smirk back at him, loving his laughs. "Why, whatever do you mean? I made the BFG laugh. I was running out to tell the townspeople of my achievement," I tease.

Furrowing his brows and fighting a smile, he asks, "What the hell is a BFG?"

I'm giggling uncontrollably at this point when I explain, "BFG means Big Friendly Giant. And I called you that because

I have a feeling that you, big guy, are exactly that once you crack that thick outer shell you've got."

He laughs again. "You've got me there, Angel. Now get on downstairs before D has a heart attack or wears a groove in the floor," he says as he finally releases my hips.

Before I head downstairs, I need him to understand something. So, I turn around to face him.

"Need somethin', Blake?" he asks, brows scrunching together in confusion.

"Umm.. yeah. I just need you to know that even though I'm willing to hear him out, that doesn't mean I'm ready or willing to forgive and forget yet. I have seven years of built up hurt and resentment. I can't let it all go in a day, even if it hurts him to be kept at arm's length." I trail off quietly, waiting to be asked to leave. Or to be told I'm not worth the effort.

He steps closer to me, gently brushing a lock of hair behind my ear.

"I respect you more for your honesty than I would if you just gave in for the sake of keeping the peace with an old friend. I won't pretend to know how you feel, but please know that any one of us is always willing to lend a shoulder to cry on, or a hand to hold when things get hard. You were worth every minute of searching, Blake," he murmurs.

Whispering out my thanks, I realize I really am thankful to have met these men, even under the less than stellar circumstances. I'm blushing like crazy when I run downstairs and just as my foot hits the bottom, there's a knock at the door. I don't see any of the guys around. So, after checking the peephole and seeing the pizza guy, I open the door, my stomach growling in anticipation.

The guy is probably my age, and maybe only 4 inches taller than me, making him close to five foot eight. As soon as I get the door open fully, he leers at me and I can *feel* his eyes on me like a physical touch. So even though I've had a shower *and* a bath today, I feel dirty.

Licking his lips in an over-exaggerated way, he makes a show of inhaling deeply. His voice is nasal and high when he speaks. "Damn, girl. I thought *I* was the one bringing the snack. I didn't realize you already were one."

He smirks at me widely, leaning in to tug on a lock of my long hair. My mouth drops open in shock as I quickly smack his hand away. When Rook did it, I liked it, and it made me feel comforted. When this guy does it, I get the urge to vomit for the second time today. Leaning just the tiniest bit closer to read his name tag, I try my best not to give in to the panic beginning to claw at my throat from the unwanted touch.

"Listen, Kenny, is it? I'm really not—"

Suddenly, a vicious growl comes from behind me and I'm enveloped in the scent of fresh, spicy gingerbread as a toned arm wraps around my waist. Kenny's face has gone completely white, but that doesn't stop him from opening his mouth again. Clearing his throat and squaring his scrawny shoulders, he lifts his chin at the Alpha behind me.

"Listen, buddy. I don't know who you think you are, but it's not really fair to assume one Alpha can handle a fine piece of ass like this during a heat. I mean, look at you! You'd probably break—"

He doesn't get a chance to finish his sentence before the man, who I'm guessing is Kaspian, steps out from behind me and punches him in the face. Hard enough to knock him out right there on the porch. He's shaking out his hand when he turns back to look at me. His lips are set in a straight line, but his eyes are guarded like he's worried I might be upset with him for that show of violence.

You'd think after being hit my whole life I would be, but I'm not.

My perfume blooms in the small entryway as he slams the

door closed. Sucking in a deep breath, his dark brown eyes dilate so far, they're almost black. The only true difference between Kaspian and Kairo seems to be their eye color. Where Kai's are a honey brown with golden flecks and seem to radiate light, his twins are twice as intense and such a deep color you almost can't tell they're brown. With him reacting to my perfume like this? You would never be able to tell they were brown at all.

His scent deepens in response to mine, surrounding me with the smell of gingerbread and sweet icing. It reminds me of that old children's story about the witch who lived in a gingerbread house. You know, the one with the bratty kids who stuff her in an oven or something. I giggle, picturing this giant man in a witch's hat and bent over a cauldron.

He smirks, stepping directly into my space and using the knuckle on his pointer finger to tilt my head up. He leans so close his lips brush my ear as he speaks, sending my giggles to a screeching halt as I shiver.

"What's so funny, Trouble?"

Letting out another breathy giggle, I open my big mouth and blurt out, "I was just comparing you to that old witch who lived in a gingerbread house and wondering what you'd look like in a witch's hat."

I slap my hand over my mouth as he backs up just far enough to look me in the eyes, raising his eyebrows at me.

"We're going to circle back to that, because I think the guys need to hear the way your brain works too, Little One. But first, I wanted to apologize. I don't know what you've been through, and I hit that punk in front of you without considering that it might trigger you in some way. Are you okay?" he asks quietly.

Needing to reassure him, I tentatively bring my hand up to cup his jaw, marveling at the scratchy feel of his stubble against my palm. Lowering my voice and pulling his face in to meet mine, I say, "RIP pizza delivery guy." And wink at him.

This time I was trying to make someone laugh, but it still startles me when he lets out the loudest laugh I've ever heard. It's so loud that all four of the other guys come running in with confused looks on their faces, which just makes me laugh harder as we turn around to face them. Tears are streaming down my face, and I'm leaning back on Kaspian, who's also still laughing as he holds me against his chest.

Achilles steps forward. "Uhh, does somebody wanna explain why y'all are laughing like lunatics, Blake is crying, and I just got a call from Pete's Pizza wondering where their delivery boy is?"

We once again burst into hysterics, and Kaspian laughs so hard he starts coughing and falls on his butt, taking me down with him. So now I'm sitting in his lap on the floor, gasping for breath as I try desperately to calm down and explain what happened.

"So… just know it wasn't my fault."

Four sets of eyebrows raise at my statement as I stand. I smile sheepishly at them, acutely aware of Hades standing there with a mix of emotions playing across his face. Not wanting to dissect those at the moment, I go on.

"The delivery guy, Kenny—" Kaspian lets out a growl at that, making me roll my eyes. "Anyway, like I was saying before I was so *rudely* interrupted," I pause, giving him a side eye. He just winks back at me, unbothered by my glare. "The delivery guy knocked and none of you were around, so after checking the peephole, I opened it. He said something kinda sleazy. Kaspian knocked him out, and I gave his eulogy. See? No big deal."

I was fully expecting the shocked expressions and dropped jaws, but what I wasn't expecting was the growl that sounded like it was torn straight from Rook's throat. I think I might be a little twisted inside… Because as soon as he growls and starts to stalk towards me like a predator seeking its prey, my perfume explodes out of me, and my panties are instantly soaked. My face flames when they all groan, knowing my reactions and scent are a lot stronger than they normally would be because of the drugs.

He stops less than an inch from my face and bends down so his nose is practically touching mine. Growl subdued to a low rumble in his chest, he pins me with a look that makes my Omega instincts preen at the protectiveness in his icy gaze.

"Angel, what's the first thing we learn as kids? The one rule every parent drills into their kids' heads before they go out in public?"

My cheeks flush because *I don't know.* The only thing my parents ever told me was to cover the bruises and keep my mouth shut. And Phil just kept me locked in the basement. I must be showing my confusion on my face because understanding dawns in his eyes as he seamlessly switches tactics and lowers his voice so only I can hear. I think the guys must know we need space because they all leave the room, muttering about warming up the pizza and picking out a movie.

"Blake, one of the most important things we were taught as kids is to avoid strangers. I know you're an adult, but we're only a few miles from where the twins rescued you, and I don't want to risk somebody findin' out where you are. I'm beggin' you. For your safety and my sanity, please be careful at all times and stick by one of us when we leave, okay? Can you please do that for me, Angel?"

My eyes are misting over at the care he's taking while explaining something so simple to me. He's not making me feel stupid or sheltered or weird. He's being honest because he's worried… about *me.* Nodding quickly and sniffling, I throw my arms around his shoulders and whimper as he purrs and hugs me back hard.

"I'm so sorry, Rook. I didn't know. Except for the year I had Hades, I was kept locked up away from people my whole life. I didn't think. I just wanted to help."

He wraps his arms around me even tighter and holds my head against his neck so I can breathe in his creamsicle scent while he purrs. After a minute of silence while I calm down, he speaks.

"Blake… please *never* apologize for how you grew up. They did those things *to* you. You didn't ask for them or deserve them. From everything Hades has told us, you were the sweetest, sassiest kid he'd ever known. Meeting you now, even with your broken heart, I'm inclined to agree. And listen, Angel, whenever you're ready, I'd like to hear all about your childhood, okay? We will go over everything you should have learned growing up and we'll do anything you missed out on because of the shitty hand you were dealt. And we'll start right now. Is there anything you always wanted to do as a kid but never got to?"

I take a minute to really think about it, and only one thing comes to mind.

Turning to Rook, I tell him, "I want to learn how to swim."

CHAPTER 6

BLAKE

The big guy took my idea and ran with it. He kissed me on the forehead and sent me off with the guys to eat my pizza, (which was even better than I remembered). Only to show back up an hour later with bags full of pool toys, a bathing suit for me, and arm floaties. I gaped at him as he walked in the door carrying bags full of pink plastic and foam, completely unashamed.

He didn't want to start swimming last night since it had already been dark, so instead he led me up to his room and requested I use it to sleep in. Rook's face turned bright pink when I asked him why, and seeing this huge, intimidating man blush melted my heart a bit.

"It's just... well. You slept in Kai's room last night and that's totally fine. My instincts are just demanding I keep you safe after everything we talked about tonight, and I would really like it if you would stay in here. I can either stay on the floor or I can room with D, whatever you're comfortable with. I wasn't sure if you would be nervous staying alone in a new place now that you're clear-headed. But if I'm overstepping or being too Alpha, please just—"

I stop his rambling by stepping close and hesitantly wrapping my arms around his middle. "Rook?"

He clears his throat and hugs me back, letting out a deep sigh. "Yeah, Angel?"

Giving him a small smile, I tilt my head back to look up at his pretty eyes. "I would love to stay in your room with you."

His eyes go wide and he chokes. "Wait, really? You'd let me stay in here with you?"

Nodding quickly, I start to explain, "I trust you, Rook. I've been here less than two days and you've done nothing but show me you'll put my needs first. Even when you were asking me to talk to Hades, you made it clear that you respected my need to wait. You haven't pushed me on it once. And when I told you I didn't know something most *children* know, you explained it to me in the gentlest way possible without making me feel dumb. I'm not ready to talk about everything, but if I can make you feel better by sleeping in here, then I'm going to. And honestly, I am nervous. So, I would really like it if you would stay. Please."

The smile that takes over his face steals the breath from my lungs. He looks like I just gave him the world, when all I did was agree to let him comfort me and soothe his instincts. We get ready for bed separately. He gives me one of his t-shirts and a brand-new pink toothbrush. Then, he heads off to the bathroom in the hall, leaving me to use the massive bathroom attached to his bedroom.

After brushing my teeth and throwing my hair into a messy bun, I put on a pair of boy shorts. The soft navy-blue shirt is absolutely *covered* in Rook's orange creamsicle scent. I bring it to my nose, breathing it in so it fills my lungs and eases my nerves. It's so soft, but not like it was made that way, more like it's been through the wash so many times it lost all structure. I know it has to be one of his favorites, and the fact that he wants me to wear it makes me feel all warm and fuzzy inside.

A knock on the bedroom door startles me out of my thoughts and forces me to pull the shirt away from my nose and hop into the bed. Getting under the covers and calling out that I'm decent, Rook walks back into the room. His eyes darken, and his nostrils flare when he sees me in his shirt. The vanilla in his sweet creamsicle scent deepening until it's almost caramelized in its intensity.

"Good lord, Angel. You look better in my favorite shirt than I do. I may have to insist you keep that." His eyes trail down my upper body, making me shiver despite the thick comforter covering my legs.

With a tilt of my head, I study him, wondering why he would want me to keep his favorite shirt. "But... it's your favorite. I can't keep something you love so much. Why would you want to get rid of it?"

Smiling softly, he sits down on the edge of the bed facing me so we're only inches apart.

"You are the first person I've ever met, aside from my family and this pack, that hasn't asked me for anything, even once. And you don't *expect me* to take care of you or buy you things. Growing up wealthy the way I did, I never knew if people wanted to be around me for *me,* or if they were just trying to get something from me. I know you're not like that, though, and it makes me *want* to do things for you. Especially when those things involve seeing you in my favorite shirt." He ends his speech with a sexy smirk.

At this point, I think my cheeks may be permanently pink with how much I've been blushing, and I grab his hand, looking up at him through my eyelashes.

"Rook... I want you to know I would *never* expect anything from you. And I have some money saved up, so you don't need to feel you have to buy me things or buy my lo— affection." I say, quickly changing what I was about to say, because what kind of crazy person falls in love in two days?

He may look pretty and smell incredible, but that doesn't mean I love him.

His eyes soften, and I'm pretty sure he knows what I was about to say, but again he doesn't push. Getting up off the side of the bed, he makes a bed on the floor using an air mattress I didn't see him bring in.

When he's finished, he turns back to me and says, "Let's get some sleep. We'll start your swimming lessons first thing in the morning."

I nod, laying down and curling up on my side so I can see him down on his makeshift bed. Leaning up, he turns out the lamp and rolls to face me. After a few minutes of silence, he speaks.

"I know you don't expect anything, Angel. That's why I'm going to do everything in my power to give you the world."

He reaches up and twines our fingers together, and I fall asleep with his hand in mine and a smile on my face for the first time in seven years.

I'M TRYING to work up the courage to walk out there in a bathing suit. Rook picked me out a modest one-piece, saying I was already going to be vulnerable in the water, and he didn't want me to feel exposed on top of that. He also said that once we got back to their home in Lockwood, we would go shopping since my wardrobe currently consists of clothes I grew out of five years ago. I'm not gonna lie; I cried after trying to refuse and being firmly but gently shot down. Nobody has ever put my feelings or needs first before, except for maybe Hades, before he left me.

But I'm not going to think about that today, or the

looming heavy conversation. Today I'm going to enjoy what I was told by Kairo and Kaspian would be "the most epicly amazing, Olympian-level swimming lessons in the history of water". I couldn't help but laugh at their antics, because they had been going out of their way all morning to make me laugh.

It started with breakfast when the twins started a food fight, managing to peg Hades in the face with an over-easy egg. I probably laughed harder than I should have but come on. He deserved it a little. I also caught a wistful smile on his face when I laughed, so I don't feel too bad.

Rook let me try his coffee since I'd never had it before, and I think I might be in love. He told me we would try new coffee in every place we go, because apparently, we're going places. I don't really know how or when it happened, but apparently this pack of gorgeous men has taken me in as their own, and I'm starting to think it might not be so bad.

"WHAT IF I DROWN?" I don't mean to whine, but it comes out anyway.

Rook snorts, looking at me with a single eyebrow raised. "Angel, we've been over this no less than a dozen times now. Not a single man in this pool would let you drown. Hell, neither would the two saps sitting over there pretending not to watch your every move."

He points to Hades and Achilles, who are currently perched in beach chairs and, if I listen to Rook, pretending to read while actually watching me. When all five men came out in just their swim trunks half an hour ago, I nearly fainted. I'd never seen a man shirtless before, let alone five of the most perfect men I've ever seen. But did I say that? Or something equally nice?

No.

The first words out of my mouth are, "Wow, there are like, SO many nipples out right now." At which point I proceeded to slap my hands over my fire engine red cheeks and consider drowning myself in the shallow end. Of course, the guys laughed like hyenas for a solid ten minutes before we could actually start lessons. Then we did fifteen minutes of water safety at the edge of the pool. Which leads me to right now. With me sitting on the ledge at the deep end whining because I'm too scared to jump in, despite there being three very handsome men there to catch me.

Kas pulls on my big toe gently. "Come on, my dry little duckling, we need to know you can at least keep your head above water. Although I don't think any of us would let you out of our sights long enough to fall into water... but some of the bathtubs back home are pretty deep." He smirks at me.

I giggle. "Did you just call me your dry little duckling? That's weird."

He chucks my chin softly. "Yeah, but it got you to smile and stop panicking, didn't it?"

These men are terrible for my intentionally hardened heart. If I'm not careful, I might fall in love with them. And the thought of falling in love kind of gives me hives. Or... it did three days ago.

Jolting when his hand strokes my cheek, I nod. "Alright, let's do this."

THREE HOURS LATER, I've successfully done five laps of the pool and my fingers and toes all resemble raisins.

I pop up at the end of the pool and see Kai holding out a towel for me. Letting him pull me up, I wrap my arms around his neck in a hug.

"I did it! Thank you, guys, so much for teaching me and being so patient. You have no idea how much it means to me."

Kai hugs me back tight before letting me move to hug his brother as he says, "You don't need to thank us, Sugar. We did this as much for you as we did to alleviate our own fears."

Moving from Kas to Rook, I'm practically giddy with excitement. "Either way, you gave me a skill I always wanted but was never able to learn. I'm so happy," I say, smiling up at all three of them.

Suddenly, I'm scooped up and thrown over Kas' shoulder, causing me to squeal with laughter.

I can hear the smile in his voice as he says, "Come on, Swedish Fish, let's go get some lunch."

We all settle on Thai food for lunch because when I told them I'd never had it before, Achilles called it blasphemy and proceeded to order enough food to feed an army.

"Trust me, ma douce fraise, you live with five grown men now. We'll finish it all and then ask you if you want dessert," he says with a laugh.

I thought he was kidding. But they dig into the food the minute it arrives, and each has a second plate before I even finish my first. As soon as I took my first bite of Pad Thai, I let out a loud moan that had more than one of the Alphas in the room letting out a low growl.

I sheepishly shrug my shoulders and swallow before I speak. "Sorry. I didn't realize how delicious it would be. I think Pad Thai and egg rolls might be my new favorite foods. I know this place isn't home, so are there any good Thai places near your house? Where exactly is it, anyway?" I ask, taking a drink of my Thai tea.

The guys all look at Rook, who clears his throat. "So... here's the thing. Our pack house is in Lockwood."

I choke at that, coughing and spraying orange liquid out of my mouth. Thank whoever built this house that they put in hardwood. "I'm sorry, did you just say you live in *Lockwood*? Like… across the country, Lockwood? What are you guys doing here if you live there? You're not working, right?"

The guys all look at each other with some sort of silent communication and eventually turn to Hades, who looks apprehensive as he faces me. Taking a deep breath, he locks eyes with me.

"I think it's time we had that talk."

CHAPTER 7

HADES

I'm sweatin' like a sinner in church waiting for Blake to decide if she's ready or not. The strawberry in her scent, which has been strong since she got here, is souring the longer we sit here. It's obvious she doesn't want to do this, but she needs to know what really happened. Not to mention all the lengths we've gone to in order to find her cute ass. Her minuscule nod has me letting out a sigh of relief. "Would you mind if we sat out back on the swing by the pool? It's not too cold out, but I can grab a blanket if you want."

To my surprise, it's Kaspian that hops up. "I'll grab you a hoodie, little popsicle. Hang tight for a sec."

He sends a wink in her direction, earning him a beautiful giggle. I'm hoping after this long overdue conversation we can finally get to know each other again. Honestly, though, even if she's not ready, that's fine. I'll wait forever for this girl.

Kas comes bounding back down the stairs with a hoodie in hand. "Come on, Frosty. Arms up," he says as he drapes the hoodie over her head.

Through her continued giggles, she finally asks the question I'm sure we're all wondering. "What's with the random nicknames, Kas?"

He actually looks kind of sheepish when he answers. "Well... all the other guys have cute nicknames for you, and that's awesome, but I love seeing you laugh. And you laugh every time I use some weird, random nickname on you. So, I'm gonna keep it up until something sticks." This former Olympian, six-foot four Alpha, is blushing and nervous in the face of this tiny redhead who's a good foot shorter than him and a hundred pounds soaking wet.

Blake looks positively giddy. "That might be the sweetest thing I've ever heard." She pops up onto her feet on the couch, putting her just high enough that she can stand on her toes and kiss his cheek. "Thanks, giant egg roll." She winks, turning toward the sliding door that leads to the pool as Kas barks out a laugh and the other guys chuckle. Turning back to me, she raises a single eyebrow. "You coming or what?"

And god *damn* if that sass doesn't make me want her even more.

I don't want to piss her off by smirking, so I just nod my head and follow her out to the swing. I sit down first, and she sits down a good foot away from me, curled up as tight as she possibly can be in the corner, with only her face peeking out of the blanket. It reminds me so much of that first night so many years ago that it almost makes me cry.

Sucking in a few deep, steadying breaths, I begin to explain everything starting from that night. How I went to meet the guys, but the police picked us up and they kept me out of the home. How the Beaumonts asked if they could adopt me and how they had lined up some friends to foster and eventually adopt Blake so we wouldn't be separated. When I get to that part, she cries. Hesitantly, I scoot a little closer and link my pinkie with hers. She doesn't look thrilled, but she also doesn't pull away, so I'll take the win.

I pick back up with the story starting with the next morning when we went to the house. How Dianne told us she had followed me out the night before and was now missing, and her eyes go wide. A gasp gets caught in her throat and she chokes, looking at me with understanding dawning on her features. She knocks my pinky away and twines our hands together, tears rapidly falling down her cheeks.

"Hades, that next morning when I woke up to find you gone, Phil told me you had been adopted and chose not to come back to the house because you didn't want to see me again. Dianne had kicked him out, and he took me. I was chained in an abandoned warehouse for three weeks before he talked her into letting him live in the cottage out back. He kept me locked in the basement there until I escaped, and the twins found me," she sobs out.

I'm. Fucking. Wrecked.

"You were here the entire time?" I whisper, tears forming in my own eyes.

She gives me a tiny nod. "When you didn't come back for me, I assumed Phil was telling the truth, and I just… gave up. I followed his rules, accepted his punishments, and stayed silent in that basement until I turned eighteen and knew he couldn't legally get me back. I was *so* angry with you for leaving me, but memories of our year together are what kept me sane. Some nights when Phil was passed out drunk, I could sneak onto the roof of the cottage and lay there to look up at the stars and wonder if you ever did the same. If you ever thought of me at all…"

Tears are dripping down my face and I make no move to wipe them away, *needing* her to see how sick I feel. That I didn't know. I didn't know that she was right *fucking* here the whole damned time. I grab her and pull her onto my lap, desperately needing the contact. She stiffens up momentarily, but she must need comfort as much as I do because she relaxes quickly and tucks her face into my neck as I keep explaining.

"Blake… Shortcake. I didn't know. If I had had any idea you were still here, the guys and I would have done *anything* to get you out of that house. We spent the last seven years searching all over the world for you. Rook was already eighteen and had access to his trust when the Beaumonts adopted me, and he helped me co-found our company so we would have better resources to find you. I know Phil isolated you for a long time, but have you heard of the Omega Haven Project?"

~

Blake

MY MOUTH PARTS IN SHOCK. "*You* founded the OHP? I've seen your company on the news so many times breaking up Omega trafficking rings."

He nods, pulling me tighter into his chest. "Me and my pack. Shortcake, we founded the OHP to find *you*. I will thank every god there is that we've been able to help find and rescue Omegas all over the world, but I will always be more grateful that it brought us back to you. I will never forgive myself for not knowing you were under my nose the whole fucking time. We've been back to Asheville no less than a dozen times since you went missing, and if I had known…"

I reach a hand up, just barely covering his mouth with my hand. "D… you couldn't have known. The basement was completely soundproofed. There were industrial strength scent blockers on all the doors and windows, and he only fed me once every few days, so I would be too weak to fight back or try to run away. You aren't responsible for the actions of that monster. I'm not going to lie. It might take some time to let go of almost a decade's worth of anger and resentment, but knowing the truth helps take away the worst of the sting."

Knowing what I do now, I can feel my anger receding quickly, and I drop my hand as I sink further into him. I don't know how long it will take to gain back that trust, even if it was never really broken in the first place, but I'm willing to try. He pulls my face into his neck as he runs his fingers through my hair, and I just breathe him in. His rich caramel apple scent in my nose and lungs makes me feel like I've been slowly drowning and finally broke the surface to breathe. I suck in deep gulps of air, wanting to sear his scent into my nose permanently, so I never have to be without it again.

Burying his nose in my hair as a deep purr starts up in his chest, he whispers, "I missed you so fucking much, Shortcake. I don't know if you're ready for this yet or if you ever will be with me, but now that I have you back, I need you to know that this pack wants you. We want you to be our Omega. I'm sure you're not ready for any kind of bond or lifelong commitment. So instead, please consider this my pack's formal request to court you, Blake Wilder Connolly. Let us prove to you, let *me* prove to you, that we can be the men you deserve."

I'm stunned... but then again, am I really? From the moment I woke up in this strange house with these strange men, I've felt at home. The only time I ever felt truly at peace was when I was with Hades or surrounded by his scent, and now I've felt that with every single member of this pack. Even Achilles, which from what I understand, isn't common to feel with Betas. With a sudden moment of shocking clarity, I turn my face to his.

"D... are we scent matched?" I ask him quietly.

He rewards my question with a blinding smile and a burst of deep caramel in his scent as he nods frantically. Then shocks the heck out of me when he leans forward and kisses me on the lips hard, just once. And it's over too quickly for me to even process that it happened.

I bring my fingers to my lips, trying to wrap my head around the fact that Hades, the boy I loved so much as a child, just gave me my first kiss. I don't even think he realizes it.

"God, Blake. I've suspected it for so long, since after you were taken, really. I took your stuffed animal with me when I moved to Lockwood with the guys because it was the only thing I could find that smelled like you. And when that finally faded, I literally bought in bulk strawberry shortcake scented candles. When the guys and I bought our house a few years ago, I put one of those candles in every room of the house, so I always felt like you were with me. I would even leave them burning while I slept. The guys were so worried I was going to burn down the house they found me a shortcake scented pillow shaped like a strawberry."

Kiss forgotten for now, I gasp, laughing. "Stop it. No, they did not." That has to be the cutest, saddest thing I've ever heard.

He nods, clearly happy he could get a laugh out of me after such a heavy conversation. "They did. And I take that fucking thing *everywhere*. In fact, hold on. I'll be right back."

He sets me gently on the swing and sprints into the house, flipping off the guys who are all crowded onto one couch, pretending not to listen. I give them a small finger wave and a wink, causing several of them to chuckle as Kas rolls his eyes playfully back at me. Less than a minute later, Hades comes sprinting back out of the house. He dives onto the swing, causing it to swing violently as I squeal until I'm thrown sideways back into his lap.

When I finally right myself, the overgrown child is giving me a cheeky grin and holding up a giant stuffed strawberry with eyes and a mini angel food cake hat. I gasp in delight when I notice it even has green eyes like mine and suspicious looking brown dots that I think are meant to be freckles. Leaning in to get a closer look, I snort before laughing loudly.

"Did you... really... draw freckles... on the strawberry's eyes... with... a brown sharpie?" I wheeze out between bouts of laughter.

He looks a little embarrassed now, but he's still smiling when he answers shyly, "It smelled like you. I wanted it to look like you, too."

God, that's too cute.

"Does it have a name?" I ask with a smirk when my laughter finally dies down.

Looking at me incredulously, he asks, "Did you really just ask me that, *Shortcake?*"

I have another lightbulb moment. "You named your strawberry Shortcake?" I ask, my eyes misting over as he nods. I swear, I'm not usually this weepy, but I think Kai said moodiness was a side effect of the meds I'm on. That reminds me, "Hey, would I be able to see a doctor before we leave? I know you guys said a nurse saw me while I was... asleep... but I would like to see a doctor and be fully conscious."

Throwing me a mildly concerned look, he calls out for Kai.

A neatly styled blonde head pops out of the door. "Yeah?"

Hades runs his fingers through my hair again as I hold Shortcake Junior to my chest, enjoying the softness of it. "Would you mind calling that concierge service back and seeing if they can get a doctor out here tomorrow morning for an appointment for Blake? The earliest one they have available."

Achilles pops his head out. "Uhh, so about tomorrow." He grimaces. "I just got a call from Amelia, and we're needed at HQ, like, as soon as possible. The jet will be here tomorrow at two."

I feel an irrational spike of jealousy when he says another

woman's name, and a tiny growl slips out of my throat. All three men look at me in shock before Kai's eyes widen in realization. Walking over to me and cupping my face in his large hands, he calmly reassures me, correctly guessing the reason for the sudden shift in my mood.

"Sugar, Amelia is a female Alpha in an all-female pack. They've been bonded to their Omega, Jane, for over ten years. I swear you will *never* have anything to worry about with us because we only want *you.* You'll get a chance to meet everyone we work with if you want. OHP only employs bonded men and women for the safety of the Omegas we rescue. Which means we're invited to lots of family dinners and holidays, and now we have an Omega to brag about. If you'll let us."

Hades glares at him from over my shoulder. "She hasn't actually given an answer yet, you dick. Don't pressure her."

Rolling his eyes, Kai lightly growls back. "I would never, and you know that. I know y'all just made up, and that's great, but that doesn't mean you get to act like an overb—"

"Yes." My whispered word cuts off their argument and is followed by absolute silence.

All three men turn to look at me, but it's Achilles who speaks from directly in front of me. "Yes what, Blake? Be very specific about what you're agreeing to here."

I give the men a big, cheesy grin as I say, "Yes, I would like to accept your formal request to court me, however that may look to you, both individually and as a pack."

It's silent for another minute before absolute *chaos* erupts. I'm picked up and swung around by Kai as Kaspian and Rook join us outside with twin looks of confusion on their faces.

"Somebody wanna fill us in?" Rook asks.

I peek at them over Kai's shoulder and, as casually as possible, respond, "I'm not really sure what happened. It's all a bit of a blur. One minute I was holding Shortcake Junior overreacting to hearing Achilles say another woman's name, and the next thing I know I've accepted an invitation of courtship from a group of crazy ass men who searched for a stranger for seven years." I smirk at them, waiting to see when it clicks.

I'm not disappointed.

Rook steals me out of Kai's arms to give me a bear hug while Kas shoves his twin in the pool, curling himself around my back to hug both of us. If this is what pack life is like, even some of the time? I can't wait.

CHAPTER 8

KAIRO

*B*lake and I need to be up bright and early this morning to meet with the doctor, and I'm quickly learning that our girl is *not* a morning person. Leaning over the side of the bed, I stroke my hand down the side of her perfect face as she grumbles at me.

"Come on, Sugar. You've gotta get up. I need you up and at 'em before the doctor gets here to take your blood and whatever else you wanted done." She gives me the cutest damned grunt in response, turning onto her back and peeking one eye open as I start to pull the covers off.

Shaking her head and crooking her finger at me, I lean down, thinking she just wants to whisper so she doesn't wake up any further.

Boy, am I wrong.

The minute I'm within reach, she wraps her arms around my neck and *pulls.* How someone so small can get so much leverage is beyond me, and before I even have a chance to catch myself, I'm on top of her and we're touching from chest to toe. I would normally say head to toe, but considering she only reaches my chest on a good day, we'll go with that.

As I chuckle and move to roll off of her, I get a *strong* hit of her scent that goes straight to my dick, and without conscious thought, I groan and grind myself into her pussy. With only two thin layers separating us, I can feel the heat coming off of her core, and I growl, forcing myself to pull away. Blake hasn't been this forward once since we met her, and reaching up to feel her forehead, I can feel that she's burning up.

My eyes widen. "Oh shit. Sugar, I think you're having a mini-heat flare."

She moans, trying to grind herself against my thigh. "Kai… I need you."

I grab her chin firmly and force her to look into my eyes. Her pupils are huge, but she's definitely coherent, which erases my last reservations about this. If she were lost to the fog, I would've talked her through it without touching her.

"Blake, I need you to tell me with your words *exactly* what you need right now. Have you ever done this before?" I ask gently and without judgement, needing her to know I don't care one way or another.

Her cheeks flame, and she looks embarrassed. "I've never done any of this before," she whispers.

My brows raise and I decide that while we need to take care of this flare-up, we can do it in the gentlest way possible. So, I ask her the most important questions first. "Sugar, have you ever had an orgasm before?" She shakes her head, writhing slightly on the bed. I nod, expecting as much after her confession. "Have you touched yourself at all? Ever?"

Shaking her head again, her voice is quiet as she replies. "No, I was too scared to do it with Phil right upstairs and even if he left, I didn't want to risk him scenting anything when he came back." Her cheeks are on fire right now, and I doubt it's from the sudden surge of hormones raging through her body.

I nod. "Okay then, Baby. If you're okay with it, here's what we're gonna do. I'm going to start by kissing you," I say, leaning in close so my lips brush hers as I talk. "Has anybody kissed these pretty lips before?"

She nods slowly, her eyes lighting up as she bites her lip. "Hades did last night, just once. It was quick, and I don't think he realized it was my first kiss," she says shyly.

Smirking, I brush my lips against hers gently. "He's an idiot, but he's a lucky idiot. We're all so happy to have you here Blake. You're everything we've ever wanted and more. Thank you for staying and for hearing him out, but most importantly, for trusting me to care for you right now."

Her eyes are misting over, and I don't want this to be tainted with tears, so I sit back on my heels and look down at her, lowering my voice as I command, "Strip, Sugar."

I'm not using my Alpha bark at all, but she still immediately complies, making my dick throb. I wonder if she'll be so compliant every time we're in the bedroom, or if she'll want to take charge sometimes. The thought makes me shudder.

God, I hope she wants to try dominating me.

I've only ever had one-night stands, and even those were only before we began looking for Blake. Because of that, I have never once felt comfortable enough with someone to bring up my fantasies. Now definitely isn't the time for that, either, but I'm hoping it will be soon. The stigma around Alphas can be hard to deal with for someone like me. I'm completely comfortable being dominant when I want or need to, but it shouldn't make me less of an Alpha to want my Omega to dominate me in the bedroom sometimes.

Blake shedding her clothes quickly snaps me out of the fantasy of my sweet girl ordering me onto my knees for her. Within a minute, she's fully naked underneath me, and I've never seen anything more gorgeous in my life.

I groan, taking in every inch of her. "Goddamn, Sugar. You are absolutely stunning."

She blushes, a whine slipping out of her throat as reaches

for my neck and drags my face down to hers in a deep, messy kiss. I can tell she's new at this and that, combined with her scent that's currently saturating the room, has me hard as a fucking rock. But this is about her, not me. I can take care of this in the shower later. Taking one last long pull from her strawberry flavored mouth, I scoot back even further on the bed. I pull her thighs wide and up over my own, so she's bared completely to me.

"I want you to do what feels the best for you, okay Blake? This is about helping *you* discover what feels good without worrying about what anybody else thinks."

She nods frantically. "Okay. Just *please* touch me, kiss me, *something*. It hurts, Kai," she whimpers out.

I cover her hand with mine and guide them to her soaked slit. Gently gliding our fingers through her slick, I slide them up to her clit and begin rubbing slow circles around it, my fingers showing hers what to do. She mewls, and I increase my pressure, causing her noises to grow in volume until she's moaning loudly. Taking my fingers away, I encourage her with my words to keep going, to find what feels good.

"That's it, baby. You're doing so good. Do you want to try a little more?" I ask, bringing my fingers back to her pussy that's absolutely gushing slick now. She nods again, but I need to hear it out loud. "Words, Sugar. I need your words."

She whines. "*Yes*. Yes, please. I think…"

I can tell that she's close, so I coat one of my fingers in her slick and slide it into her tight pussy. Gently thrusting in and out, I encourage her to take what she needs from me.

"Good girl, keep rubbing your clit for me while you ride my finger." Leaning over to kiss her, I slowly add another finger. I can feel her clenching around me, and I groan into her mouth. She's panting hard and her eyes fly open to meet mine.

"Kai, I can't, it's too much," she says. Her head is thrashing on the pillow, so I grab her chin and force her to meet my eyes.

"Yes, you can, baby. Let go. I promise I'll be right here to catch you." I try to reassure her, but I can see her letting her mind take over. I don't want this experience to be ruined for her by overthinking.

I quickly lean down and kiss her hard, stroking my fingers against her top wall, and she falls over the edge, calling out my name and soaking my fingers. Still kissing her, but more gently now, I watch as she comes down from her orgasm and the mini-heat begins to recede.

I slide my fingers out of her slowly and immediately suck them into my mouth to see if my girl tastes as good as she smells. My dick twitches *hard* at the intense strawberry short-cake flavor and I know I'll be taking a cold shower later. She gasps, and I stroke the fingers of my clean hand down her flushed cheeks as I smile down at her.

"You did so good, Sugar. I'm so proud of you. How do you feel?"

Smiling up at me, her voice is croaky when she answers. "I feel amazing. Thank you so much, Kai. I don't think I could have done... *that*, without your help."

I have to hold back my chuckle at her shyness even after what we just did. "You can cover me in your slick anytime, Blake. And I do mean *any* time," I say, waggling my eyebrows at her.

I'm expecting another one of her sweet giggles, but instead she furrows her eyebrows. She sits up on the bed and her eyes widen at the mess on the sheets underneath her. Glancing up at me nervously, she says, "I'm so sorry. I'll clean the sheets, I promise. I didn't know I would do... *that*."

Leaning forward to grab her chin, I bark out, "No," in the firmest voice I can manage without yelling.

The tone of my voice causes her to jump, which instantly

makes me feel like shit. I curse. "Shit, I'm sorry, Sugar. I just meant no; you're not going to apologize for making a bit of a mess while giving me such an incredible gift. You trusted me with something so personal and intimate, and as your future Alpha, I feel like I'm on cloud fucking nine being able to help you like that, Blake. Your body producing slick when you're turned on is completely natural, and I never want you to feel guilty for that, baby. Okay? Your slick lets me know I'm doing my job and pleasing you, and *I love it.*"

My sweet girl looks so relieved when I explain I feel like punching myself for scaring her like that. She doesn't linger on it or make me feel bad, though. Instead, she just crawls into my lap and hugs me tight, kissing me on the cheek.

"Thank you, Alpha," she says sweetly.

I take one last deep breath of her scent before standing up with her in my arms. She wraps her legs around my waist, laughing, as I take her into the bathroom and turn on the shower. I gently set her down, giving her a sweet peck on the lips. She reaches for the band on my shorts, but I gently push her hand away.

"No, Sugar. This morning was just for you. And honestly, if you touch me right now, you're gonna miss your appointment and D will murder me."

Her light giggle is music to my ears, and the pout she aims my way just about melts every last resolve I have.

"Aww, don't worry, babe. I won't let big bad Hades hurt you. I promise."

"Oh thank goodness. I feel so lucky to have a tiny warrior defending my dishonorable actions," I say, smirking at her and loving that she called me babe without even realizing it. She rolls her eyes and yelps when I smack her cute little ass. "Get in the shower, tiny. I'll wait for the doctor downstairs, so just come down whenever you're ready."

She salutes me sarcastically, and I fucking *love* the sass on this girl. "Yes, Sir," she says mockingly.

And even though she was kidding, I think I may have just found a new fantasy for us to try.

CHAPTER 9

ROOK

Blake said her appointment this morning went well, and she seemed really excited as she walked the doctor out. I didn't ask for specifics, even though I was dying to know why she wanted to see someone before we left. She spent the last few hours helping us pack up the house and was surprised when we didn't deep clean until I told her we hire a local cleaning company whenever we use a rental. Leaving their tip on the table with the house keys, we hop in the car and begin the two-hour drive to the private airstrip.

Achilles and Blake are in the very back of the SUV since they're the smallest, and after spending the first hour staring wide eyed out the window, she faded fast. Now she's leaning against his shoulder, fast asleep. I know she was up late last night, and after her and Kai's... activities this morning, I'm sure she's exhausted. The flight is about ten hours nonstop, so she'll have plenty of time to sleep on the plane too. I want her to get enough rest since we'll touch down at Heathrow in the morning and head straight to HQ.

Kai is in the seat next to me and keeps turning to look at her, and I finally decide to bring up this morning.

"Dude, did you not get a good enough look this morning?" I ask him, smirking.

He looked like the cat that got the damned canary when he came down smelling of thick strawberry syrup this morning. I was jealous for a few minutes, but the look on her face when she walked down the stairs nearly knocked me on my ass. Blake was *glowing* and any momentary jealousy I felt went out the window. I would give anything to always see her that happy.

Turning back to me after looking at her again, he's got this dopey smile on his face that makes me grin.

"I don't think I've ever been this happy in my life." Kai turns around in his seat to look at Hades. "D, I know you always told us she was the one, but I'm not sure I believed you until I met her. That girl is too sweet for this world, and there's so much she's been sheltered from in her life. I just want to wrap her in bubble wrap and never let her go," he says, looking more concerned by the second as he no doubt thinks back to what happened this morning.

Earlier that morning

Kai comes bounding into the kitchen in only his shorts and we all let out groans at the intensity of Blake's scent that is practically *dripping* off of him. He's smirking as he pours coffee for himself and grabs another cup for Blake, setting it in the fridge. Kaspian introduced Blake to flavored iced coffee over breakfast yesterday and she's been drinking it like water since.

Kas gets up from his seat, scowling at his twin. He shoves him roughly out of the way. "Don't you think you've done enough for her this morning? Let me make her damn coffee how she likes it." As Kairo opens his mouth, likely to bicker back, there's a loud thud on the front door. He glances at

Kaspian, who looks around at all of us, before shaking his head and sighing. "I'll go get it."

Kai turns back to us and smiles softly. "Y'all know how he gets when he feels left out. We'll just need to make sure everyone gets to spend some one-on-one time with her while we're in London. And we KNOW Kas is gonna call dibs on taking her on the Warner Brothers Harry Potter tour. I don't know if she's seen the movies or not, but he's gonna beg her to go with him since none of us will." He laughs.

Suddenly, we hear Kas growling and cursing loudly before he shouts, "Guys! Get the fuck out here, *now*."

He's not as expressive as his brother when it comes to his emotions, so the terror in his voice gets me moving. I make it to the door first, gagging when the smell of rotten fruit reaches me before the sight does. Smeared across the door and the steps of the porch there are dozens of rotting strawberries with a piece of tattered cloth smashed into them. Covering his nose with his shirt, Hades' eyes widen, and he grabs the edge of the cloth to unfold it.

"That motherfucking piece of *shit*. I'm gonna kill him," he snarls out, a vicious growl building in his chest.

Achilles is the last to make it to the door after making sure Blake is still safely upstairs and away from this. Whatever *this* is. His eyes go wide as he gags at the smell. Covering his nose with his hands steepled over his face, his voice comes out muffled as he asks, "Is that a *shirt*? Why is it here covered in rotten strawberries, and why is it all... holey?"

I didn't notice before, but he's right. The shirt looks ancient. It's so thin, it's basically see-through, and it's littered with holes. The neckline is so stretched out I can't see how it would stay on a person. It takes me a second to notice Hades is absolutely frozen, just staring at the shirt with a single tear rolling down his cheek.

Crouching down next to him, I rub my hand across his shoulder. "What is it, D?"

He looks at me as another tear falls and whispers, "It's my shirt."

Of all the things I expected him to say, that wasn't even in the same stratosphere of possibilities that had crossed my mind.

"I—*what?*" I choke. "What the hell do you mean, it's *your* shirt?"

Back to staring at the shirt again, he's quiet for a minute before answering in the same small voice.

"When Blake first came to the foster home, all she had was a small backpack with a few clothes and her favorite stuffed animal. She never asked for anything, or complained because she didn't have something. She was just content with what she had. I mean, God, she even gave me her *only* stuffed animal because I had nightmares. And she absolutely refused to accept gifts because she said they always came with strings. About a month before she was taken, the sleep shirt she wore every night got caught on a nail that had been sticking out of that rickety ass roof. It tore straight down the middle of her back and just barely missed her skin, but the shirt was ruined."

He gives us a sad laugh.

"You know she didn't say one negative word? She didn't cry, or whine, or say anything about how her only sleep shirt was ruined. She looked up at me with those beautiful eyes and laughed, saying, 'I'm so glad that didn't scratch me. Phil and Dianne never would have let me go to the doctor for a tetanus shot.' She threw the shirt out the next day and I knew she wouldn't ask for another one or accept anything I gave her, so I grabbed one of my favorites and left it on the ground. I never did that, so when she asked me about it, I said it was too small for me and I needed to toss it when I got home from the rink.

"I came home late that night and she was fast asleep wearing my shirt. I had never felt so good in my life than I did being able to give her something she needed. From that night on, I let her think she 'stole' it, and she was so damned cute thinking she got away with something. I can't believe she kept it all those years." He finishes with an incredulous tone.

I'm still rubbing his back as I look at the rest of the guys, hoping they're on the same wavelength as me. This had to have been the foster father.

Achilles clears his throat. "I'm going to call the pilot and have them on the runway a few hours earlier. We need to get Blake out of here as soon as possible." With that, he brings his phone to his ear and walks back into the house.

Kai is just grabbing the hose to spray down the door and porch when the doctor shows up. I'm thanking my lucky stars he had the forethought to ask for a female doctor. My instincts are riding me hard to have my Omega within eyesight and make sure she's as safe as possible. Having another male around her right now might tip me over the edge and into feral territory.

I take a deep breath as Kas greets the doctor and Hades takes the shirt inside to bag it up so we can have some friends of ours look for fingerprints or scent ID. Silas, Owen, Grayson, and Beckett O'Connor are Alphas we've known forever who also happen to work for the Designation Bureau. Whenever we need something looked into under the table, we go to them. They're good friends, and I fully trust them to handle something so important.

Part of me wants to go find this fucker right now and end his life. The rest of me knows spending the rest of mine in jail would hurt Blake, so we'll save that as a last resort.

I'm brought back to the present when D growls, "I fucking know. I can't wait to get her out of the... oh *shit!*" he yells.

The sound is so jarring it makes Kas jerk the wheel slightly before he manages to right the car, and Blake startles awake. Eyes wide and wild, she whips her head around in a panic. Achilles gently cups her face in his hands and whispers soothing words I can't make out in her ear until she snaps out of it, looking sheepish.

"Sorry, guys. I didn't mean to fall asleep. What happened?" she asks quietly.

Kas is still grumbling in the driver's seat. "I'd really like to know, too. What the hell, D? Blake could've been hurt," he says angrily.

Hades looks slightly distraught when he says, "We can't take her out of the fucking country. She doesn't have a passport." I chuckle at the look of panic on his face, and he growls at me. "What the fuck is so funny about that, you dick?"

Rolling my eyes, I say, "It's funny, because finding Blake has clearly made you forget who we are. I called Si the day after we found her and had them rush us a passport. It'll be waiting for us on the jet."

His face flushes lightly. "Oh."

Blake's eyes are once again wide behind us. "Wait... where exactly are we going? I thought... you said *HQ*. I assumed that meant Lockwood. Why would I need a passport to go there?" she asks, sounding slightly panicked.

Kai's eyes light up and he throws her a wicked smirk as he turns back to look at her. "Oh no, Sugar. We're headed to London."

CHAPTER 10

BLAKE

In the last week, I've gone from being locked in a nearly windowless basement to sitting on a massive private jet, preparing to fly to *England*. With my childhood best friend and his pack, all of whom want me to be their Omega. This has to be a dream. Things like this don't happen to girls like me. Needing to know for sure, I reach down and pinch my thigh, hard.

"What the hell, Shortcake? Why did you just pinch yourself?" Hades grabs my hand and pulls it away from my leg, cupping it in both of his gently.

My cheeks flush. "Umm... I just... can I plead the fifth?" I whine.

All the guys chuckle at that, giving me a collective, "Nope."

I groan loudly, burying my face in my hands. Peeking out between my fingers, I see Kas sitting directly across from me on one of the couches, giving me a little smirk, and I take a breath.

"I was just thinking about how this doesn't feel real. You guys don't feel real. Less than a week ago, I was being held captive in a basement. Now I'm sitting on a *private jet* with five of the most gorgeous guys I've ever seen, waiting to be flown to their company's international headquarters in England. A place I've always dreamed of going, but knew I would never be able to. I just... I feel like I'm not bringing enough to this pack."

A loud growl that comes straight from Rook cuts my rant off, and the rest of the guys stare at him wide-eyed.

He stands, holding out his hand for me. "Come on, Angel. You need a nap," he says.

Taking his hand, I let him see my confusion at his sudden change of subject, but follow him anyway.

I glance back at the guys and see them all chuckling as Hades winks at me and mouths, "Good luck, Shortcake."

Still tired even after my car nap earlier, I don't fight Rook as he pulls me into a surprisingly large bedroom at the back of the plane. Closing and locking the pocket door, he looks sheepish when we're finally alone.

"I'm sorry for getting all growly out there. My instincts have been on high alert since you agreed to court us, and I don't want to push you too far, too fast. I'm desperately trying not to scare you off by being too protective or overbearing," he says anxiously.

Gently pushing him to sit on the edge of the giant bed, I cup his face in my hands, the tips of my fingers barely grazing his cheekbones. I look him directly in the eyes as I speak. "Rook, listen to me. There is *nothing* you could say or do to push me away now. I've known you for less than a week and yet I can't imagine not seeing you every day, or not sleeping in your shirt, or hearing you call me angel. The only reason I was ever hesitant is because things between Hades and I felt unsettled, but they don't now. I'm happier than I've ever been, and I met my scent matches. The only thing that could make it better is being this pack's Omega."

His jaw drops, and he chokes on air, beating on his chest as he coughs. I curl my lips in, trying not to laugh as I reach behind him and gently pat his back. "You alright there, big guy?" I ask as a small giggle escapes me.

Gaping at me, his voice is incredulous. "Angel...you *know* we're scent matched?"

I roll my eyes at him playfully. "Well, *duh*. I hoped, but Hades confirmed it last night when we were talking."

His entire face lights up as he beams the biggest dang smile at me and *wow*. I didn't think he could get any more attractive, but I was clearly wrong. His gorgeous ice blue eyes are so bright they're practically clear and the tops of his cheeks are flushed. Even the tips of his ears are pink, exposed only because he has his chin length hair up in a tiny bun on the top of his head.

Grabbing me around the waist, he pulls me into his chest to give me a tight hug. I immediately bury my face in his neck to get a deep inhale of his orange creamsicle scent. The orange must be what shifts with his mood, because right now it's sweet and so intense, showing me he really is happy.

"God, Angel. You are everything this pack needed and so much more. So fucking perfect for us. I don't know what we did right in life to deserve you, but I thank every deity there is for bringing us Hades and helping him lead us to you." He nuzzles his nose into my hair, kissing the top of my head.

I snuggle further into his chest, his scent lulling me into a relaxed calm. "I worry I won't be enough for you guys. You're so smart and talented. I mean, you run a multi-billion dollar company, for crying out loud. I'm just a girl with a terrible family history, less than $1000 to her name, and enough baggage to fill this plane."

He snorts, pulling my chin up so I can look at him through sleepy eyes. "You, my silly, beautiful Angel, do not owe us a single damned thing. We aren't perfect by any means, but you're helping us soothe all of our rough edges. Kai and Kas are fighting less. Achilles is actively hanging out with us and participating in conversations, and Hades is smiling more now than I've ever seen."

Noticing he left himself out, I stroke my finger down his broad nose and ask, "What about you, big guy?"

He kisses the tip of my finger, making me giggle. "You set me free, Blake. You showed me I'm worthy of love and affection just for who I am. Not because of what my money can offer people. You never ask for anything, and you fight me when I try to give you things. You make me talk about myself and you pay attention to my needs. I have never felt so seen in my life as I do when I'm with you. I've been hearing about you from D for *years*, and I always wondered how he could love you so much in such a short amount of time. *I get it now*, Angel. You're impossible not to love."

Tearing up, I throw my arms around his neck and squeeze him as tight as I can, leaning down to whisper in his ear, "You're impossible not to love too Rook."

He beams at me, leaning in to kiss me. His kiss is soft, but deep, and absolutely perfect. "Will you take a nap with me, Angel? I know you're still tired and honestly, I am too," he asks sweetly as he helps me off his lap.

I nod shyly, slipping out of my jeans and sweatshirt. I'm still in a long-sleeved shirt and my usual boy shorts, but he stands there frozen for a minute, just staring at my legs.

I sit down on the edge of the bed and cross my legs, startling him and earning me a sheepish smile and a shrug. "Sorry, sweet girl. You're too pretty not to stare at."

My cheeks flush and I shake my head, my jaw dropping when he strips off his shirt and gives it to me.

"You wanna sleep in that, Angel? It's soft, and it's too warm back here for long sleeves."

I'm distracted from answering his question as he takes off his joggers, so he's standing in front of me in just his boxer briefs. I quickly snap my eyes up to see him smirking at me, still holding out his shirt.

Clearing my throat, I take the shirt from him and mumble, "Thank you," while slipping it on. I turn around and crawl over to the other side of the bed, and I hear him groan from behind me as I slip under a comforter that feels like clouds. Raising my eyebrow at him, he quickly shakes his head and climbs in after me. As soon as he's under the covers with me, he reaches up and turns off the light, sliding the little window shade shut to block out the midafternoon sun. When the plane begins to lift off the ground, I jump, startled that I didn't notice it moving at all before now. Rook turns me on my side, my back to his front, and pulls me tight against him. His huge body completely cocoons mine and I instantly calm down as I'm surrounded by my Alpha's scent.

Sighing in contentment, I grab his hand and thread our fingers together over my ribs. "Night, Alpha."

Roaring purrs are my response, and as I'm falling asleep, I hear him whisper, "Goodnight, my love."

CHAPTER 11

ROOK

I wake up what can't be more than a couple of hours later to Blake moaning in her sleep. At first, I think she's having a nightmare, but I quickly realize she's burning up. We don't have a thermometer on the plane, so I get up and open the bedroom door a crack to see if Kai is awake. Luckily, he is, and he's the only one. Kas and Achilles are sharing one of the couch beds, snuggling in their sleep. I chuckle at that and snap a quick picture of them to show Blake later.

Hades is on the other couch bed, and Kai is sitting at one of the small tables working on his laptop. I walk up behind him and tap on his shoulder to get his attention, since he has headphones on. He raises an eyebrow at my lack of clothes but when he sees my expression, he snaps into what we like to call his "doctor mode". He was the kid genius you always hear people talking about in awe. Graduated high school at nine, med school at seventeen, and he finished his residency right before we found Blake. He's now our Medical Director at OHP.

"I think she has a fever. Her whole body is on fire and she's moaning and wiggling around on the bed. Is there anything we have on board to give her?" I ask him, hoping he brought his bag.

He barks out a laugh before quickly stifling it, checking to make sure he didn't wake the others. Grinning at me, he chuckles. "Sorry, man. She does have a fever, but she doesn't need medicine. She needs a little vitamin *D,* if ya know what I mean." He winks at me.

It takes me a second to catch up, and when I do, I blush.

Kai nods again, still chuckling. "It's probably another mini heat from the meds. You'll need to help her through it. Try to remember, she's as new at this as you are. It might be good for y'all to experience that together."

I nod. "Right, okay. I can do this. Thanks, man."

He's smiling like an idiot at me and whispers, "Good luck, dude. And have fun!"

I lock the bedroom door again and crawl back into bed with my girl. She immediately rolls over and tosses her leg over mine, trying to pull me to lie over her. She gasps, and it quickly turns into a breathy moan as she tries to grind herself against me. If she doesn't stop soon, I'm gonna blow in my boxer briefs and embarrass myself.

"Blake, Angel. You've gotta stop," I say gently, running my fingers through her vibrant red hair.

Her eyes pop wide open and she gasps, apologizing profusely while struggling to sit up. I move my body so I'm straddling her hips, which unfortunately pushes my already hard cock up on her stomach. My knot's just barely beginning to inflate at the base of my cock. I'm already thick around, but my knot is almost twice the size when it's fully inflated. Blake is tiny, but Omega bodies are made to take knots, and I trust her to tell me if something hurts.

She gulps, apologies forgotten, before glancing at it and whispering, "Jesus, Rook. Are they all that big?"

I half laugh, half choke as I answer, "I'm not sure Angel,

but I don't think so. I'm a big guy, and I feel like it's probably proportionate. Sorry if I made you uncomfortable. If it helps, I've never been in this particular position before."

It's her turn to choke, cheeks red and eyes bright as she stares up at me. My cheeks flush when I realize how that sounded.

"God, sorry, no. That's not... I mean, it's true, but not in the way it sounds. Jesus, I'm fucking this all up. What I'm trying to say, Blake, is that I've never done *any* of this before," I say quietly. My voice tapers off near the end of the sentence as embarrassment washes over me in a tidal wave.

Looking at me blankly for a minute, I can see the moment when what I was trying to say dawns on her and she gasps. "But... *how?!* You're gorgeous, and smart, and thoughtful, and funny, and clearly, you're not lacking anything in the physical department..."

She's rambling, and it's so goddamn cute I can't help but lean down and seal my lips over hers. When she opens her mouth on a gasp, I slip my tongue in to massage hers gently, and she tastes better than my wildest dreams. Seeming hesitant, she pokes her tongue out and slides it across my lips, causing me to let out a sound that's half growl, half groan as she once again tries to grind herself against my shaft.

"The guys will be able to hear us, Angel, but do you need your Alpha to take care of you, anyway?" I ask my sweet girl, tilting her chin up so I can look in her eyes.

She nods, looking nervous. "I-I've never done anything like this before. I don't know what to do," she whispers.

Knowing I get to touch this incredible woman sends a bolt of lust straight to my already aching cock.

"You just lay back and try to let go, Blake. Let Daddy Rook take care of his needy Angel."

I have no clue where the fuck that came from, but the thought of Blake calling me *Daddy* makes me fucking shudder.

Thoughts of trying to breed her, rut her, and claim her as *my Angel, my Omega,* have me half feral. My cock is weeping precum into my boxer briefs, leaving a wet spot on the front where I'm currently grinding the head against her clit.

Her pupils blow wide, and she nods frantically. "Yes, please."

I growl, leaning down to tear her soaked boy shorts off of her, exposing her bare pussy. I shuffle down the bed until I'm at eye level with her pretty pink cunt.

"Do you shave, Angel?"

She nods. "It's just more comfortable for me. It's a lot of work, but I prefer it this way… If you don't like it, I can—"

I lick a long stripe up the center of her pussy, her sweet strawberry and vanilla taste *exploding* on my tongue.

"I don't want to hear any of that, Blake. You do what you want with *your body.* If you want to be shaved bare, or wax, or hell, get laser hair removal so you never have to shave again, that's fine. If you want to let it grow and never shave again, that's fine too. I am going to worship my girl, regardless of what your hair looks like down here. Got it?"

Nodding again, she smiles. "Thank you, Rook."

I pop up to kiss her lips, making sure to thrust my tongue in so she can taste herself and know that I'm about to have the best dessert of my life. Pulling away and sliding back down the bed, I growl against her pussy.

"Enough talking, Angel. I haven't had dinner yet, and I'm *starving.*"

Inhaling her scent as deeply as I possibly can, I lean in and fucking *devour* her. I've never done this before, so I'm trying to pay close attention to her reactions as I go. Flattening my tongue, I lick over her clit a few times until I get a wild moan out of her. While I'm doing that, I bring one hand up and gently slip a single finger inside her, finding her hot and dripping.

Groaning, I thrust against the bed, desperately trying to get some friction against my throbbing cock. I might need to start every day with my face buried in my girl's delicious pussy. I finger her gently for a minute before slowly adding another finger, causing her to whimper and moan at the stretch, and I try to soothe her.

"Shh, Angel, you want to be able to take Daddy Rook's cock, don't you? Take a deep breath and try to relax those muscles for me. That's it, good girl," I coo as she relaxes, and her moaning gets louder. I don't know what she and Kai did this morning, but I'm quite a bit bigger than he is and my fingers are a lot thicker, so I'm trying to be gentle.

I curl my fingers upwards to try to hit the spot I've read about. I'm instantly rewarded with a gush of slick that tastes like the best fucking dessert I've ever had. Licking up every last drop, I dive in with renewed vigor on her clit, alternating between licking and sucking as I continue to stroke her g-spot.

"You're doing so well, sweet girl. Are you gonna come for Daddy?" I start to thrust into the bed faster, so close to falling over the edge myself, but I *need* to get my girl there first.

"Oh god, oh Rook, I'm so close. Please, I just—I," she cries out.

"I know, Angel. I'm right there with you. Be a good girl for me and come *now*." I use my Alpha bark as I gently bite down on her clit, and she detonates.

"Oh god, *YES, Rook*! Holy shit," she calls out as she drenches my face and the sheets in her slick. Hearing her call out my name as she comes is enough to set me off.

"Oh, fuck, Angel... *Blake*." My voice is a hoarse cry as I come with hard jerks of my cock into my underwear.

Sitting up and kissing her, I try to hop out of bed to clean us both up when she shakes her head at me, pulling me back down on top of her. "I need more, Alpha."

I try to pull back so I can ask her if she's sure, but she yanks me forward and bites down on my neck, *hard.* The bite, combined with her scent, like a cloud around us in the small room, is nearly enough to send me into my very first rut.

Gently pushing her back onto the bed, I lean down and pull her shirt off, nipping at her gorgeous tits as I do. She moans. "*Please*, Daddy. I want this, and I want it to be with you."

She begs so beautifully; I know I'll give her anything she wants. "Are you absolutely sure, Angel? I'm on the edge of a rut. If we go all the way right now, I don't know if I'll be able to stop myself from claiming you."

Her eyes widen, and she whines again. "Rook, I may be having a flare-up, but *I am not in heat.* I am perfectly capable of consenting. So please, for the love of God, *fuck me.*"

I growl, yanking her down the bed and shoving my under-wear off at the same time. I'm barely hanging on to my sanity, but I still manage to ask, "Do you want to use protection, love?"

She beams at me and lifts up her arm, showing off a small bandage.

My eyes widen. "What the hell is that? Are you hurt? Jesus, Blake, you gotta tell us when stuff happens!"

She's giggling wildly now. "Relax Alpha, it's a ten year birth control implant. That's why I needed to see the doctor this morning. It's 100% effective, even during heats." Her eyes turn molten with heat when I growl and purr at the same time, grinding the head of my cock into her soaked slit.

"You ready, Angel? This might hurt for a second until your body takes over."

She nods frantically. "*Please Daddy,* it aches," she whines.

That one whine is enough for the rut to fully take hold.

I notch the head of my cock at her entrance and slide in as slow as I possibly can, pausing every inch or so to let her adjust. When I'm maybe halfway in, she groans and pushes me onto my back, climbing on top of me. She lines herself up and takes my entire shaft in one drop of her hips, ripping a groan out of my throat. She's so fucking tight I have to grit my teeth, so I don't blow my load five seconds into this.

Blake leans down and kisses me, whining again as she bounces on my cock. I've never been this hard in my life, and she feels *incredible*.

"Look at you, riding me so well. Such a good girl, Blake. Just like that." I gasp as she bounces faster, and I lick my thumb before rubbing it over her clit.

She moans long and loud as I rub her clit, and she tightens around my shaft.

"That's it, Angel. Are you gonna come for me? Are you gonna come all over Daddy's cock?" I ask her, sitting up to bite her pretty pink nipples.

She keeps grinding on me, breathing heavily and panting out, "Oh god, Rook I'm close. Please, I need…"

"You gonna come for me, Blake?" I ask as I bite down hard on her nipple and pinch her clit at the same time.

She goes off like a fucking rocket around me, and I'm lost to the fog. I flip her on her back and rut into her, completely losing track of time.

"You ready to take my knot, Angel? You gonna be a good girl and come on Daddy's knot this time?"

"*YES, Daddy!* Please, give me your knot. I need it," she sobs out.

I thrust into her a few more times, my knot forming quickly. Before it fully inflates, I thrust into her one last time, *hard.* My knot slips in, and she screams out another orgasm as I come so hard, I black out. When I come to, I feel a strange giddiness in my chest, and when I lick my lips, I taste blood on them. My eyes fly open in shock, and I look down to see Blake with a bite where her neck meets her shoulder. *My bite.*

"Oh my god. Blake, Angel, I am *so sorry*. I blacked out, and I didn't even check with you first. Jesus Christ, I'm the worst Alpha in the world." I'm on the verge of a full-blown anxiety attack, and my breathing speeds up as I realize I probably just ruined this for my entire pack.

Two tiny hands cup my face, and suddenly my Angel's lips are on mine. She kisses me hard and fast before pulling back and looking me straight in the eyes. "Do you regret it?" she asks quietly. I can see the insecurity shining in her eyes and my heart sinks.

My eyes widen. "God, Angel, not even for a second. I could never regret having a bond with you, but we're on a plane, for god's sake. You deserved to be asked, and courted, and a fancy hotel with flowers and the entire pack worshipping your gorgeous body."

She smiles at me. "I love you, Rook."

My mouth drops open as my brain shuts down for a minute. When I snap out of it, I kiss the hell out of her, thrusting my tongue into her mouth and rolling on my back to pull her on top of me since we're still locked together.

"Fuck, Blake. How the hell did I end up with someone like you? I love you so goddamn much. And everything that just happened is *so* worth the ass kicking I'm going to get from the rest of the guys when they find out I accidentally bonded you. Jesus," I say, shaking my head.

Her aggressive growl shocks me out if my musings.

"*Nobody* is touching my Alpha. You warned me you might not be able to help it if you fell into a rut and I went in knowing we could come out bonded. I wanted this, *Daddy*," she says, smirking.

My still hard dick twitches inside her, and we both groan.

"Come on, Angel. Let's try to get some more sleep before the yahoos out there barge in and try to steal *my Omega*," I say, turning us on our sides and running my fingers through her hair.

We're quiet for a bit before she giggles lightly and asks, "Who do you think will crack next?"

I chuckle back quietly. "Kaspian, definitely. And probably on your first date."

She leans back a little and looks at me with a single brow raised. "Wanna bet?"

Smirking, I say, "Betcha five bucks and an orgasm, Kas breaks next, and in less than three days."

Kissing me one last time before she snuggles down into my chest, she murmurs, "You're on."

CHAPTER 12

ACHILLES

We landed in London super early this morning and drove straight to the hotel to sleep. Blake and Rook slept the entire plane ride, and honestly, we were all more shocked than upset when he finally 'fessed up about *accidentally* bonding her. On the fucking plane. But she was so happy none of us wanted to ruin it by teasing them, even if the other Alphas were jealous as hell. She also threatened to not speak to us again if we were mean to Rook, so that shut us all up real quick.

Her eyes are still closed when I approach the bed to wake her up this morning, so she startles when I crawl on top of her. She stretches her arms above her head, pushing her hair up off her neck as she does.

I catch a glimpse of the shiny silver scars of her bonding mark from Rook before she moans in satisfaction from her stretch, making my dick perk up in my boxer briefs. I quickly adjust myself, already annoyed by the confining fabric. Unless I'm in jeans, I prefer going commando.

Blake opens her eyes to stare up at me with a look of contentment on her pretty face, and I can't resist lowering my body to grind against hers as she stretches. She moans, eyes going wide. Her eyes are always incredible, but right now, still sleepy and lit with desire, they're *breathtaking*.

I smirk as I lean down to kiss her on the forehead. "Careful there, ma douce fraise. You keep making noises like that and we'll be late for work. Go take a quick shower and I'll go get you some food."

She beams up at me with wide, happy eyes. "Are we seriously about to go to work in *London?* Oh man, can I have chocolate chip pancakes before we go?"

I chuckle at her rapid thought process, even as my heart aches for her. This girl couldn't be any sweeter if she tried, and as of last night, she's officially ours. Helping her out of bed, I lean in to whisper in her ear, brimming with pride at the way she shivers and sways forward. "Anything for you, mon cœur. Now get that cute ass in the shower so we can head out. You've got an hour before we're late," I say, smirking at her and smacking a noisy kiss on her cheek.

Smiling to myself, I turn to head into the living room so I can order my darling strawberry girl her pancakes. The first thing I see is Rook pacing quickly with a concerned frown on his face, talking on the phone. He's a serious guy normally, but this is a whole other level. I can't help but wonder if it's something bad or if his new bond is intensifying his feelings about something trivial. No matter what he's hearing, it's clearly not good.

Stopping directly in front of him, I wait for him to let me know what's going on, since I can only hear bits of the conversation from his end. It isn't long before he hangs up and turns to me.

"We need to grab the rest of the guys *now*," he says, a bit of growl slipping into his voice.

I nod my head. "You got it. Give me a sec. Blake should be in the shower if we need privacy."

He nods, and I rush to the other two rooms down the short hallway, banging on the doors. "Pack meeting *NOW*," I say it as quietly as I can while still letting them hear how serious I am.

Less than a minute later, the entire pack is gathered in the large living room of our suite. We have a home here in London, but because this will be a short trip and we want Blake to be able to experience as much as possible, we're staying at The Savoy.

Rook is still pacing and muttering to himself, so I look around at the other guys and shake my head, letting them know I have no idea what's going on. Finally, he sits down on the coffee table in front of us, his hands steepled in front of his face as he takes a deep breath. "So, I just got off the phone with Pack O'Connor, and they requested an urgent meeting *without* Blake. Like, they want to meet at HQ right now. One of us needs to stay back and take her sightseeing for a few hours while we get through this meeting."

Kas, shocking all of us, lifts his chin. "I want to take her to Warner Brothers today. It's forty-five minutes by car and a two-hour tour, which puts us back here by noon. We can meet up with y'all, have lunch, and show her around the facilities and show her off."

Clearing his throat, Kai looks at his brother like he's an alien. "Dude... are you sure you're okay missing this meeting?"

He rolls his eyes at all of us. "If y'all think I'm gonna miss a chance to take our Omega to my favorite place in the world, you're wrong. I trust y'all to fill me in or record the meeting, but this is exactly what I need right now."

Hades nods. "I'll make sure to take notes if we can't record, but come on. It's Silas, Owen, Grayson, and Beckett. We know these guys; we *trust them* to handle the important stuff. Whatever they're gonna tell us, it's because we need to know, but we all know they've got it under control."

"Exactly. So, I'm gonna go finish getting ready, and then show our girl the wonderful world of witchcraft and wizardry." He smirks, walking backwards and shooting finger guns until he rounds the corner.

Laughing in surprise at his attitude shift, I shake my head. "And on that note, I'm gonna go tell Blake there's been a slight change of plans."

I walk back into the bedroom to see Blake tossing Rook's shirt on the bed and I mentally make a note to give her one of mine. I groan when I notice she's only wearing a towel, and she turns back to look at me, smiling shyly and covering herself. Walking up to her, I gently pull her arms down by her sides and kiss her puffy pink lips.

"Mon cœur, you *never* need to feel shy with me. I may not be one of your Alphas, but I'm ready to be your Beta if... *when* you're ready to claim me. I'm yours, sweet girl."

She's blushing now, but instead of shying away from my declaration like I expected her to, she pops up on her toes and gives me a sweet kiss. Before she can pull away, I run my tongue along the seam of her lips before slipping it into her mouth. She moans softly, bringing her hands up to the back of my head and scratching her fingers gently on my scalp. I groan loudly, practically purring into her mouth as my knees buckle and I fall back to the bed, bringing her down on top of me as gently as possible.

"Oof." She giggles as we land. "Sorry, are you okay? I hope I didn't hurt you!"

She sits up, so she's straddling my hips, and I have to name different dinosaurs in my head, so I don't get a boner like a fifteen-year-old having his first make-out session.

Velociraptor, T-rex, Brachiosaurus, Dilophosaurus, Chicken...

Blake looks down at me like I'm crazy. "Did you just call

me chicken? I thought weird nicknames were Kaspian's thing?" she asks.

Shit, I said that last one out loud.

I'm blushing now. "Uhh... what are the chances you'll let me out of here without explaining why I just said chickens?" I ask her with a big smile, making sure to pop the dimple in my right cheek that always got me out of trouble as a kid.

Rolling her eyes at me, she drops down, so her elbows are on my chest. She leans her head in her hands and gives me the sweetest smile. Just as I think she's going to let me off the hook, she boops me on the nose.

"Less than zero percent. But bonus points for having a cute dimple," she says smugly.

Holy shit. I am in so much trouble with this girl.

She leans back and crosses her arms, giving me a stare I'm sure she thinks is intimidating, but really makes her look like a mildly annoyed kitten. There's not a chance in hell I'm ever telling *her* that, though.

Taking a deep breath, I smooth my face into some semblance of serious and pin her with a look. "What you say in response to my next question could make or break our relationship. Are you prepared for that?"

She looks curious but not scared, so I doubt she's buying my bullshit. She indulges me anyway and says, "Hit me with it, Ace."

Quirking my brows at her, I wonder where the nickname came from, and I remind myself to ask her later. Getting serious again, I look her straight in the eyes. Then, with every single ounce of composure I can muster, I ask, "Do you believe chickens are dinosaurs?"

Her eyes are wide as saucers as she blinks owlishly at me. "Maybe..." she says slowly, dragging the word out into several long syllables. "Ace... do *you* believe chickens are dinosaurs?"

I nod solemnly at her. "I don't just believe it. They *are*."

CHAPTER 13

BLAKE

*A*chilles' question is so unexpected I have no idea what to say, but I'm trying desperately not to laugh. I only manage to be silent for another minute before my face splits and then I'm laughing so hard I can hardly catch my breath.

"You're… insane," I say as I finally get my laughter under control.

The next thing I know, The spicy scent of gingerbread surrounds me as Kaspian steps up behind me, pulling me to lean further back against his chest. It startles me, and I tighten my towel around my chest, all too aware that I only have on panties underneath.

I don't own a bra because of the whole "captive since I was eleven" thing, and I feel like I should probably get one at some point. I don't get a chance to feel shy about my lack of clothing, though. Cupping my throat, he tilts my head back so I can see his gorgeous, dark brown eyes and smirking lips.

"What's so funny, my little crumpet?" he asks, his smirk widening into a full smile as he leans down to kiss my forehead.

Giggling, I back up to slide off of Achilles' lap. "Did you

know dinosaurs are actually chickens? Ace told me so," I say, looking over my shoulder at his sprawled form. He's still stretched out on the bed and his shirt has ridden up so I can see his drool worthy abs and just a hint of tattoo on his ribs. The thought of licking them distracts me so much I don't hear the guys break out into raucous laughter at my statement.

I'm brought out of my fantasy when Kas gently uses a finger to turn my face back to his. "You done drooling there, Neil?"

My nose scrunches. "Huh?"

He rolls his eyes playfully. "You wound me, B. Neil Armstrong was the first man on the moon, and you were just spacing out. Ipso facto, Neil. But speaking of nicknames, did you just call Achilles, Ace? And if so, *why?*"

The reminder makes me giggle again as I nod. "Yeah, I did. One of the movies that played most often at night was Ace Ventura, and Phil would fall asleep on the couch with the TV blaring. So even though I've never actually *seen* the movies, I can quote them almost word for word. When Achilles just randomly brought up chickens, and then told me they're dinosaurs, it just made me think of something Ace Ventura would say. So now he's Ace," I say, smiling back at him as he groans and covers his face with his hands.

A shuffling sound comes from behind me and I roll my eyes when I see that at some point, the rest of the guys came in without me noticing. They're all snickering, some hiding it better than others. But it's Hades that finally cracks and a full belly laugh comes out of him, which sets them all off.

"Dude... why the *fuck* were you talking about chickens with our gorgeous Omega straddling your lap?" Hades gets out between chuckles.

The man on the bed, still hiding behind his hands, lets out a snort, followed by another deep groan. "Godfuckingdamnit, *fine.* I'll tell y'all." Finally uncovering his face, he looks at me.

"You were sitting in my lap and looking all fucking gorgeous, and I was trying to not immediately get a boner like a teen…"

Rook barks out a laugh. "Newsflash, you *are* a teen."

Glaring over at him, Achilles snaps out, "*Anyway*. I was trying to get control of my damned body so I could talk to our girl, and I started naming dinosaurs in my head and because a chicken *is a dinosaur*, I named that one too. Only… I guess that one was out loud."

Everybody is silent for a minute while we process his words. I roll my lips to hide my laughter, and once I can speak, I say, "So when I asked you *why* you said chickens, and you changed the subject… I guess you could say you *chickened out?*"

The guys and I all howl with laughter the second I finish my question. Kas and I are leaning on each other and he's laughing so hard he has tears building in his eyes. Ace is scowling at me, but I can see a playful glimmer in his eyes, and I think he's just happy to see me happy.

Kas finally stops laughing and wipes his eyes. "Alright, little comedian, you and I are gonna paint the town green today, baby. You ready?" he asks, giving me the sweetest smile.

I smile back but look at all of them. "I thought we were going to work? I want to see what you guys do and meet people." Okay, I'll admit. I'm pouting just a little. My bottom lip quivers just the slightest bit, which causes Rook and Kai to cover their eyes immediately.

Leaning to the side and mumbling to Hades, "D, Jesus Christ, give the girl whatever she wants. Just make her stop with the look," Rook begs as Kai nods in agreement, still covering his eyes.

Kas rolls his. "Pout-pout fish, do you like Harry Potter?" he asks.

My pout disappears as my jaw drops. "Like? Did you just ask me if I *like* Harry Potter?! Does the ocean *like* salt? Do flowers *like* the sun? Do you *like* breathing? It is *ESSENTIAL.* Those books got me through my entire seven years of cave dwelling. *Like* is an understatement of world ending proportions."

All the guys' eyes are wide, and Kas is positively *beaming* at me.

"You're in luck then, Slytherin. We have a tour of the Warner Bros HP film studio in just over an hour and we need to leave now if we're gonna make it on time. Especially if we want to get Butterbeer before the tour starts," Kas tells me excitedly.

"Holy shit. Where are my shoes?!" I start running around frantically, pulling on one of Kas' hoodies I swiped from his suitcase last night and dropping the towel once I have it on. It's practically a dress on me, but it smells like gingerbread cookies and the sweetest vanilla icing, so I'm wearing it. Quickly tying my shoes, I pop up from the ground. "Ready!"

All the guys are just standing there grinning at me from the doorway, so I cock my hip and raise an eyebrow at Kas. "You can't promise me Butterbeer, and then drag your feet. Let's go!"

Chuckling, he turns into the living room and snags a set of keys I didn't notice on the coffee table.

"Yes, ma'am."

"I'M SORRY, but you absolutely cannot convince me that rats haven't taken over the sewer system. No matter how clean or magical a place may seem. You just know they're down there fighting for dominance over the frogs," I tell Kas emphatically as we're finishing up the guided part of the studio tour. Apparently, we get to explore after this because he pulled some strings for us.

I love that no matter how excited or loud I get, he doesn't get mad or tell me to quiet down and quit embarrassing him, even in public. I love that he's having as much fun as I am. Kas seemed really nervous when we left the hotel, and I was worried he had changed his mind about going and didn't know how to tell me.

We've been driving about fifteen minutes and I've been gently peppering Kas with questions for the last ten. He keeps giving me short answers and seems so anxious. I just really hope he's not second guessing our date. Turning to me with a blush staining his high cheekbones, he shyly admits he has really bad anxiety. So as much as he loves going on this tour, he usually ends up having an anxiety attack at some point during it.

"Being in public and around people triggers it the most, which is why I spend so much time at home," he explains quietly. I smile at him and grab his hand, squeezing tight. Hoping to distract him, I start talking about a few of the only movies I was allowed to watch as a child.

The first movie I brought up makes him fidget nervously, and I don't hesitate to ask him why.

He sighs dramatically, and I hold in a giggle because that is such a Kai thing to do, but I don't want him to think I'm comparing him to his twin. "I don't want you to laugh at me," he says with a pout. He pouts, and it's so freaking cute I have to fight to focus on his words.

"Baby," I say gently. "I'm not gonna laugh at you. Just tell me."

Sighing again, he glances at me for a long moment before speaking. "I don't think you know this, but Kai and my last name is Sparrow," he says dejectedly. My eyes widen, immediately knowing I'm about to break my no laughing promise. "Our parents have always told us we were conceived during a pre-heat Pirates of the Caribbean movie marathon. And trust me, I know how ironic that is. Our mom is absolutely obsessed with Johnny Depp. So, when we were born, they decided to pay tribute to the reason for our existence and named us Kaspian Jack Sparrow and Kairo Johnny Sparrow. We've never told anybody our middle names. Even the guys don't know." He looks straight into my eyes as he says the last bit.

I'm trying desperately to hold myself together, so I don't break my promise. I roll my lips inwards and I'm holding my breath, but I can feel my eyes watering with the effort right as Kas looks over and scoffs. "You can laugh, you brat."

Breaking out into a fit of wild giggles, I bring his hand to my lips and kiss it. "I'm so sorry," I get out between breaths. "I swear I'm not laughing at you. It's just so cute! I can't wait to meet your mom."

He's smiling softly at me now. "She's gonna love you, giggly goose. I can't wait for her to meet our girl."

I keep talking about kids' movies the entire car ride. Just as we're pulling into the studio, we realized that one we've both always liked features a pet rat that saves the sewer rat community in London from a flood during the world cup. The fact that we're in London right now has me absolutely convinced it's going to come true right under our feet and we won't even know it.

"I fully agree, Rita. But the real question is, do you think there's a frog King? Or would they have evolved into a democracy by now?" he asks seriously. Kas and I have been playing and joking all day, and it's a side I never expected from him. He's so funny even when he's quiet about it. I just feel like he thinks he has to make himself fit into this mold of only being the quiet twin because Kairo has such loud thoughts and feelings. Seeing this goofy side of him is so attractive I can feel myself getting turned on, and my perfume floods from my body. Kas' pupils go wide, and he leans in to sniff my neck. We've been sitting outside one of the shops in Diagon Alley, finishing up our delicious Butterbeer and talking for maybe fifteen minutes and we're completely alone. Perks of being super rich, apparently.

"Sweetheart." He pauses, still sniffing my neck. "Are frog kings your kink? Maybe your permanent nickname should be

Princess if you have a thing for royalty." He chuckles lightly as he strokes his fingers lightly down my cheek.

My cheeks flame red. "What? No, don't be weird. I was just thinking it's so nice to talk to someone else about the stuff I like. How much fun it is to see you talk about something you're passionate about, especially when it's the nerdy and geeky stuff I love, too. It's really... um... sexy." I gulp. I'm getting more comfortable talking about sex, but it's still really awkward trying to flirt when you have zero experience.

My nerdy Alpha groans, burying his face in my neck. "B, you calling me sexy in that sweet voice of yours has got to be one of the biggest turn-ons I've ever experienced." Lifting his head up, he looks around quickly before standing up and grabbing my hand, pulling me to stand with him. "Do you trust me?" he asks quietly.

Immediately, I nod my head. "More than anything." And it's the honest truth. Two weeks ago, I never would have said I would trust a man, let alone five of them. But meeting my scent matches has overridden some of my trauma and I *know* I can trust my men. *My pack.*

He nods, a mischievous grin playing on his lips. "Good, then come with me, and be very, *very* quiet."

CHAPTER 14

HADES

The guys and I arrive at HQ to meet Pack O'Connor less than a half an hour after Blake and Kaspian leave for their tour. We're all a little on edge, considering we don't know why they requested this meeting, or why it has to be without Blake. She's been gone less than an hour and I miss her so much already. Even though I know I'll get to take her to the eye with Achilles later while the guys catch up on work here at the office.

We walk into the meeting room to see the other men are already seated and looking haggard, which is unusual since they're some of the most professional and put together guys I know. My stomach is in knots and I'm suddenly dreading whatever they're about to tell us.

"Hey, y'all. Welcome back to London. It's been forever since we've seen you!" Silas, the oldest of the brothers, says, coming around the table to greet us.

The O'Connors grew up right down the road from us in Lockwood. When they all started talking about branching into private security, we offered them jobs at OHP as consultants. They're not allowed to work directly with the Omegas since they're unbonded, but it works for them and their skills. They've been in London holding down the fort while our local pack is on parental leave. The other men follow their brother, and we exchange hugs and handshakes all around. Looking at them, I can tell something is off, and I have a feeling whatever plans we had later are about to be cancelled.

I take a seat at one side of the large rectangular table, eyeing the rest of my pack until they do the same. "I hope you know how much we appreciate you looking into this… situation for us."

Owen, who's only a year younger than Silas, answers me. "We were more than happy to do it when you asked us… but I think we have a personal stake in this now, too."

I know I'm not the only one who's confused, and I'm proven right when Kai snaps at him. "What the hell are you talking about, Owen? And why are we here without Blake?"

The four brothers give each other a look I can't decipher, and I notice tears in Beckett's eyes. He's the youngest of the O'Connor's and the most stoic, so to say I'm surprised by his show of emotion in front of us is an understatement. We've known these guys since we were kids, and the last time I saw Beck cry was…

"Holy shit," I say, shock rolling through me as I finally start to put the pieces together. The red hair, the eye color, her age. "We found her? I knew her all this time? My Blake is *Blakely O'Connor?*"

They all look a little misty-eyed now, and even I can feel myself getting choked up. Turning to my pack, I try to keep it together long enough to explain. "Do y'all remember when Beckett's twin sister went missing after preschool one day? He had been home sick, so Mrs. O'Connor arrived a few minutes later than normal to pick up Blakely, but when she got there, nobody knew where she was. We helped them search for *months.* Rook, your parents even funded the search parties when the police declared it a cold case six months later." Covering my mouth with my hand, I turn back to our friends to see them all crying or nearly there.

Beckett sniffs and clears his throat. "We had the shirt y'all sent us examined for DNA, and two matches came back from the Bureau. One for a Phillip Morris, who is a known trafficker, and the other was linked to our sister's cold case." He breaks out into huge, wracking sobs.

Grayson, the last of the O'Connor brothers, pulls Beck's head into his chest and rocks him back and forth like you would a small child. Which is probably exactly how he feels right now. Looking up at us with tears running down his own cheeks, he says five words that are going to change my Shortcake's life forever.

"Blake is our missing sister."

CHAPTER 15

KASPIAN

I'm trying to be gentle as I drag Blake deeper into the set, but good god, I am nearly *drowning* in my need for this girl. She was so excited to come today, and we've learned so much about each other. I'm used to the guys not liking the things I like, or teasing me for them, so the fact that my Omega likes them? I'm about to lose it.

She let me geek out about my favorite books and movies the entire tour, and not only actively *listened* to me, but she *got it.* She likes them all too. Or she likes the idea of them, since she wasn't really allowed TV as a child. I'd get down on one knee right now if the guys were here, but since they aren't, I'm not leaving without at least my bite on her.

Pulling her into a corner of the dark alley, I gently grab her throat and push her up against the fake brick facade. "I was planning on waiting a bit before I asked you this, but you made me fall in love with you in less than two damned hours today, Blake. I know we're scent matched, and even though that doesn't necessarily always mean the match will work, *ours will.* I want you to be mine, B. *My* nerd buddy, *my* partner in crime, *my* Princess, *my* Omega." I say the princess part with a tiny smirk, and she gives me a mock glare.

She's so fucking cute.

Surprising me, she pushes herself up onto her toes as she grabs my sweater and yanks me down to meet her lips. She slips her tongue into my mouth, and I go *wild.*

I grip her thighs in my hands and lift her up, so she can wrap her legs around my hips, not breaking the kiss for even a moment as I press her back against the wall. Using the wall for leverage, I let go of her leg with one hand and cup her face, tilting it to the side so I can slide my tongue in deeper. Her strawberry shortcake scent is filling the space around us, and she tastes even better than she smells.

"I want to be yours, Kaspian," she says, pulling back so her lips brush mine as she speaks. "Today has been one of the best days of my entire life, and it's barely halfway over. Seeing you away from the rest of the pack and in your element has shown me everything I need to know about you. You told me you spend your life in Kai's shadow, always the quiet one, the one who's afraid to be left out, but I see you. You're passionate and smart and so kind to everyone you meet, even with the grumpy face you're always making."

I feel myself scowling at her last comment, proving her point. Her giggle is the sweetest thing in the world, and I hope I get to hear it every day for the rest of my life.

"It's only been a week since we found you, Princess, and already I can't imagine my life with you. You're right, I am used to living in Kairo's shadow. I don't resent him for it. He's just always been loud and outspoken and funny, and sometimes he's my voice when I get anxious. I know he occasionally takes it too far, and sometimes he speaks for me when I don't want him to, but it comes from a good place," I tell her, completely confident that even though I'm talking about him, she would never tell Kai any of this if I don't want her to.

Needing to express my gratitude to this perfect woman, I kiss her deeply. She moans as I lick my way into her mouth, gripping her ass tighter as she grinds against me. We get lost in each other for several minutes until my lungs are begging for oxygen.

Pulling back, I continue as I catch my breath. "I don't talk about my anxiety with anybody but the guys, and even they don't know how bad it gets sometimes. Being around you is the only time I don't feel like the walls are closing in, B. You make me feel seen, but not like there's a spotlight on me. I can breathe when I'm with you. I've been wondering how Rook was ready to bond with you so fast, but Princess, I'm *there*. I need you to be mine in every way, no matter how fast it is. You're already my Omega, but will you take my bite too?"

Giving her a minute to process everything I just dumped on her, I squeeze her thighs and drop playful kisses all over her face. I kiss her cheeks, her forehead, her nose, and by the time I get to her eyelids, she's giggling and pushing me back.

I assume she backed off to answer my question, so when she stays quiet and slides off of me before dropping down to her knees, I'm a bit lost. My confusion is short-lived because the second she runs her hands down my thighs and licks over my erection that's throbbing behind my jeans, all rational thought is gone.

"To answer your earlier question," she says, looking up at me through her lashes with affection shining in her eyes. "I was terrified to come to London, and to come here today. I spent the last seven years locked in a basement and it doesn't feel real that I'm free and safe. And I still haven't wrapped my head around the bond with Rook, but I've never been happier," she says sweetly before unzipping my jeans. She pulls them down just enough so she can lap up the precum dripping from the head of my cock.

Jesus H. How can such a sweet mouth be capable of such sinful things?

She pulls back the barest inch and continues. "You're giving me space to figure out who I am outside the basement, and you're holding my hand while I do it. You listen to me, and always ask my opinion on things. Even things as simple as food. I just… I don't think I need to know every detail about you to love you. The scent match helps, but I fell in love with you for *you.* It might be soon, but I want to be your Omega, Kaspian. I want your bite."

Growling, I yank her back up to my lips, kissing her fiercely and sliding my hands under her thighs to pick her up again. I'm so lost in the taste of her I don't notice that I'm feeling only the bare skin of her ass underneath my hands. I groan deeply. "Princess, are you not wearing shorts under my hoodie?"

She shakes her head slowly, a blush spreading from her cheeks down her neck before disappearing under the sweater.

"Naughty girl, Princess. I'm gonna have to punish you for that later," I say, nipping at her bottom lip.

Her pupils are huge, but she looks a little nervous. "I'm s..sorry Kas. I didn't know I couldn't do that. I promise I'll put on pants if we can stop at the hotel before we go to OHP." She almost looks near tears, and I let go of her ass to cup her face.

"Blake, Princess, take a deep breath and then look at me," I say gently. She takes several before looking me in the eyes. "I was just kidding, baby. None of us will *ever* hurt you. I swear. Something I hope you'll let me teach you is that when I say punishment, I mean something that is going to bring you pleasure, never pain. And if you ever don't like something we say or do, or you find a trigger you didn't know you had, you tell us right away. The word punish is clearly a trigger right now, so we'll avoid that, okay? You're safe with us, Princess. And you can wear and do whatever the fuck you want."

She looks relieved now, and I let out a breath. "Thanks, Kas. I needed to hear that. I've just had too many people punish me in my life for pretty much everything I did, and with you guys, I don't feel like I need to be careful all the time. I worried I got too comfortable and finally messed up," she whispers, her eyes downcast again.

"B, look at me." She does. "You have complete free rein with us. You can wear, say, do anything, and we will *never* treat you like you aren't an equal. That means no real punishments, no yelling, and no pain. *Ever.* We love you too much to treat you like those pieces of shit ever did, okay?"

Nodding, she reaches up to kiss me gently. "Got it," she whispers against my lips. "Can we get back to the fun part now?"

Chuckling darkly, I slide my hands back onto her bare ass, only slightly covered by her underwear that look like tiny shorts. "Oh, you mean this?" I lean down to put my lips next to her ear. "Or do you mean like *this*?" I ask as I slide my hands to her inner thighs and rip her panties in half, only leaving the thick band across her hips intact.

She gasps, letting out a quiet moan. I give her a tiny test smack on one perky cheek. "Do you think you can be quiet, Princess? Or do I need to find a way to keep you quiet?"

The spank caused her to moan again and grind her hot pussy up my shaft, which is hard as steel behind my jeans. I reach down with one hand to free myself the rest of the way.

With flushed cheeks and her perfume thickening in the air, she bites her plump bottom lip. Looking up at me from under her long eyelashes, she whispers, "I think I need you to keep me quiet, Kas."

I tip my head back and groan. "Fuck me, Princess." I reach up higher and tear her panties clean off her body before pulling them out and holding them up between us. "Are you sure you're okay with this, B?"

Her eyes go wide and instead of answering me, she opens her mouth. My dick jumps against her ass, and I need to be inside of her *now*. I ball the panties up and gently put them in her mouth. "The second you start to panic, you spit those out or pinch my side, okay?"

She nods, nothing but trust in her gorgeous green eyes. I reach down between us to play with her clit and find that she's already soaked and ready for me.

Thank fuck for Omega biology.

Wetting my thumb with her slick, I roll her clit between my fingers, reaching down to slide one inside her. Her moans are muffled through the panties in her mouth and the sound drives me to the edge of my sanity. Pumping my finger in her a few more times, I lean down to run my nose up the side of her neck, inhaling her incredible scent.

"You ready for this, Princess?" I ask her quietly, a purr rumbling through my chest when she nods and leans her forehead against my chin.

I line myself up with her entrance and slide into her slowly, giving her plenty of time to adjust to my size, but also giving myself a second so I don't immediately come. Unlike my brother, I've never gone further than some heavy petting with the only girlfriend I ever had. And even that only lasted three weeks.

Moaning loudly, she spits the panties out. "Oh my *god*," she cries breathlessly. "What is that?"

Smirking down at her, I lick up her neck and nip her ear before I answer. "*That*, my Princess, is called a Jacob's Ladder piercing. I waited so long for my first time that I figured it couldn't hurt to get something to add a little extra *pleasure* for both of us."

Her eyes widen, and she gives me the most breathtaking smile I've ever seen. "I love you, Kas."

My breath hitches, and I can't hold back anymore.

Thrusting into her as deep as I can, I slide my hands up to play with her perky tits, surprised to find she's not wearing a bra. "No bra either, B? You really are a naughty girl," I whisper in her ear. Cupping them in my hands, I pinch the nipple on one as I gently squeeze the other, earning a whimper from Blake as she tightens around me.

Still thrusting into her at a steady pace, I drop my hands back to her ass and spread her open even further. Dipping a finger down and gathering some slick on my pointer finger, I slide it up to circle her back hole gently.

She rears her head back, eyes wide and a little apprehensive, but as soon as I add a little pressure and speed up my thrusts, she absolutely *melts* beneath me.

Leaning in for a deep, licking kiss, she uses whatever leverage she can find to bounce back on me, causing my finger to slip inside her the barest amount. She immediately freezes and lets out a loud moan, making me slant my mouth over hers so I can keep all of her noises to myself.

I speed up my thrusts as my knot swells, and I know I'm close. Reaching around to play with my gorgeous girl's clit, I whisper in her ear.

"Are you gonna come for me, Princess? I want you to come all over my cock while I bite you and make you officially mine. Can you do that for me?"

She's crying out loud now, but I can't bring myself to give a single fuck when I'm so close to the edge. Picking up speed, I thrust one finger in her ass as I use the other hand to pinch her clit and she comes screaming. I can feel her clenching around me, and I need my knot in her now. "Look at me." My voice is right on the edge of an Alpha bark. "Are you ready for my bite, B?"

"Bite me, Alpha. Make me yours," she pants out.

I give her a deep kiss, sucking her bottom lip into my mouth. Thrusting one, two, three more times, my knot slips into her at the same time I bite down on her lip just hard enough to draw blood and seal the bond. She comes again, dragging me over the edge with her.

My knot is pulsing, my cock shooting rope after rope of cum into her tight pussy. It continues on for what feels like forever. Her aftershocks cause me to jerk repeatedly inside of her until my knees finally buckle and I land on my ass with my Omega on top of me.

Feeling her giddiness in my chest, I smile as I lean up to tend to her mark, licking across it to speed up the healing process. The bond is absolutely lit up with her happiness and contentment, and I've never felt so whole in my life.

I can even feel echoes of the bond she shares with Rook. It's similar to the pack bond we share, but also so different. Like right now, I can feel his joy at our bonding and his envy wishing he was here for it.

Cupping my sweet girl's face in my hands, I pull her in for a deep kiss, licking her bite again. "You're officially my bonded Omega, Princess. How do you feel?"

She sighs, leaning her head against my chest as we wait for my knot to deflate. "Full," she mumbles wistfully. I chuckle, knowing she didn't mean it literally, but also unable to think of anything else since I'm still locked inside her.

Her head lifts, and she rolls her eyes. "I didn't mean it like that, god you're such a guy." She giggles.

"True," I say. "But I'm *your* guy."

Her eyes light up and she looks so happy I can't help but kiss her again. "Kas..." she starts. "Was this really your first time?"

I feel my cheeks flush as I nod. "Yeah, it was. And I'm so beyond glad I waited for my girl. There's nobody else I would have ever wanted to share this with, and now I get to share it with you for the rest of our lives," I say, nuzzling into her neck.

My knot finally releases us, and I feel a flood of our combined fluids rush out onto my pelvis. My heart stops and my eyes are wide as saucers. "Blake..."

Startled by the sudden shift in my tone, she meets my eyes with concern. "What happened? Are you okay? You're not having second thoughts about the bond, are you?" she asks in a panic.

I choke. "Princess, what? *No.* Absolutely not. I could never regret bonding with you. And I'm so, so happy. Perfectly fine. I just realized we didn't discuss protection, and you're so young. We haven't even discussed kids yet. Holy shit, I can't believe I did that."

Her surprised giggle isn't what I'm expecting at all, so I just stare at her with wide eyes.

"That doctor's appointment I had before we left?" she asks softly, and I nod to show I know what she's talking about.

Bringing my hand up to the inside of her right bicep, she pushes my fingers into what feels like a small bone. I look at her in confusion until she laughs and explains.

"I had a semi-permanent birth control implant put in. It's good for ten years and extra strength to withstand heats," she says. "I'm sorry I didn't bring this up before we bonded, but I don't want kids of my own. I do want kids someday, but instead of having babies, I want to foster teenagers. Kids like Hades and me who just needed someone to love them and care for them. I wish I had found people like the Beaumonts who took him in and raised him as their own, even though he wasn't a little kid. I want to be that pack for someone."

Relief flows over me in waves, and I have so much fucking appreciation for this woman in front of me right now. Tucking her hair behind her ear, I bend down so I'm in her line of sight.

"Princess, you have no idea how happy you just made our entire pack. We've discussed doing the *exact same thing.* And

Hades was always so sure you were going to be our Omega, it made us even more determined to find and foster the older kids who need it most when we were bonded and settled. The fact that you want that too? It's incredible. *You're* incredible, Blake. I love you so goddamn much."

She smiles at me. "I love you too, Kas." She licks over the fresh bond mark on her bottom lip, and I groan.

"Alright, Trouble. Let's get going before we're late to lunch and the cavalry arrives to rescue you from Nerdville."

Gifting me with more of her sweet giggles, she nearly makes my heart explode with her next words. "I'll follow you to Nerdville anytime, Alpha."

CHAPTER 16

BLAKE

The drive to Omega Haven Project Headquarters feels like it takes no time at all. Kas holds my hand the entire way back as he effortlessly navigates the busy London streets, and it's beyond hot.

I keep subconsciously biting my lip and then shivering when I scrape my teeth over my new bond mark. I nearly had another orgasm when he insisted on tending to it again before we left the studio.

I was so worried we would be yelled at or get into trouble for our little tryst, but nobody ever came looking for us or said anything when we left. Kas explained their pack is extremely well known for their work with the OHP, and, because of their money, they're given a lot of special privileges they try not to abuse.

Soon enough, we're pulling up at a beautiful old building in the middle of what looks like a quaint shopping district. My jaw drops as I turn to look at my Alpha after he parks. "*This* is your London headquarters? It's gorgeous here!" I'm bouncing in my seat, eager to go explore. "I feel so underdressed. I mean, I don't even have a bra on," I say, pouting lightly.

He turns to look at me, cocking his head to the side. "Yeah, I meant to ask earlier, why *don't* you have a bra on? Not that you have to wear one, because you don't. I was just wondering."

My cheeks flush bright red and I mumble, "I don't have one."

His eyes widen slightly. "I'm sorry. What was that?"

Sighing in frustration, I turn to face him fully. "I don't have one, okay? I've been kept in a basement since I was eleven, and I definitely didn't have boobs then. I could go buy myself one now, but I wouldn't even know where to start or what to do…" I trail off, embarrassed at my lack of knowledge.

"Blake. Look at me, Princess," he says softly, lifting my chin. "You don't need to feel ashamed for not knowing or having something. You said it yourself; you were locked in a basement for god's sake. But you have us now, and your pack isn't gonna let you go without anything. After the tour, we'll go get lunch and then get you some new underwear. How does that sound?"

I cringe slightly. "I don't want you to have to spend money on me. I have a bit saved up that I can use to get a few things I need."

He scoffs and gives me an incredulous look. "Princess, we're your *pack*, and while we don't like to flaunt it, we have more money than God. If we want to take you out and buy you pretty underwear, or lunch, or a fucking *car*, please just let us. It soothes our Alpha instincts to take care of you, and you don't need to spend your own money when everything we have is now yours, too. We love you, Blake, and that means taking care of your every need and want." He pauses for a second. "Wait a minute, how do you have money saved up?" he asks curiously.

I'm blushing hotly now. "Oh...um.... So, every time Phil got a little too drunk and passed out in his chair, I would take some money out of his wallet and hide it. I was planning my escape the entire time I was in that basement. I know it was wrong to steal but..."

He interrupts me. "No. Absolutely not. B, you did what you had to do to survive, and he owed you so much more than the bit of money you took. Never apologize or feel guilty for what you had to do to survive that hellhole." He kisses me. "I'm so damned proud of you."

Trying not to cry, I quickly change the subject. "Can we go inside now? I'm excited to meet people and see what you do."

I'm sure he can feel my anxiety through the bond, so he just nods and gives me another quick kiss before getting out and opening my door for me. We walk in the front entrance so he can explain a little about the history of the building. When we get to security, they take my picture and give me a special access card.

Wrapping my hands around Kas' bicep, I look up at him and ask, "Kas, why do I get a special access card when I might not ever be here again?"

He raises his eyebrow at me and pulls us to a stop, gently grabbing my cheeks in his big hands. "Princess, I don't even know where to start with that. First thing, we'll be here once every few months." My jaw drops open in shock and he nods. "We come here as often as we can to support our staff. Now for the second thing, you, my sweet B, get that special access card because you're an owner now. Being an owner means that card gives you access to every single building owned or used by the OHP."

My eyes are wide as saucers at this point as he leads me to the elevators and scans my pass against it, pressing the highest button. Turning to me, he smirks and gently chucks my chin, so I snap out of my shock.

"What do you mean, I'm an *owner?*" I hiss. "I've known you guys a week, and I've never been a part of the OHP. How can I be an owner?"

He still has that infuriating smirk on his face. "You're cute when you're angry. Like a feisty little kitten." He chuckles. My brows furrow and I scowl at him as he tosses an arm over my shoulder. "You're our Omega, B. Everything we have is yours now. Do you want to work at OHP with us?"

My scowl lessens as I think it over. "Yeah. I think I would really like that. Especially if I can work with the kids you rescue in some capacity. I would love to take some youth psychology courses somewhere too, so I can really help them," I say softly.

I'm overwhelmed at the opportunities I might never have gotten if I hadn't met these men, and I can feel myself getting anxious. Just as my breathing speeds up, Kas stops the elevator and picks me up, so my legs wrap around his waist. He tucks my face into his neck and purrs loudly as hugs me tight. One hand burrowing in to play with my hair.

Kissing the top of my head, he speaks into my hair. "Princess, I can feel you spiraling. You don't have to decide everything right now, or even in the next year, okay? We just found you, Blake. Let's enjoy some time as a newly bonded pack and learn everything we can about each other. Before the pressure of things like school, work, travel and eventually fostering keeps us apart more than an hour a day."

My chest finally expands with a full breath as his scent relaxes me, and I smile shyly up at him. "Thank you, Alpha."

Growling, he pushes the button to start the elevator again. Then he kisses me on the nose before licking over his bond mark, pulling a moan from me as our scents thicken in the small space. "You're welcome, Princess. I love you."

Shivering, I say, "I love you too."

The doors finally open to the rest of our pack, looking

anxious. Hades rushes me, pulling me from Kas and wrapping me up in a tight hug. "Thank God you're finally here. Are you okay?"

Confused, I gently push on his chest a bit so I can glance around. Rook is rolling his eyes, and Achilles is standing close to the elevator, smirking as his chest rises on a deep inhale.

"Umm... I'm fine? I was with Kas," I say slowly. "Are *you* okay?"

His eyes are wide and wild as he takes in deep lungfuls of my scent, his heart racing beneath my palm where it rests on his chest. "I... no. Not really. We have some news for you," he says softly.

It's my turn to panic now, a whine slipping out as I turn to look at my bonded Alphas. They moved to stand together and have been talking quietly since Hades grabbed me. When my panic spikes in the bond, their gazes dart to mine and they rush over to pull me between them. They purr at the same time, soothing me instantly.

Rook turns to look at Hades. "You couldn't have waited a minute to bring it up?" he hisses quietly. "They just got here, and Blake needs to eat," he says, more softly this time.

Hades looks like a lost puppy as his gaze moves between the three of us, and he clears his throat before reaching a hand out for me. I take it, letting him pull me into a hug. "I'm so sorry, Shortcake," he whispers. "I didn't mean to scare you. I promise it's good news, but Rook is right. Let's go get some food and meet a few people and then we'll talk, okay?"

I nod slightly, even though the thought of eating right now kind of turns my stomach. Suddenly I'm scooped up and thrown over a slender shoulder, and I let out a small shriek.

Achilles chuckles as he lightly taps my butt. "Come on, mon cœur. Let's go get some pizza. Our team ordered it in for lunch and it should be here by now. Plus, you can meet Amelia!"

~

ONE VERY DELICIOUS slice of pizza and several of Amelia's homemade cookies later, I have a new friend. Amelia is an incredibly sweet female Alpha who's in her thirties and smells like the ocean. I took to her the second the guys introduced us and her bonded Omega Jane, and I have already planned dinner the next time we're in town.

We're all walking to a conference center when Kai gently grabs my elbow and holds me back as the others head into the room ahead of us. Hades glances back with a sad look on his face and my anxiety spikes again when I remember they have something to tell me.

"Don't look so nervous, Sugar. I promise everything is okay," he says.

My eyes are tearing up from nerves. "Kai, what's going on? Why does D look so sad? You guys are freaking me out and I don't like this feeling," I whisper, trying my best to hold back nervous tears.

As long as I can remember, I've been an anxious crier. When I lived with Phil, I had to hold it in until he was asleep. On nights I knew he was going to come home drunk, I would cry for hours beforehand because I needed a way to release the building anxiety.

My happy Alpha's eyes widen when he sees my tears, and he cups my cheeks in his warm hands.

"No no no no none of that, Darlin'. Please don't cry," he whispers in his smooth southern accent as he peppers my face with kisses. I let out a small giggle at that, my anxiety lessening for a moment.

Leaving one last sweet kiss on my nose, he backs up the barest inch to look in my eyes. "What do you remember from your childhood, Blake? Before you were in foster care, I mean," he asks quietly.

My brows furrow, and I try to think of what I actually remember. "Umm… honestly? Not much. My parents were pretty awful, but they homeschooled me, so nobody ever knew. Any time we'd go in public, I had to wear long shirts and pants and sunglasses to hide the bruises from their 'punishments', even in the middle of summer."

Kai lets out the start of a vicious growl before clearing his throat. "Sorry," he says. "I hate that you were ever treated like that, Sugar. And knowing you were just a little girl makes me sick." Taking a deep breath, he pulls me gently into his chest. "If you don't mind me asking, how did you end up in foster care? Did somebody see something?"

I'm shaking my head before he even finishes his question. "No, there was a fire at the house…" I say slowly, trying to remember details of a day I tried hard to forget, but had vague nightmares about for years. "I was locked in my room because I had gotten sassy with my mom a couple of days before about school."

A chorus of growls sound out from behind me. Whipping my head around, I see the rest of my pack standing there, clearly having heard every word. My cheeks burn with embarrassment and Hades steps up to hug me from behind.

"Shortcake, please don't feel embarrassed. We want to know everything about you, and you know we'll never judge you. Your story can't be any worse than mine," he finishes quietly. And he's right. He was mistreated by the only parent he ever knew and then abandoned. At least mine didn't abandon me on purpose.

Nodding, I continue. Sweet looks from each of my guys give me the courage to finish my story. "So, I was locked in my room, and it started to get really hot, which I remember thinking was weird because they never turned on the heat, no matter how cold it got. I went to try to open my door, but my hand got burned really bad and I started crying. I tried hitting my door with my chair because it was the only solid thing I had, but the chair broke. I was so small and weak from being hungry for so long."

The men growl again at that, and I wince, not having meant to let that part slip.

"It was really smokey, and I was starting to panic because I didn't have a way out or a way to call 911. My window was nailed shut, so I used a piece of the chair to break the glass. The house was really old, so thankfully the glass broke easily. I could hear sirens and see neighbors standing around, but nobody was looking at the attic window. I guess over the noise, nobody heard it break…" I trail off, lost in thought for a minute as memories of that day threaten to overwhelm me.

I'm jolted back to the present when Kai lifts my chin. "Stay with us, Sugar. You're not there anymore. You're safe. We've got you," he murmurs. My eyes water, and I give him a small lift of my chin. With a nod, he encourages me to go on.

"The attic was on the third floor, and the fire was so fast. It had already spread through the door. I was ten years old and scared I was going to die. After another minute, I knew help wouldn't make it in time, so I climbed out the window and held onto the ledge as long as I could before my arms gave out and I dropped. Thankfully, one of the men standing around had noticed me and was able to catch me before I hit the ground. My hands and arms were cut and bloody. I had bruises from the day before, and I'm sure I looked like a wreck. The man didn't care that I was getting blood all over his clothes. He still held me the entire time until Social Services got there. Even as the paramedics checked me over, he insisted he be allowed to stay with me…"

The guys all look a little confused, and looking back, I can see why they were confused. Rook looks the most troubled.

"Angel," he asks, "did you know that man?"

I shake my head. "No, but he seemed so angry. Not *at* me,

but *for* me. I remember him flashing a badge and trying to stay with me even longer. But because they couldn't find my birth certificate, he said his hands were tied, and I had to go with Social Services," I say quietly. "I only know his name because he kept repeating it. He just kept saying he wanted me to know the name Roman James in case I ever got in trouble with the police or needed help."

He sucks in a breath, eyes wide. "Blake… I think that man was my uncle."

CHAPTER 17

BLAKE

I'm gaping at Rook for several long seconds before a slightly hysterical laugh bubbles out of me, causing him to look at me in alarm. Tears are building in my eyes as I stare at him, the laughter receding slightly when I see his face that had just been shocked turn grim.

"That's not funny, Daddy," I whisper as he moves closer.

I thought I was quiet enough that nobody but him would hear me, but I'm quickly proven wrong when Hades chokes behind me. He sends himself into a coughing fit as he moves away from me, brushing off the others' concern. My cheeks are flushed when I turn back to see a small smile playing on the big guy's lips.

He leans down, getting right in my ear so only I can hear him. "I love it when you call me that, Angel. *Especially* when we're in public." Lightly sucking at his bond mark, he leans back and winks before sobering.

"I wasn't kidding, Angel," he speaks loud enough for the other guys to hear this time. "I know it's been a long time, but was he super tall? With black hair, features similar to mine?

He would have had a fresh scar or a bandage through his left eyebrow."

My jaw drops open. "Holy crow," I whisper. "How… how is that possible?"

Shaking his head, he takes my hand. "I don't know, Blake. But we're gonna go home and find out. I promise."

I'm distracted from answering when I catch the faint scent of strawberries and chocolate. It triggers something in my brain that I can't quite latch on to, tears immediately springing to my eyes and rolling down my cheeks.

Kas is by my side in seconds, cupping my cheeks in both hands. "B, what is it? What just happened? Your scent just took a nosedive," he says frantically.

I shake my head quickly; the scent getting stronger. "I—"

"Hey," a new voice says. "Are y'all alright out here? I thought we were gonna meet… Blake." The stranger stops abruptly less than two feet in front of me, tears filling his light green eyes the minute he sees me behind the guys. "Oh my god… I thought… I didn't really think it was you," he chokes out through sobs. He looks so familiar and actually, he looks just like me. With the same eyes, red hair, and freckles covering his face. Although he has a lot less than I do, and he's probably close to a foot taller than I am.

Another man comes rushing up behind him, bringing the familiar scent of peaches with him. This one is even taller than the first, with dark russet hair and a thin layer of facial hair the same color. "Beck, you good, brother? You're all over the place in the bond right… now." He stops speaking and his jaw drops open as the man, Beck, I guess, turns the newcomer's head towards me. "Holy shit… Blakely?" he whispers. "Is that you, bug?"

I step back, using Kas and Rook as human shields. I don't know what's going on, but I know their scents, and I don't know why. I can feel panic beginning to creep up my throat as my breathing becomes erratic.

My head is shaking as I step back. "I don't... I don't know you," I squeak out through my tears. "My name is Blake, not Blakely. I don't..." I stop, taking a deep breath as strong arms wrap around me from behind. Closing my eyes, I catch another whiff of their scents and something about them mixing together urges memories forward that I'm not sure are real.

Loud Sunday morning breakfasts, fighting my brothers for the last chocolate chip pancake.

Holding hands with Beckett and skipping on walks to school with mama.

Daddy Ben holding me on his shoulders at the rodeo so I can see the horses.

Grayson gently pulling my pigtails and telling me I'll always be his very best friend.

Silas helping me with my backpack on the way to school.

Owen holding me as I cried when I fell off my bike and scraped my knee.

Mommy's new friend picking me up from school because Beck was sick.

Falling asleep in the car because I was getting sick, too.

Waking up alone, sick, and scared.

Crying for Mommy and Daddy. For Beck and Gray and Si and Wenny.

Ellie telling me she was my new Mommy now, that my family moved away and didn't want me anymore.

Bruises, hunger, tears, and pain. So. Much. Pain.

My hand comes up to cover my mouth as a loud sob escapes, my other hand squeezing Rook's arm so hard I'm worried I'll draw blood. He squeezes me tight and sends love and calm down the bond as he leans down to whisper in my ear. "It's okay, Angel. I can feel your confusion, how scared you are. You were barely five when you were taken, and we all looked for you for years, Blake. But you're remembering now, aren't you? You know them. Deep down inside."

I'm nodding, and I couldn't stop the tears if I wanted to. I give my Alpha's arm one last squeeze and step out of his embrace. Both of the men in front of me are crying openly and I can't take my eyes off of them as the pieces click into place inside my brain. Buried memories of the only time I was ever happy in my life. My *real* family.

"Beck?" I whisper, facing the man I now realize must be my twin. He nods as I turn my head to the man standing next to him, who's inching closer to me slowly. "Gray?" I guess. He has the same pretty brown eyes I remember wishing I had, because I couldn't stand the color green.

They both nod and we all just stand there for a second.

And then the dam breaks.

I don't know who reaches first, but suddenly I'm in their arms and it feels like *home.* Not like it feels when I'm with my pack, but like my soul has been hurting for so long and these men are the balm to my childhood pain. The small pieces I didn't even know were missing until now. We're all crying as we pull back and each of them grabs a hand like they're afraid I might disappear again if they don't.

"Jesus... I can't... I can't believe you're here. That our best friends found you. That D *knew* you all these years, and we didn't know. Holy shit, we have to go home." Beckett's eyes are wild as he looks toward my pack. "We have to go home and bring her to Mom and Dads'. It can't wait." He's rambling, talking as fast as he can, like he's afraid they're going to fight him on it.

Achilles moves to the side to catch my eye, raising his brows. I can practically hear the unspoken question, so I give him a minute nod, needing him, needing them *all* to know I want to go home.

He nods back at me and claps his hands together. "Alrighty then, y'all. D, you find a team that can cover the O'Connors. Rook, I need you with me to pack up the hotel and get the flight arranged. Kai, I need you to fill everyone in on why we're leaving and grab anything we may need for the flight home. Kas, you stay with notre cœur and facilitate the reunion with the other yahoos." He winks at me, walking over to kiss me on the forehead. "And you, ma douce fraise, be good." Booping me on the nose, he runs off to do whatever things my sweet Beta does to keep us all on track.

Beck and Gray escort me into the conference room where the other two are on a call with a client who's apparently been very picky about how she wants her security set up.

"Although honestly, I think she just uses it as an excuse to flirt with us. Victoria has been a pain in our asses since we were kids," Grayson says. "It's been worse since you guys left. You should probably keep her away from your new pack member when y'all get home." He directs this at Kas, who rolls his eyes and scoffs.

"She couldn't get our attention even when we were kids. She's sure as hell not gonna get it now that we have an Omega," he says grumpily. His face transforms into a smile as soon as he turns to me. "I'm so excited to have you in our home finally, Princess." He gives me a light kiss, causing the two men in front of us to gag dramatically.

I roll my eyes as we walk into the conference room, letting out a quiet giggle. The second I do, the two men hunched over the table next to a phone whip their heads up to stare at me, eyes wide and mouths parted. The one I think is Silas quickly ends the conversation with their client.

"Sorry, Victoria, we have to go. We'll schedule a meeting soon," he says gruffly as he hangs up the phone.

Standing up straight, I see that he's probably as tall as Rook, and has dark brown hair with the faintest tinge of red in it. Gray gently tugs my hand and pulls me to stand in front of my other brothers.

God, that's weird to even think. I have brothers! A whole family!

Snapping myself out of my musing, I look at the two wide-eyed men in front of me. Silas looks the most different out of all of them. He's huge and bulky with muscles. His dark hair is cut close to his head, and he has a serious look on his face that's kind of intimidating when you combine it with his dark eyes. Owen looks exactly the same, just older. Honey brown eyes that are glowing with joy, piercing through one eyebrow and in both ears. Lots of tattoos, and lighter russet hair that's closer to mine and Beck's than the other two.

It's Owen who steps forward first, looking at me like he's not sure if I'm real. "Blakely... sorry—*Blake*... is it really you?" he asks quietly.

My eyes are filling again, but I don't cry this time. "Hey, Wenny," I murmur. His eyes light up even as they glisten with tears, and he pulls me in for a tight hug.

Leaning in, he whispers loud enough I'm sure everybody else can hear. "I can't believe you're here right now. We missed you so much, Strawbs." He chuckles, using a nickname I vaguely remember from before I was taken.

Silas is the last to approach me, seeming hesitant. I don't make a move towards him, wanting to give him time to process however he needs to. I mean, I'm sure I'll have a breakdown on the flight home when the shock wears off. For now, though, I just want to scream that I have a family that cares about me. That I wasn't unloved and unwanted my entire life until the guys found me.

I watch emotions play across Si's face too fast for me to decipher. He finally settles on what I can only describe as elation as his face breaks out into a massive grin showcasing perfect teeth. He rushes forward and steals me from Owen, spinning me around as he laughs.

"Holy shit," he says as he sets me down and pulls me in for a tight hug. I look up to see his eyes watering. "Our baby sister is alive. And *bonded* to our best friends." He turns to Kas, leveling him with a scary look. Kas looks like his typical stoic self before he breaks into a huge grin and comes to hug both of us.

"Guess we really are family now, huh *bro*," he chuckles as he leans over to ruffle Beckett's hair.

My pack finally comes strolling back in a little while later as I'm giving my brothers a general overview of the last thirteen years of my life. There's enough growling and Alpha energy in the room that I'm slowly retreating into myself, my Omega nature not used to this amount of angry Alpha all at once. Achilles seems to sense the tension when he walks in. So, he scoops me up out of my chair and sets me in his lap, pulling my face into his neck so I get his calming lemon bar scent that's purely Beta.

"There you go, Pretty Girl. I figured you'd be ready for a nap and some calming Beta cuddles right about now," he murmurs gently. To the rest of the guys, he speaks louder. "The plane is ready when we are, and I think today has been a lot for all of us. I'm gonna take Blake and get her set up in the bedroom so she can rest before the next big emotional reunion. The rest of y'all, are you flying with us or separately? We have a team to cover your positions for as long as you need."

It's quickly decided that my brothers will fly separately on the other jet so they can pack up their flat and hopefully be home shortly after us. Achilles carries me out to the car where he buckles me in between him and Hades. The last thing I remember is laying my head on D's shoulder with a smile and sucking in lungfuls of his delicious caramel apple scent.

CHAPTER 18

ACHILLES

We made the half hour drive to the airport, boarded the jet, got through takeoff, and had been flying for three hours all as Blake slept peacefully in my arms. D came to the room and joined us in the bed for a nap maybe an hour ago, and Blake is just now waking up.

Stretching, she unintentionally grinds her perky ass against my growing erection, causing me to groan low in my throat. Her head whips around and there's a blush high on her cheeks. Glancing back at Hades to make sure he's asleep, she turns over to face me.

"Sorry," she whispers, running her hands down my chest and over my abs, visible underneath my cropped tee.

She doesn't stop until she reaches the band of my sweats. Tracing her soft fingers back and forth across the skin of my lower abdomen, she stops at the tattoo peeking out from above my waistband.

I hear her quiet gasp as she looks at me with questioning eyes. I reach down to pull my sweats down a few inches, exposing the V on my hips and the top of my pubic bone. As well as the fresh tattoo Blake is currently gaping at.

"But…when did you get this?" she whispers. "And *why?*"

Grabbing her hand, I kiss each fingertip between words. "I wanted to get something for my Omega. I know you can't technically mark me or bond me like you can with the others, but I needed a mark, too. So, the day after we found you, I snuck out and got a strawberry for you. All it took was one hit of your delicious scent, one small conversation. I'm all in, ma jolie fraise. Forever."

Her eyes are wet with emotion, but she reaches up to kiss me, immediately slipping her tongue into my mouth and pulling a moan from me. I reach down to pull her on top of me, and she wastes no time grinding into my rapidly hardening cock. We're so lost in each other that when she lets out a startled gasp followed by a long moan a few minutes later, it takes me a few seconds to realize why.

Hades has pulled her shorts down and is licking her from behind, *while* she's grinding on top of me. None of us have ever shared a girl before, considering most of us were virgins until this sweet Omega walked into our lives, and I didn't realize just how hot it could be. Looking up at me, he cocks an eyebrow, silently asking if I'm okay with this. I respond with a small nod and turn back to Blake.

"Do you want this, Pretty Girl? Do you want D and I to make you feel good?" I ask her.

He runs his hands from her ass up her sides to rest over mine on her hips. "Yesss," she hisses out. "Please, I need you both."

Lifting her off of me, he sets her on the ground and barks at her to strip. I'm about to go off on him for using his Alpha bark on her when Blake shocks the hell out of me by immediately complying.

Her eyes glazing over with lust and her perfume blossoming throughout the small room. Not a trace of fear in her expression. It's a good thing this plane is ours, because at this rate we'll never get her scent out of here.

Not that we'd try.

In seconds, our Omega is naked in front of us and my heart feels like it's going to beat out of my chest. I'm stunned speechless at how insanely fucking gorgeous she is. D smacks her ass, and she lets out a little yelp, turning a cute glare his way. He just smirks at her, grabbing her hips and guiding her towards me.

"Why don't you help your Beta get undressed, Shortcake? He's looking a little shell-shocked by your perfect body," he says smugly.

I never expected my Pretty Girl to get this confident this fast. She saunters over to me sexily before pecking me on the lips and pulling the half shirt off over my head.

She pauses to stare at it for a second before turning back to me. "I really like that shirt on you," she murmurs, a light pink blush marring her freckled cheeks.

I let out the closest thing to a growl I can and pull her face to mine, kissing her deeply. Swiping my tongue over hers, my dick jumps in my sweats when I get a taste of her perfect strawberry shortcake flavor. The deeper I kiss her, the clearer it becomes. Bright tangy strawberries, sweet fluffy angel food cake, and rich vanilla whipped cream. All mixed together in a flavor that's perfectly fitting for ma fraise chérie.

My Darling Strawberry.

I feel Hades come up behind her and pull her hips back, forcing her to lean even further into me as she grips my hair for stability.

"Ohhh my god. Please don't stop," she whimpers out.

He stops whatever he's doing, pulling a whine from her. He chuckles. "Aw come on, Shortcake. You're practically a platinum member of the mile high club now. Let's take advantage of your newfound sense of adventure. There's no time for whining when our Beta looks like he's feeling a little neglected. Why don't you see if he tastes as good as he smells?" The smug bastard throws a wink my way when he sees my blush.

I'm not into guys necessarily, but I'm also not *afraid* of them either. If a little touching or flirting happens while we're trying to make our girl feel good, I'm gonna go with the flow and enjoy it.

What can I say? My pack is hot. A little heteroflexibility never hurt anybody.

She looks nervous, and D must be able to tell even while not being able to see her face. Stripping off his own clothes until he's completely naked, he winks at me again and leans in to whisper in our girl's ear. "You need a little help, Love? Here, start like this."

He puts his hands over hers and slides them up my legs to the waistband of my joggers. Curling their fingers into the band on either side, he helps Blake tug them down slowly.

Hearing her quick intake of breath as my painfully hard cock springs free almost sends me over the edge before she's even touched me. I gasp and toss my head back, trying desperately to control myself and let her explore.

"Oh my god," she breathes, leaning in even closer to inspect the four bars that line the underside of my shaft. "You have them too," she whispers under her breath. "When did you get these?"

I can feel her breath rushing across my sensitive skin and it's taking everything in me to stay still. Suddenly remembering she asked me a question; I blow out the breath I'd been holding. "I got them for my birthday last year. D went with me and held my hand." I chuckle, remembering him teasing me about never getting through TSA again. "The fucker never lets me forget it, either." I smirk at my pack mate before something about what she said comes back to me. "Wait… what do you mean, I have them *too*?" I ask.

Her cheeks flush an even deeper shade of red and she giggles nervously. "Oh… umm… Kas also has them," she murmurs.

Looking behind her to D, I can tell we're both shocked.

"What the fuck?" he chokes out around a laugh.

I roll my eyes and shoot him a glare I don't really mean. "Listen, can we talk about Kaspian's dick bling later? I'd love to get back to focusing on our girl now, *Alpha*," I say mockingly.

Heat takes over his eyes as he leans down to nip at our girl's ear. "You hear that, Shortcake? Our Beta's getting impatient. Should we give him some relief?" he whispers.

Blake's gaze darts between us before finally settling on me. "Can I touch you?" she whispers as D slides their hands from my knees to my pelvis, stopping just shy of where I need to be touched.

Reaching one hand out to cup her perky breast, I lick my bottom lip and give her a heated look. "Pretty Girl, you can do *whatever* you want to me, just please touch me. I'm dyin' here, Sweetheart." My voice is hoarse with desire.

Her cheeks are on fire, and her pupils are blown out. "Will you tell me if I do it wrong?"

Hades lets out a laugh at that, pulling her in for a dirty kiss that makes my dick jump, bumping into their hands on my hip. Licking across her mouth one last time, he pulls back. "See, love? Anything you do, anything *we* do, is going to be good for our Beta. Do you need help starting?" he murmurs against her lips.

She nods shyly.

"You good with both of us touching you, Lee?" he asks quietly.

I nod frantically. "I don't care who touches me right now,

as long as somebody fucking touches me before I explode," I grind out, my breaths coming faster the closer they get.

Sliding their hands up, he curls them hand around my shaft, letting her feel the piercings as he gently pumps up and down my shaft. My hips thrust up to meet them on each downward stroke.

"Jesus, fuuuuck. Harder, *please*," I beg.

Squeezing harder, D is still whispering instructions into our Omega's ear. "That's it, gorgeous, squeeze him harder. In fact, why don't you try tasting him while I taste *you*?"

CHAPTER 19

HADES

I never thought I would see one of my best friends lose his virginity. And I sure as *fuck* never thought I would get turned on seeing him fall apart for our Omega, let alone *touching him*.

He's always joked about being flexible in his sexuality and I honestly thought he was kidding. But no. He's currently naked and writhing on the bed as I watch our Omega suck him into her mouth. She moans like his dick is the best thing she's ever tasted while I guide her hand to cup his balls. I'm so hard I can barely think straight, and all I want to do is bury myself in my sweet Shortcake.

Leaning down behind her, I let her play with her Beta while I go to work on her perfect pussy. Taking a deep inhale, I immediately focus on her clit, licking in gentle circles. She moans around Achilles, causing his hips to buck off the bed.

"Godfuckingdamnit. I'm sorry, Pretty Girl. I didn't mean to go so deep," he grinds out. "You okay?"

She pulls off his cock with a pop, and everything is silent for a moment. "Umm I'm fine... was that bad? Did it hurt you?" she asks.

I whip my own head up, blinking owlishly at Lee with my jaw hanging open. He's staring back, just as wide eyed as I am.

"Shortcake, do me a favor? Take Lee as far down your throat as you can without gagging," I ask her.

She looks confused, but does as I ask, slowly lowering her mouth onto him until her nose touches his lower abdomen. Achilles lets out a loud moan as she hums around him, clearly still enjoying his flavor.

"Holy shit Blake. Did one of the other guys teach you how to do that?" I ask, shocked at her lack of gag reflex.

My sweet girl shakes her head but doesn't come up for air, and Lee's moaning gets louder as I watch her instinctively swallow around him.

I need to be inside her *now.*

Scrambling back behind her, I dip one finger inside her, quickly adding a second when I feel how wet she is. I thrust my fingers inside her for a few minutes, putting pressure on her front wall. As soon as she clenches around me, I pull out, earning an adorable whine out of her. I lean forward to nip at her neck.

"You ready to take my knot, gorgeous? I've been waiting for this since the minute I kissed you on that swing," I say, licking up the side of her neck.

"Mmhmm," she mumbles around our Beta.

If I keep watching her suck his cock, I'm gonna blow before I even make it inside her. Lining myself up with her entrance, I push in slowly. She finally comes up for air and lets out a long moan. Thrusting into her faster, I wrap her hair around my fist and gently guide her head down to Achilles' cock, encouraging her to take him back down her throat.

"That's it, baby. Such a good girl, sucking your Beta's cock like that. You gonna make him cum down your throat?" I ask her, trying my best to get them both there before I explode and lock myself inside the heaven that is my Omega.

"I'm really fucking close, Darlin'. Swallow around me just like that," he moans loudly, wrapping his hand in her hair with mine. I lace our fingers together, helping him work her over his cock while still pounding into her from behind. The sounds of our skin slapping together echoing around the cabin.

Leaning forward, I take her hand again and guide it from the base of Achilles' dick further down to the space between his balls and his ass. I whisper in her ear loud enough so he can hear, "Stroke your fingers along here, love, and watch."

She does as I say while I guide her, and he loses it.

"Oh fuck, oh shit, goddamnit D. Blake, baby, I'm gonna come. That feels too fucking good," he chants frantically.

He tries to pull her off of him, but she doubles down and takes him even deeper, if possible.

"Fuck, fuck, fuuuuuuck yes. Swallow every drop, Pretty Girl," he groans loudly, panting as his hips thrust up to meet her puffy lips.

"How does he taste, Shortcake?" I ask when she pulls off him, moaning loudly as I change angles to hit the perfect spot. I *need* her to come before I knot her. I need this to be as good as possible for her.

"So freaking good," she whimpers. "Wanna taste?" she asks with a wicked smirk I've never seen on her cute face before.

Taking a second to think about her request, I realize I kind of want to say yes. So, I use the fist still buried in her hair to yank her face to mine. I plunge my tongue deep into her mouth and tasting her sweet strawberry shortcake flavor mixed with his tart lemon bar. I'm still not into dudes, but *fuck*, they taste good together.

A sound that's half growl, half purr comes out of my throat. "Fuck, man, you need to taste that," I tell him.

He smiles at me, sitting up on shaky arms to lick into her mouth as I pound into her from behind. Smile morphing into a wicked smirk, he slides off the bed to kneel at our feet and suddenly I feel a tongue at the base of my cock, licking over my knot and her clit. A sound I'm pretty sure I've never made before comes out of me when he repays the favor by stroking his fingers along my taint.

"*FUCK*," I shout. My knot is swelling bigger than I've ever felt it, and I need to lock into her *right now.* "Blake, Shortcake, you ready for your Alpha's knot?"

"Yes, please. Knot me, Alpha," she sobs out. Achilles must have his tongue on her clit because her legs are shaking, and he puts his hands over mine on her hips to hold her up.

I thrust into her once, twice, a third and final time. I'm coming so hard I see stars, roaring out my release as my knot slips past her tight entrance and locks us together.

Achilles speaks from beneath us. "Come for me, Pretty Girl. All over your Alpha's knot and your Beta's face. Come *now.*"

Blake falls apart with a scream, her legs giving out beneath her. Mine aren't too steady either, so with Lee's help, we guide our sweet Omega to the bed before collapsing on either side of her. Both of us pepper kisses all over her face and upper body.

I know we need to clean up, but they're so warm and cuddly. Achilles has his arm around Blake's waist and against my stomach, and it's comforting being wrapped in their scents. I wish the rest of the pack was in here, too, but we'll be home in the pack bedroom soon.

Just as I'm drifting off to sleep, she gently clears her throat. "I know it hasn't been long, and there's so much going on right now, but I want you both to know I love you," she murmurs. At my sharp intake of breath, she reaches up and twines our fingers together, bringing them to rest just under her breasts. "It's true," she continues, "I love all of you so much. And Achilles, I know I can't bond with you like I can the others, but…"

"I'll bond you both," I blurt out. Lee sits up on one elbow, staring at me with wide eyes, his mouth open in shock.

"We're not… we don't…" he stutters out, unable to complete a full thought.

I grab his hand with my free one, twining our fingers together over Blake's hip. "I know," I say. "I love you, Lee. I don't think I love you as more than a friend and a pack mate, but giving you a bond with our Omega and becoming your Alpha too? As far as I see it, this is just another way to bring you closer to the pack. Not all bonds are sexual, and ours doesn't have to be either unless we've got Shortcake between us. Let me give y'all a real bond."

His eyes are bright with unshed tears as he looks from me to Blake. "Do you want that, ma jolie fraise? Do you want to bond with me? I know I'm not an Alpha, but…"

She cuts him off with a finger over his mouth. "Baby… *of course* I want a bond with you. You were one of the first faces I saw when I came to this pack. The first person to tell me how happy you are to have me here. *I love you*, Achilles. I want to be yours in every way possible," she says, getting choked up. Looking up at me, she kisses me lightly on the mouth. "Will you make us yours, Alpha?"

My knot is starting to deflate, but I'm not ready to lose that connection yet. Surging forward, I grab her hand, bringing it to my mouth and kissing the fleshy part of her palm right underneath her thumb before sinking my teeth in. I feel the bond snap into place and lick over the wound before pulling Achilles forward. I place a gentle kiss where his neck meets his shoulder before doing the same to him, cementing the bond between the three of us. After tending to both of their wounds, I finally pull back to see tears in both of their eyes. Blake pulls us both in for a hug and kisses away the tears I'm surprised to feel on my own cheeks.

"I love you both. Thank you for giving us this, D," Achilles says, gratitude shining in his hazel eyes.

I squeeze his hand before we all snuggle into each other, and I pull a blanket over us. As I drift off to sleep, the only thought in my head is how lucky I am to have a bond with the girl I've loved most of my life, and one of my very best friends.

CHAPTER 20

BLAKE

e landed in Lockwood early the next morning. The guys wanted to take me straight to my parents' house after we stopped at their house for quick showers and breakfast for all of us. My brothers were less than an hour behind us and were planning on meeting us there.

What I've seen so far of my pack's house is *gorgeous*. It's like someone took my dream house and dropped it in this adorable, gated community.

The house is a massive modern antebellum style with a huge wraparound porch and second-floor balcony. The siding is bright white, leading down to black painted brick at the bottom and black storm shutters. There are also flat overhangs on each side of the roof that would be perfect for stargazing. I haven't seen much of the inside, but what I have seen is full of natural light and soft colors. The guys all promised me I could explore more later.

There wasn't a lot of fanfare surrounding our new bond marks, but they did seem pretty surprised Hades bonded us both. Rook just gave us all a really proud look. When I pulled him aside to ask him why, he said that he was proud of Hades for taking Achilles' needs into account during a moment he could have made only about him as the Alpha.

The love these men have for each other is incredible and I feel so freaking lucky to be a part of this pack. Kai pulled me back as we were walking out the door, nipping at my ear and whispering that he had plans for us tonight.

I definitely had to hide a shiver after that.

About an hour later, we're all fresh, clean, and fed before going on the short walk to my parents' house. Apparently, all four packs live on this street, which was the main draw when the guys bought their first house here.

My brothers come sauntering out of the house next to my pack's. Beck sprints at me, picking me up in a tight hug before somehow maneuvering me onto his back for a piggyback ride.

"I slept almost the entire flight home, and I woke up in a panic thinking you were a dream. That I was going to step off the plane and still be missing the other half of my soul. I'm so dang happy it wasn't a dream, Blakey," he murmurs, sounding choked up.

I squeeze him tightly around his neck. "I'm happy it wasn't a dream too, Becky." He scoffs playfully at that, causing me to giggle. "I never thought I would know what it was like having a family who actually loves me and cares about me. In less than two weeks, I got a pack, a whole gaggle of brothers, *and* parents who are about to find out I'm still alive and okay. I'm terrified that I'm going to wake up someday and still be in that basement, or worse. I don't want to lose you guys again," I finish in a whisper.

He squeezes my legs where he's holding them under my knees. "If we have anything to say about it, Short Stack, you'll be *begging* us to leave you alone with your new pack. Trust me, we have thirteen years of being annoying brothers to catch up on. You'll never get rid of us at this rate," he says, loud enough for the others to hear.

His words spark a lively debate between all nine guys about a visitation schedule. How they probably shouldn't show up unannounced if they want to avoid seeing one or more of them naked.

They're all still arguing like children as we approach a pretty white house with blue shutters and huge dogwood trees out front. Memories play out in front of my eyes as we approach, and I lean over to catch Grayson's attention.

"Did you fall out of that tree and break your arm when we were kids?" I ask him quietly. His eyes mist over, and he puts his hand on my back as he nods.

"Yeah, Bug. I did. I was chasing your wild ass, and you somehow managed to get down before I even reached the top. When I looked down to find you, I lost my footing and fell. That was maybe a week before you were taken, and you spent that entire week doing everything I asked because you felt so guilty that you got me hurt. I never really blamed you, you know. You had us all wrapped around your tiny finger from day one." He chuckles. A single tear rolls down his cheek as Beck purrs happily beneath me.

Silas is the first to the robin's egg blue door and doesn't bother knocking, just walking straight in and taking off his shoes. Owen, who walked behind me on the way here, gently takes mine off and sets them on the shoe rack by the door. Setting me down, Beck moves me in front of him and puts his hands on my shoulders to keep me steady as I shake with nerves.

"Hey Mama," Si yells out. "We need you and Dads in the living room now, please."

Gray leans in close. "Wait for it, all the families are here for Sunday barbecue, and we didn't tell them anything. This is going to be amazing. Just be prepared for non-stop crying," he murmurs. Tears are evident in his own eyes and are quickly building in mine, so I have no doubt he's telling the truth.

"Good grief, Silas O'Connor. They're already in there. There's no need for you to…" she trails off as she rounds the corner and spots us, her eyebrows rising in mild shock until her gaze lands on me.

She's a small woman, maybe an inch taller than me, with a slender build. Her hair is a slightly darker red shade than mine and Beck's, and her eyes are brown, crinkling at the corners. She has what look like laugh lines around her mouth and you can tell she smiles a lot.

"Oh my word…" she whispers as she drops the vase of flowers she was holding, shattering it against the smooth brick flooring in the foyer. "No… it can't be. This isn't… how…" Her words cut off on a loud sob and suddenly four enormous men are rushing into the room and surrounding my mom.

I take a tiny step forward, Beck following right behind and twining our hands together.

"Hi, Mama," I choke out, tears racing freely down my cheeks.

The four men stiffen before turning slowly. Two of the four, a set of identical twins, stare at me with eyes the exact shade of mine and Beckett's.

The largest of the four stares blankly at me before his face crumbles. He puts his giant hand over his mouth before breaking out into gut-wrenching sobs that are so loud, I nearly have to cover my ears, backing further into Beck.

He's the largest man I've ever seen, towering over everyone in the room, but maybe only an inch or so taller than Rook, who is already six and a half feet. He's got the same dark russet hair as Grayson and kind brown eyes that glitter like amber in the midday sun. Despite his sheer size, he's not somebody I would be afraid of if I ran into him on the street.

"Daddy Ben?" I whisper, recognizing the huge man in front of me as the one who carried me everywhere as a child even when Mama told him he was spoiling me.

He nods, and Mama comes forward, stopping less than a foot away. "Blakely, baby, is that really you? How are you here?" she gets out between hiccuping sobs.

I'm nodding before she even finishes her question, but it's Owen who answers for me. "It's a long story, but the Beaumonts found her, Mama. We already did the DNA test in London, there's no question Blake here is *our* Blakely," he finishes, crying softly.

I'm startled when the twins, Luke and Liam, come rushing at me. They look exactly like Beck and I, so I know one of them has to be my biological father. With slim builds, bright red hair, green eyes, and a million freckles between them, Beck is their spitting image. I guess I am too, but the girl version.

I don't have time for my natural defensive reaction to take hold before I'm crushed in an embrace between the two. They're rocking me back and forth, both crying, and then we're surrounded by another set of arms. Looking up through my tears, I see it's our last dad, Sebastian, or Daddy Bas.

He looks exactly how I remember. Dark blonde hair and dark green eyes that look hazel sometimes. He's tall with an average build, not super muscular, but not skinny either. His facial expression is hard to describe, but the closest I can get would be pure, unfettered *joy*.

Their scents wash over me in calming waves. Liam's sweet tea and summer breeze, Luke's rain and fall leaves, and Sebastian's coconut ice cream scent.

"Let go of my baby girl so I can hug her. Y'all make better doors than windows, so open the hell up," Mama barks at them, no power behind the words like an Alpha would have. She's an Omega too, so hearing her bark at them and seeing them immediately comply is pretty funny.

My humor is quickly forgotten because the second she gets her arms around me, I'm five years old again and sobbing in my mama's arms. Her vanilla coffee scent overwhelms me with safety and comfort. I feel someone behind me and catch the scent of the ocean, and I know it's Ben. A smell I had forgotten until now.

We're joined by a gorgeous woman with dark hair and features, with eyes that remind me of Rook's.

"What's the holdup in here, y'all? My babies are home, and I can't even get a hello when you walk in the door?" she asks. Everything from her expression to her voice screams serenity. If this is who Hades got to grow up with after he left, I'm so grateful.

"Mama," Rook and D say at the same time, each kissing her on a cheek and hugging her. "There's someone we want you and Dads to meet," Rook continues. Her eyebrows furrow for a second before she finally takes in the scene in front of her. Gasping, her hands come up to cover her mouth.

"Blakely? Sweet girl, is that you? Boys, somebody better fill me in right this second or I'm fixin' to send y'all back to etiquette classes right this minute. *CONNOR, SPENCER, AARON,* get y'all's asses in here right now!" she yells. Her voice is so loud I have zero doubt every single person outside can hear her. Rook quickly comes back to my side when I flinch, and he pulls me into his arms.

"Mama, can you please watch the volume? Blake here isn't used to much noise at all, but especially not loud ones," he says quietly, still holding me tight to his chest.

His mom's eyes widen, and she apologizes in a whisper. I'm holding back a giggle at her overcorrection while she continues nodding for a solid minute until the men, I assume she just yelled for, come rushing in.

Confusion is clear on their faces until they see Rook and Hades, and then there are wide smiles on all three of them. That is, until they see me, and then the joy morphs into shock faster than I can blink.

"I'm sorry—I feel like I missed somethin' here," the tallest one says.

"Dads, this is Blake, but I think you might remember her best as Blakely O'Connor," Rook says. There's a giant smile on his face as he watches his parents process the information being thrown at them.

"Or as you may *also* remember, *my Blake*," D cuts in smugly.

Every adult in the room is gaping like a fish before the room explodes in chaos. I'm enveloped in a group hug with all four of Rook and D's parents as they all ask the guys endless questions about *who, where, how, why, when* and *why didn't they call?*

They explain with a shortened version of the story who I am and how I came to be with their pack. And just as everybody settles down, six more people file into the house, wanting to know what all the noise is about. The two women walk in arm in arm and stop dead when they see me wrapped up in a hug with Rook and his mom, Amy.

I'm wrapped in *another* round of hugs and sweet words while I learn from Rook that these are Achilles and the twins' mothers, Sarah and Lynn. Sarah is a sweet Beta with gorgeous light brown skin and hair and big brown eyes, while Lynn is blonde Omega with pretty brown eyes and light bronze skin.

We make introductions all around and we finally get everybody to sit down with their food at a massive table outside. I recount a somewhat edited version of my story with my pack around me for support. Throughout the story, the table shakes with growls from all the Alphas and I can't lie and say it didn't make me nervous. Kas feels it through the bond, so he picks me up, and I tell the rest of my story from his lap.

I tell them about how I was kept in a basement and on my eighteenth birthday, finally managed to escape, only running into Kas and Kai by sheer luck and great timing. I tell them about our trip to London and meeting my brothers for the first time. And finally, I tell them how we rushed back here so I could see my parents again.

By the time I finish an hour later, every single person at the table is crying and telling me how happy they are to have me here. Ben gets up the minute I finish my story to make a call and comes back a short while later with a detective in tow.

"Blakel...*Blake*, this is Detective John Benson. He's the one that was on your case all those years ago, and the only one who never stopped searching."

Detective Benson looks like he might cry, so even though I'm nervous, I walk up to him and shake his hand. When I get close enough, I can smell that he's an Alpha, and I relax further. Unfortunately, because of everything Phil put me through, I seem to be more cautious around Betas than Alphas.

"It's nice to meet you, sir. Thank you for not giving up the search for me, even after so many years," I say quietly.

He clears his throat. "Miss Blake, it was my absolute privilege to be able to search for you even after we exhausted every avenue. Your parents, and now your brothers, are very dear friends of mine. I'm so sorry we didn't find you sooner, Darlin'."

Shaking my head and smiling, I tell him, "The past is the past. I escaped, and in doing so, found my pack. There's no point in dwelling on what might have been. I'm just so happy to be home now."

He opens his mouth to speak when the front door slams open, startling me enough that I jump, biting my cheek.

"Oooow," I whine. My pack is on their feet in seconds, surrounding me and peppering me with questions. I roll my eyes. "You guys, the door startled me, and I bit the inside of my cheek. I'm *fine*. Promise," I say, smiling at their overprotective tendencies.

Rook opens his mouth to speak when suddenly slender arms come around his middle in a hug from behind. We're all momentarily frozen in shock when a sultry voice purrs, "I didn't know my favorite boys were back already. I missed y'all so much."

That seems to knock him out of his shock, and he pushes her arms off before coming to stand behind me, wrapping me up in his big arms and resting his chin on my head.

"Victoria. Didn't know you were in town," he grunts out. His tone is nothing short of curt and it lessens some of the jealousy I can feel building in my chest.

"When Daddy told me y'all were coming home, I decided to cut my trip short to come see you." Her voice is dripping with sweet southern honey, and it's grating on every nerve I have.

The other guys are all still surrounding me. Kas is scowling like he'd rather be anywhere else. Achilles and Hades both look angry, and Kai's normally expressive face is totally blank.

Rook snorts under his breath. "It's actually great that you're here," he says enthusiastically, and a growl builds low in my throat until he tightens his arms around me. Her face lifts into a wide smile, showcasing perfect white teeth that look like they belong in a toothpaste commercial. "This is our Omega, Blake."

Her jaw drops open. "Your *WHAT*?" she screeches loudly, forcing me to cover my ears.

Kas smirks, stepping closer to me. "Our *Omega*," he enunciates dramatically. "You know, not a Beta or an Alpha? The one who completes a pack and gets the bonding, heats, marriage. The whole nine."

She scoffs. "I know what an Omega is, Kaspian. Are you sure she's not just another Beta tagalong you picked up?" she asks, sending a sneer toward Achilles. "She looks like she's twelve at most." She rolls her eyes.

Several growls sound out at that, causing her to cringe backwards. Her cloyingly thick apricot scent souring.

"What exactly did you just say about our daughter?" Ben's voice growls out, surprising me. I forgot he and the detective were still here, and my cheeks flame knowing they're witnessing this. His question was aggressive enough that it alerts the others who were still outside, and now all the packs, including my brothers, are in the room.

"What's going on, honey?" my mom asks, coming over to rest her hand on my dad's shoulder. Luke, Liam and Bas all come to stand next to my pack, looking between us in concern.

Victoria freezes in her tracks, staring around the now crowded room. "What do you mean your *daughter*?" she asks, her voice getting shrill.

Kai mirrors Kas now, looking smug as all get out. "Oh, did my brother forget to mention the best part? Blake is *Blakely O'Connor*. We finally found her. Isn't that incredible?"

Her face is getting red, and she looks like she might explode. "You were gone for a *week* and suddenly you have an Omega? What, did you rescue her, and she opened her legs to *thank you*? That will wear off eventually, so I would highly recommend not bonding her," she sneers.

"Get the *fuck* out," Rook growls viciously, and she shrinks into herself, fear lighting her dishwater grey eyes. "And I swear to God, if you ever speak about our *bonded* Omega like that again, there will be hell to pay. You're a spoiled, entitled, selfish brat and despite your many attempts, we wouldn't have bonded you if you were the last Omega on Earth," he grinds out.

"Ditto," Silas says, looking equally pissed. "And as of right now, your client contract with OHP is terminated, and you're banned from any property belonging to the O'Connor or Beaumont packs."

Her eyes look like they're going to fall out of her skull, they're open so wide. "You can't do that!" She stamps her foot like a toddler. "We have a legally binding contract, and y'all own practically half the city. There's no way you can legally keep me out of everything you own. Besides, the Beaumonts love me. There's no way they'll side with some temporary tramp over *me*," she says haughtily.

Achilles looks at me like he's worried I'm going to be upset, but I smile at him because the truth is, I've heard much worse. Years of Phil screaming obscenities at me every day have thickened my skin, and it's easy to see she's just mad that she can't have my pack now.

"I wouldn't be so sure about that, Victoria Cromwell," comes a deep voice from behind me. One of Rook's dads, Connor, steps forward. "Blake is our daughter by bonding, and she's proven in a few hours to have more strength and kindness in her pinky finger than you've ever shown around us. We tolerated you for your parents, but even they won't stand for the disrespect of a pack bond. Especially *scent matched* pack bonds. I think it's best that you go on home, now. Spencer, Aaron and I have a lot to talk about with your fathers on the course this week," he says ominously.

Her faces drains of color before going red again when she looks at me. "You will *never* be good enough to be a Beaumont. Sooner or later, they'll come to their senses and dump your scrawny ass for someone *worthy*," she hisses out.

Nearly every man in the room lets out a fierce growl at that, and Rook hugs me tighter against his chest as the rest of my pack crowds as close to us as possible.

Rook clears his throat. "Detective Benson? Would you mind escorting Miss Cromwell off of the O'Connors' property and informing her that threats against our Omega violate her *legally binding contract* and are grounds for immediate contract termination and being barred from any and all OHP owned properties and services?"

The detective looks positively gleeful at this turn of events as he turns to Victoria. "He's right, Miss Cromwell. And I will need to inform the owners of your home that should you set foot on any of these properties, you will be arrested and held until a restraining order is granted." The solemnity in his voice is at odds with the amusement shining in his kind blue eyes.

He escorts Victoria out, kicking and screaming about her plans to sue, and as soon as the door shuts, I'm bombarded with a dozen people checking to see if I'm okay. Their concern is so touching I can feel tears springing to my eyes and I have to blink rapidly to keep them from falling.

Achilles leans in to whisper in my ear. "You okay, mon cœur?"

Nodding, I give him a peck on the lips. "I'm okay. It's just been so long since anybody cared about me enough to fight for me or see if I'm okay. It's a lot," I whisper back.

He smiles in understanding before running his fingers over my jaw, ignoring everyone around us. "Welcome to the family, Pretty Girl."

CHAPTER 21

KAIRO

The next week after Blake's welcome home barbecue passes without incident, but with a lot of sleeping. I don't think any of us were prepared for how hard the jet lag would hit our girl after such a whirlwind trip.

Her brothers have been over here for several meals, and we've all been working remotely on her case. The problem is, her foster father has vanished and her kidnappers' bodies were never actually found after that fire that nearly killed her almost eight years ago.

Kas, Hades and I are just arriving home from another fruitless meeting with the local police when Kas cuts off from another long-winded rant mid-sentence as he steps out of the back seat.

"What the fuck is that?" he asks, sounding horrified.

I walk up behind him after locking the car to see what looks like a pile of feathers on the front door mat. Confused, I move to get a better look when Hades pulls me back.

"Don't. Fucking. Touch it," he growls out, sounding angrier than I've ever seen him.

I'm confused about the sudden change in attitude until he

grabs my chin and roughly tilts my head up. There, across the front door and written in what looks like blood, are the words, "You're mine, Omega whore."

My breath catches in my throat and a growl I've never heard before sounds from my twin. "Call Benson. Right the fuck now. Quietly go through the garage and get Rook and Achilles, but do *not* let Blake out here," he hisses to Hades.

He nods and walks off to do as Kas asked when I hear a gasp from behind us. Whipping around, I see Blake staring at the door, white as a sheet and visibly shaking.

"Blake, Sugar, go back inside. You don't need to see this," I beg her. "The police are on their way, and it's probably just a stupid prank."

She's shaking her head as her eyes fill with panicked tears. "No, this is him. I know it," she whimpers.

Kas rushes up to pull her into his chest, turning them so he's blocking her view of the door. "B, no. We don't know for sure that this is anything more than Icky Vicky playing a fucked up prank because she's jealous," he murmurs just loud enough for me to hear. Despite the terror running through my veins, I have to hold back a laugh at his use of our childhood nickname for the spoiled Omega. She lets out the tiniest giggle, and it's like the vise grip that's been around my chest since we saw the door loosens for a second, allowing me to take a full breath.

"Icky Vicky," she whispers. "I like that, even if it does feel mean."

Kas and I both roll our eyes. "She deserves it, love. She was awful to you, and she's always been a bitch to people she thinks are beneath her. Call her Icky Vicky all you want, or just try not to think about her at all. We sure as hell don't."

I smirk at her, walking forward to kiss her sweet lips. Her lips taste minty, and I assume she just woke up from another nap. Brushing her hair back behind her ears, I cup her cheeks and give her a kiss on the nose. "How are you feeling, Darlin'? Still tired?" I ask gently.

She's been a little irritable since she had her last dose of the heat suppressants earlier this week. I'd rather not add to the stress she's likely feeling after seeing the door.

She smiles widely at me. "I feel great, actually." She's practically bouncing on her toes, making me raise my brows at her in question. "Rook said we're going clothes shopping today since we didn't get to go when we were in England. I tried to tell him I didn't need anything."

I scoff, briefly interrupting her and earning me a side eye. She's so cute when she does this. I have to fight to keep my face straight. Clearing her throat, she continues on as if I didn't interrupt her and I let out a quiet chuckle this time, earning me an eye roll.

"As I was saying, I told him I didn't need anything and he… uh…" she trails off, her cheeks flushing bright pink and her scent blooming around us.

I smirk. "What did *Daddy* say to that, hmm?" I ask.

Hades let that little nickname slip earlier this week after hearing her say it in London. While most of us haven't said anything out of respect for Blake, it's pretty fucking funny to realize stoic, serious, stubborn Rook Beaumont enjoys being called *Daddy*.

Honestly, though, it kinda makes sense. Rook has always been the one to keep the pack in line. He's the oldest, and he likes things done a certain way. The more I think about it, the more I'm sure it was a natural progression for him with our sweet little Omega.

Shaking off my thoughts, I cross my arms and widen my stance a bit, not budging.

Blake sighs, covering her warm cheeks with her tiny hands. "He said I needed more than the bare minimum. If I don't let him take care of me now, he's going to take me over his knee later and give me something I would need him to take care of." As she mumbles this, her perfume gets stronger than ever in the warm mid-morning breeze.

My mouth opens slightly, a choked laugh escaping. "You like the thought of your Alpha taking you over his knee, Sugar?" I ask darkly, grabbing her hips to pull her into the borderline painful erection straining against my slacks. She looks mortified, so I pull her against me, hoping to reassure her.

My purr starts up in my chest, and she melts against me, losing some of the tension that had been lining her delicate features. I use a finger to tilt her face up so her eyes meet mine, and my breath catches at the potent mix of adoration and terror shining in her light green eyes.

"I love you, Kai," she breathes softly. "I know you're my pack and we're bonded, but I'm still so worried I'm going to wake up one day and all of this will have been a wonderful dream. When you guys say things like that, it brings back memories of the many times Phil would go on rants about how Omegas are nothing but sluts who are down for anything but really only good for one thing. I *know* you don't think that, but I guess when you grow up hearing it, it skews your perception..." she trails off, lowering her head again. My heart is aching for this precious girl and the shit hand she was dealt in life.

"Blake, look at me, Darlin'," I murmur, pulling her chin up again and planting a soft kiss on her forehead. "There are stigmas that follow every designation. Sometimes we hear them from really loud people, but that does *not* mean they're true," I say with conviction.

"You're not a slut because you enjoy sex, Sugar. Or because you like things that aren't necessarily conventional in the bedroom. It is nobody's goddamned business but ours what we do in our pack. It's like Hades bonding Achilles. Did you judge them or think they were weird because they weren't afraid to touch or because they bonded?" I ask quietly.

She shakes her head aggressively. "No, of course not. I would never judge them for doing something they wanted, especially when they did it to make me happy," she growls out. And I'm gonna have to remember to tell the guys about that, because it was really fucking cute.

The side of my mouth kicks up just a millimeter, and I kiss her deeply. Coming up for air just as we hear the detective's car pull up, I finish making my point in the same quiet tone.

"Exactly. You wouldn't judge us, and we will never judge you. We love you, Darlin'. Trust us to have your back and protect you from any more loudmouth assholes who are jealous they don't have a gorgeous, sweet, sassy Omega like you."

She beams at me, and I lean down to kiss her again when we both startle at the sound of a dramatic slow clap. Turning my head, I see my asshole brother and Rook standing there staring at us. Kas is smirking while Rook just gives us a small smile.

Kas walks over and ruffles my hair, and I let go of Blake so I can punch him in the side, forcing a gust of air and a groan from him. "Serves you right, bastard. Ruining a perfectly sweet moment with your sarcasm and poor timing," I say with a playful growl.

He flicks me on the nose with a smile before tossing his arm around my neck and turns me to face our pack mate and our Omega. He's nearly bent over in half so he can brush his nose back and forth across hers.

"I heard what you said, Kai," Kaspian murmurs softly. "I hope you know how proud I am of you and the way you are with her. I always knew things would change when we found our Omega, but I never expected it to be like *this*. You're so calm with her and you're so attentive to her needs. Not that you were a selfish ass before her, but sometimes you were so loud with your own feelings you kind of forgot about others."

I pull him in for a side hug. "I hope *you know* that I see the same things in you, brother. Don't think I didn't know about your anxiety attacks or the panic you tried so hard to keep hidden. I'm your twin. I saw it all. But I also knew you wouldn't want my help. The changes I've seen in you since we brought our girl home are something I've wanted for you for years. You're so good for each other. She's like the sunshine to your rain."

Our attention snaps over to Blake at the same time when we hear her musical giggle. I look at my twin to see we're wearing the same goofy smile.

He squeezes my shoulder tight. "I hope we never have to live without her sunshine again," he whispers.

CHAPTER 22

BLAKE

I lean back against Achilles, trying my absolute hardest to fight the huge yawn trying to break free. Rook, Achilles and I have been shopping for three hours.

I'm trying really hard not to act ungrateful but I'm tired, hungry, and I've decided I hate shopping. The other Alphas had to stay behind to talk to the detective and I'm a little embarrassed to admit I pouted when we left without them.

Rook is walking around the store looking for something he calls "house shoes". I have no idea what the heck house shoes are, but he's clearly on a mission, so I go along with it. Ace and I are sitting on a bench at the front of the store and the longer we sit here, the more I lean on my Beta.

He wraps his arm around my back and pulls me in for an awkward side hug. "You alright, ma jolie fraise? You smell a little stressed," he murmurs the question into my hair.

I sigh softly, quickly scanning my eyes around to make sure my giant Alpha is out of earshot. "I hate shopping," I mumble. "I'm so grateful for you guys and it will be nice to have more than a couple of outfits, but I'm starving and sleepy. Aside from London, this is my first trip out in public since I was a kid. I'm just not used to it."

Understanding shines in his eyes, and he kisses me on the forehead. "Pretty Girl you have to tell us this stuff, okay? I promise Rook won't be upset if you wanna go home or do something else. Trust me when I say any one of us would do literally anything to make you happy."

A grin takes over my face. "I love you guys so much. I don't know what I did to get the best pack in the world, but I'm so grateful," I say before pecking him on the cheek.

He sends a beaming grin my way. "You stay here, and I'll go tell Shoppy McShopperson over there it's time to feed our Omega before she gets hangry." He winks at me before booping me on the nose and walking away.

I quickly lose sight of him when he rounds the aisle, and he's gone less than a minute when a man slides onto the bench next to me. I nearly gag as the pungent scent of motor oil and dirt surrounds me, and I belatedly notice he's sitting much too close for comfort.

Scooting a few inches away, he immediately follows me, making my hackles rise and my anxiety spike. I turn my head, ready to ask him politely to back up, when a piece of damp cloth is suddenly thrust towards my face. I cry out, hoping my men will hear me before anything can happen.

The man rears back and slaps me hard, and I'm familiar enough with the action that I don't react beyond a small whimper, which seems to make him angry.

He brings the cloth to my mouth and snarls his hand in the back of my hair, shoving my head down into his hand. I try to hold my breath, but it only takes a few seconds for the sweet-smelling liquid to permeate my nose, making me lightheaded and dizzy.

"*HEY!*" I hear a voice bark. "What the fuck are you doing to my Omega?!"

The man in front of me jerks sideways before he releases his hold, sending me tumbling off the bench. My reactions are sluggish and I'm too focused on sucking deep lungfuls of clean air to catch myself, but instead of hitting the floor, I land on a hard chest.

I start to thrash, tendrils of panic wrapping around my heart, until I catch the scent of bitter lemons and sugar. Relaxing into Achilles' arms, I lose the battle to stay conscious and everything goes black.

~

Rook

Five Minutes Earlier

I have never in my life enjoyed shopping until today. Lee is the fashion guy in our group, and I just wear whatever I find in my closet. But shopping for my Angel? I could literally do this every day and *never* get bored.

Why is there so much cute shit for women? And Jesus, fuck, we haven't even started shopping for her nest yet!

I'm borderline panicking when a hand lands on my shoulder and I jump, startled.

"Woah there, bro. You okay? You were staring at those Crocs pretty intensely," Achilles says. Surprise is evident on his face when I whip around to face him. I grab his hand, holding it as I turn panicked eyes his way.

"Lee, we don't have anything for her nest," I blurt out. "What if she goes into heat early because of the meds that asshole foster father drugged her with? We don't have a single thing! What kind of pack are we?" I'm fully panicking now, and he grabs my shoulders, lightly shaking me.

"Get it together," he hisses quietly, looking around him quickly to make sure Blake isn't near us. "We are the perfect pack for her. She isn't supposed to have a heat for another year at least, but you're right. We don't know how the drugs will effect that timeline and we should start collecting things for her nest. But right now, our Omega is hungry, tired, and nervous, and I think we better feed her and then get her home for today."

I feel like a major jackass hearing that. My Omega needs me and I'm over here staring at fucking shoes and sending myself into a spiral over her nest, panicking about what a shitty Alpha I am. I take a deep breath and shake my head to dispel the self-obsessed thoughts and nod at my Beta.

"Let's go feed our girl, yeah?"

Smiling, he nods at me.

I've just picked up my boxes to head to the checkout counter when we hear Blake cry out, and I drop everything, immediately taking off in a sprint towards the sound. Her terror is shooting down the bond, and as I round the corner, I don't even have time to process what I'm seeing before my vision goes red.

"*HEY!* What the fuck are you doing to my Omega?!" I shout at the soon-to-be-dead asshole who thought he could get anywhere near my girl.

The closer we get, the more two things become very clear. One, this guy is clearly an idiot. And two, he's trying to drug Blake.

A ferocious growl rips out of my throat as I lunge at the other Alpha, tackling him to the side and praying Lee catches our girl. Rearing back, I punch him in the face, relishing the crunch of bone under my fist. I faintly hear Achilles in the background shouting for someone to call 911 but I lose myself in the feel of blood spattering against my shirt and neck and the pain in my knuckles.

I'm not sure how much time passes when I'm finally pulled off the sick bastard, but I hope he's dead. Or at the very least, permanently deformed. He doesn't deserve to keep breathing after touching my Omega. My instincts are on fire and I'm riding the edge of going feral when Lee's voice breaks through the fog.

"ROOK!" he shouts.

I finally stop, realizing I've been fighting the officers holding me back and Detective Benson is standing in front of me with his hand on his taser. I can only imagine how wide and wild my eyes look at I jerk out of the officers' hold and push people out of the way to get to my Angel.

Finally spotting her, I come to a dead stop, nausea rolling over me in a wave that threatens to send me to my knees. Dropping next to them, I gently stroke her hair back from her face as Lee pulls me close with one arm and hugs me.

"You alright, big guy?" he asks quietly, all too aware of prying eyes and the cameras that have gathered outside trying to catch a glimpse of the infamous Beaumont pack in a scandal. I nod in response, kissing Blake gently on her forehead.

Benson comes up behind us and crouches down, putting a hand on my shoulder and squeezing tight when I growl at him.

"That's enough of that, son. If they think you've gone feral, I'm gonna have to take you in for scent detox. You know that, so tone it down. Blake needs you," he whispers the last part, so only we can hear him.

I take a deep breath, blowing out the last of the feral fog that had been clouding my brain. "You're right. Thanks, Benson. I'm sorry if I hurt any of your guys. Once I saw that fucker with a rag over her mouth, I lost it." I can feel myself getting worked up again as I picture it, so I lean down and tuck my face into my Angel's neck, taking the deepest lungfuls of her scent I can manage.

Achilles is rubbing circles on my back, and I'm so thankful he's here with me. I've never felt this out of control in my life and his calming presence is everything I need to keep it together right now until we can get our girl home and safe.

Taking a final deep inhale through my nose and holding it, I turn to the detective in time to see his posture visibly deflate.

"Glad you're back with us, Beaumont. The basic rundown on this lowlife is that he's a low-ranking player in the trafficking scene with a rap sheet a mile long. If we can get anything out of him, I'll call you right away, but for now, go get your girl checked out by the medics out back and then head on home and hunker down. Don't go out unless you *absolutely have to* until we find out who wants Blake and why. I have a bad feeling about this, especially after her first kidnapping and then her presenting as an Omega. Not to mention the incident this morning at your place..." he trails off, a crease forming between his brow as he thinks. "In fact, maybe y'all should get out of the city for a few days. Y'all still have that cabin?"

I nod, my mind already racing with things we'll need to pack and what I can have ordered there for a makeshift nest. I'm worried this is going to set Blake back in her progress with the nightmares and touch aversion, so I need to make the cabin as comfortable and safe as possible.

I turn to my Beta, letting him see the fear in my eyes. His face softens, and he stands up, passing our Omega to me gently so I can cradle her to my chest and breathe in her scent. Leaning over, he hugs us both tightly before leaning down to kiss her on the cheek.

"Let's get Angel checked and get the hell out of here," I say gruffly. The guys are going to lose their fucking minds when we get home. I refuse to be just another captor to her, but for as long as it takes to figure this out, she's not leaving our sight.

CHAPTER 23

BLAKE

I wake up confused and alone in an unfamiliar room. My first instinct is to panic, worried I've been taken...*again.* But the room I'm in is absolutely gorgeous and smells like my pack, so my panic slowly recedes. At least until the last thing I remember before I lost consciousness makes its way to the forefront of my mind. My breathing speeds up, but I force myself to stay calm and take several measured breaths.

Rook and Achilles got to me in time. I'm still safe with them.

It's as I'm giving myself a pep talk, Kairo walks through the door. I assume it's a bathroom, given the billowing cloud of pumpkin pie smelling steam that follows him. I have to hold back a moan because he smells *so. freaking. good.* My perfume floods out of me and I can feel myself getting damp when the steam clears and I finally get a good look at my bubbly Alpha.

He's standing there in nothing but a towel riding low on his trim hips, exposing the deep lines of his Adonis belt that are covered by smooth tan skin. A single drop of water falls off his messy blonde hair onto his chest, and I follow it with my eyes as it slowly trails down before being absorbed by the towel. With messy hair and lack of his usual smart clothing, he looks more like Kas than ever.

Clearly, I was more zoned out than I thought because I blink, and Kai is in front of me. He tips my chin up with one finger and looking at me with a mixture of concern and heat in his light brown eyes. This close, I can see the flecks of gold throughout his irises and in the bright morning light, they're practically glittering.

"You alright there, Sugar? How are you feeling? Any headache, dizziness, nausea, confusion?" he asks.

I take a second to do a thorough mental inventory of my body, and honestly, aside from a little lingering sleepiness, I feel great, so I tell him that.

His smile is blinding. "Excellent… but let's tell the guys you're too tired and need to stay in bed for the day. I'm in the mood for a movie day with my Omega. You can have all the snacks and hot chocolate you want. I'm pretty sure one of your other Alphas is making you chocolate chip pancakes."

He waggles his eyebrows, booping me on the nose. Apparently, that's just a thing they're all doing now. "Let me just throw some boxers on real quick. As much as I love the guys, I don't think they enjoy seeing me naked nearly as much as you do," he says with a wink as he walks over to a large white dresser.

I stretch my arms above my head, looking around the room. It's huge and absolutely gorgeous, with tons of natural light streaming in through the tall windows, but I still have no idea where we are.

"Hey Kai?" I ask quietly. "Where are we?"

He immediately spins around with a sheepish look on his face. "Shit. I'm so sorry, Blake. I didn't even consider how waking up in a new place would make you feel. We're at our pack's cabin about an hour from home. After the… incidents yesterday, Detective Benson told us it might be better to get out of town for a while and hole up."

I nod my head, not loving the reminder of what happened, but too grateful to still be with them to let it get to me. "Thank you for doing all this to keep me safe," I murmur. "I feel like you guys have had to uproot your entire lives the last few weeks and I feel like a burden," I finish in a whisper. The guilt weighs on me and noticeably sours the strawberry in my scent.

He rushes over to lie on the bed with me, pulling me into his arms. "Hey now, none of that. We would uproot our lives a million times over for you, Darlin'. You are *everything* to us, Blake Wilder Beaumont." I gasp at his use of the pack's name, and he smiles brightly. "You like it? I think it has a beautiful ring to it, if I do say so myself. Just you wait, gorgeous. The minute you and I bond, we're gonna be begging you to marry us and make this thing official," he kisses me, tracing circles around my left ring finger.

I don't think I'm ready for marriage quite yet, but bonding with my last Alpha? I can absolutely get on board with that.

Not giving myself a second to overthink what I'm about to do, I push on his shoulder until he's lying flat on his back. Hauling myself up to straddle his hips, I finally realize I'm only wearing one of Kai's shirts. I see the moment he realizes it too, when my slick soaks his lower abs. Scooting back just a bit, I slide myself backwards over his thickening erection, feeling the slightest swelling at the base I know is his knot.

He groans deeply underneath me, and his voice is hoarse when he speaks. "Blake, Sugar, you should be resting. You had a traumatic day yesterday and..." he trails off, moaning when I rock over his hardness.

"I need something *good*, Kai. Something happy. Yesterday was terrifying, but it also reminded me we aren't guaranteed time together, and I want a bond with my happiest Alpha."

Leaning down, I lick a stripe up his chest and neck. "You want to bond with me, don't you, Alpha?" I whisper in his ear, running my hands up his chest.

He nods frantically, his pupils blown so wide I can barely see a sliver of his normal honey brown color. "You wanna take charge, Blake? Because I'll be honest, I've fantasized about it," he says huskily.

I'm shocked.

This big, strong Alpha wants me *to take control? I have no idea what I'm doing!*

He must mistake my silence for judgment, because he quickly begins to backtrack.

"I just mean... I didn't know if being in control was something you'd be interested in given your past and how little control you've had in your life. And I know it's not normal for an Alpha to want to submit. I just... I don't really fit the 'Alpha' stereotype and if that's not your thing or I'm out of line, just tell me because..."

His rambling is so cute, and the more I think about taking control over Kai, the wetter I get. I still have no idea what I'm doing, but I'll try anything once for the man underneath me who's clearly worried I'll think less of him for his desires.

Straightening my shoulders, I sit up and put my hand over his mouth. This makes his eyes widen even further as the cinnamon and vanilla in his pumpkin pie scent get warmer.

"Hush," I say sternly. Sliding off of him, I lean back against the pillows, hiding my nerves as best as I can.

I look him up and down slowly before I speak. "Stand up and take your boxers off, baby," I command quietly.

I hope I'm doing this right, and I trust him to tell me if I'm not. The truth it, this is turning me on more than almost anything has before. All the guys have taken complete control in all of our sexual encounters, and the fact that Kai trusts me to take control over his pleasure is insanely arousing.

His scent continues to get more intense as he follows my instructions. I'm dying to have his mouth on me, so as soon as he's naked, I spread my legs slightly and take a page out of my other Alpha's dirty talking playbooks. "On the bed," I command. "I need your mouth on me, Kai."

CHAPTER 24

KAIRO

This is the hottest fucking experience of my life, and it's barely even started.

Hearing Blake command me to eat her delicious cunt nearly pushed me over the edge before I even touched her, and it has me worried about my stamina. When I came clean about my fantasy of her dominating me, she was so quiet I was positive I had just fucked everything up, so I about lost my damned mind when she agreed.

I can tell she's nervous, but Jesus fuck, I can't wait to see more of bossy Blake. Diving onto the bed with no hesitation, I pepper kisses up her legs, trying to tease her to see what she'll do. She doesn't disappoint.

"I need your tongue on my pussy, *now*, Kairo."

She stumbles over the word pussy and it's too fucking cute. I can't wait to corrupt this girl beyond recognition. I hope she always has that sweet, shy side to her. Knowing she'll be able to flip that switch when we're alone has me thrusting against the mattress, desperate to get some friction on my aching cock.

I grin lasciviously at her. "Yes, ma'am." My voice is husky, lust clogging my throat.

I don't make my girl wait any longer. Leaning down, I lap at her like a starving man, licking from her clit to her ass and back again. Her moans are like music to my ears.

"God, yes, Kai. Use your fingers again, just like that first morning," she whimpers, and it's like gasoline on a fucking fire.

I growl against her slick center, immediately thrusting two fingers into her tight hole. "You're so fucking wet, Sugar. And you taste so damned good," I say. "I don't think I'll ever get tired of burying my face in your gorgeous cunt."

She whimpers as I drop back down, and I begin to lap at her with renewed intensity, desperate to taste her orgasm on my tongue. She's panting now, and I can feel her tightening around my fingers.

"Gods, *yes, Alpha*! I'm going to come. You're doing such a good job. I need some pressure on my clit, baby. I'm right there," she whines.

Moving back up to her swollen clit, I lean down and suck, *hard.* She goes off like a rocket, soaking my face in her sweet slick. Precum is flooding out of the tip of my cock and soaking the bed underneath me as I rut desperately into it.

The second her orgasm subsides, she's on her knees and pushing me onto my back on the bed. Sitting on my thighs and soaking more of me in her slick, she leans down and licks a stripe up my aching cock, sucking the head into her mouth when she reaches the top.

My back bows off the bed, the wet heat of her mouth nearly sending me over the edge. "Blake, Honey, *please.* I need you so fucking bad, I'm about to blow." I let out a whine that makes me sound like an Omega, but I'm so desperate for her I don't even fucking care.

She clicks her tongue at me. "Tsk Tsk, *Alpha.* You'll come

when I say you can come, got it?" She does her best imitation of an Alpha bark, and I have to grip the base of my cock tight to keep from coming, using my hand as a human cock ring.

"Y-Yes ma'am. I'm sorry. Please, I need to be inside you, Blake. I'm dying here." An embarrassing whimper escapes me, earning a husky giggle from my perfect girl.

Reaching down, she pulls off my shirt that I put on her before bed last night, gifting me a view of her perky tits. They're small, but I love them. Her pretty pink nipples are stiff and standing at attention as she plucks at them, scooting forward to rock over my length.

"*Fuuuuck*," I bark out in a long, low groan.

Just when I think I might actually die from the anticipation, she grips my cock in her tiny hand and lines me up with her entrance, sinking down on me. The sweet girl sighs as I let out a slew of curses, her tightness almost too much with how wound up I am.

"Sugar, I need you to move before I lose it, *please*. I'm begging you," I whine.

She must be needy again too because she doesn't hesitate, bouncing up and down on my cock that's so hard it's throbbing in time with my heartbeat.

"That's it, Kai. You fill me so freaking perfectly. I'm already so close. Play with my nipples and kiss me," she barks again.

That would be adorable if it wasn't so fucking sexy.

Leaning up, I pull her in for a deep kiss, getting as much of her flavor in my mouth as I can. I pinch her nipples at the same time, and she tightens around me.

Jerking back, her eyes are blazing and so bright. "Knot me, Alpha. *NOW.*"

She doesn't have to ask me twice.

I thrust up hard and at the same time I grab her hips and pull her down on me, my knot slipping in and locking inside her.

Using the very last bit of willpower I have, I ask my Omega permission to come inside her perfect pussy.

"Blake, can I come now? *Please?*" I beg.

She grabs my face and pulls it down to her chest. "Come with me, Kai, come now!" She cries out as she convulses around me, setting off my own orgasm while I lick and suck on her perfect breasts.

Hot ropes of cum splash against her walls in an endless wave as I come so hard, I nearly black out. Keeping my eyes open just long enough to lock onto a spot on her left tit, right above her heart, I lean in and bite down, sealing our bond.

After I tend to her new bond mark, she collapses on my chest. We're both sweaty and sticky, but I need a few minutes to get the feeling back in my legs and let my knot deflate before I carry her to the shower.

She sighs in contentment, nuzzling her face into my neck and licking over my pulse point before gently biting down. I shiver and my dick jumps inside of her, making us both moan. She shivers and I worry she's cold, so I pull the blanket over us.

"Was that okay?" she whispers. "I was so worried I was going to do it wrong. I don't have any experience outside of you guys, and I've definitely never been in charge."

She sounds so insecure it hurts my heart. Sending reassurance down the bond, I cup her flushed cheeks in my palms, nearly engulfing her whole face. "Honey, you did *so good*. I've never been that turned on or come that hard in my life. If it made you uncomfortable at all, we never have to do it again, but you should know it was the best experience I've ever had. You were perfect, sweet girl."

I can feel the relief through our bond, and I don't think I'll ever get used to feeling her emotions all the time. I put a hand over my bond mark on her chest. "I love you so fucking much,

Blake Beaumont. Now and forever," I whisper against her lips before kissing her passionately.

My knot finally deflates, so I scoop her up and walk us both to the shower, where we spend way too long after my Omega drops to her knees, worshipping me in a way I'm not sure I'll ever deserve.

~

WE SPEND the rest of the day lounging in bed, exactly like I promised her we would. Achilles delivers us breakfast in bed with a smirk and a kiss to Blake's head, and all of the guys are in and out to watch movies with us during the day.

When they're finished with remote work for the day, everybody cuddles up on the massive couch in the living room to watch one of Kas and Blake's favorite movies.

"Please don't flush me Roddy! I can't survive down there, I've gone soft!" they say at the same time, both of them cackling loudly. We're seeing a whole new side to both of them the longer this movie plays and I've never seen Kas so happy in my whole life.

He's always been sullen and off in his own world, often drowning in his crippling anxiety. Seeing him able to geek out about his favorite things with our Omega makes my heart feel like it's going to beat out of my chest.

I reach over and squeeze his shoulder, and he turns to me with a smile. We've always been good at communicating without words, so I hope he can see the love and pride shining in my eyes.

We spend the next several hours in a pack "cuddle puddle" as Blake calls it, and one by one we fall asleep holding each other. Everyone is safe, happy, and loved.

I've couldn't imagine a more perfect day.

CHAPTER 25

ROOK

The next several days after our pack movie night pass in a blur. The guys and I all have a ton of work to catch up on during the day. Blake's been happy through it all, never complaining once that she wasn't getting enough attention. She may be okay with the bare minimum after going so long with nothing, but *I'm not okay*. I feel like such a needy bastard, but I miss my girl.

She's been napping for a while now, and it's late enough I think she might sleep through the night. The back door opening startles me, but then I hear a splash, which probably means Kas is out there.

Whenever he gets anxious or he can't turn his brain off, he skinny dips. I don't know why, but it really seems to help, so I don't say anything unless he stays underwater too long.

I toss on a sweatshirt and head out back to keep an eye on him. The night air is much colder up in the mountains than it is back home.

I plop down in my chair and open the e-reader app on my phone, content to let Kas do his thing and make sure he doesn't drown. He pops his head up and sends me a small smile before going back to his laps. The back door opening startles me away from reading about Cricket's mate drama, and I turn to see my Omega wrapped up in a blanket.

"Hey Angel, everything okay?" I ask quietly, holding out my arms for her.

She skips over to me, happily falling into my arms with a sweet little sigh. "I'm fine, I just woke up, and you weren't in the room, so I decided to come find you," she murmurs, stretching up to kiss me.

This girl is everything good in the world in a tiny package. I can't believe she's ours.

"Sorry, love. I worked late and noticed Kas was out here, so I came out to keep an eye on him."

She eyes the water nervously. "Is he okay?" she asks quietly.

I nod, sending calm down our bond while tugging on my bond with Kas at the same time, hoping he gets the message to come up for air, so I don't have to move Blake off my lap. "He's fine, Angel. When he gets anxious or overwhelmed, he likes to skinny dip. Says it takes his mind off of things. He would probably love it if you joined him." I raise my eyebrows at her.

Taking my suggestion in stride, she stands up and tosses the blanket onto a nearby chair, exposing her long, lean legs. The only thing she's wearing is my blue shirt I gave her the first night she slept in my bed.

I groan. "Are you trying to kill me, Angel? You look so damned good in my clothes."

She giggles, holding out her hand to me. "Why don't you come swimming with me?" I would give this girl anything in the world as long as she never stops looking at me like that.

Smirking at her, I reach one hand behind my neck and pull my shirt off, dropping it onto the chair. "You wanna play, baby?" She nods, eyes wide and perfume blooming. "Go get in the pool with Kas, and let's play." I growl.

Stripping her own shirt off, the bratty little Omega smirks at me when it's clear I'm at a loss for words when faced with her gorgeous body. Then runs over to the other side of the pool where the steps are.

I growl again, but this time out of fear. "Angel!" I bark. "Please walk when you're around the pool. I don't want you to slip and hurt yourself." My tone is much softer this time as the initial spike of fear passes.

She looked startled when I first barked at her, but by the end of my sentence she softens visibly and smiles at me. "Sorry, Daddy. I'll be more careful."

If she wasn't getting fucked in the pool before, she is now. She knows exactly what calling me Daddy does to me, and I'm more than ready to be back inside my girl again.

The second she puts her foot on the pool steps, Kas pops his head up taking a deep, gasping breath. He looks to me in confusion and then does a double take when he sees our Omega standing in the shallow end of the pool; completely naked and with a deep frown marring her pretty face.

"Hey, Princess. What's wrong?" he asks quietly.

"What's wrong?!" she hisses. I don't know about him, but I'm completely taken aback by her tone. We've done a lot of overbearing and downright stupid things in front of her, but she's never been this angry before.

I can see his jaw open in shock. "B, what's going on? What did I do?"

Her cheeks are getting red, and she looks *pissed*.

"How long were you underwater, Kaspian..." she pauses, glancing at me. "Sparrow," she finishes, narrowing her eyes. And holy shit, I think she was about to say his middle name.

I've been trying to find out the guys' middle names since

we were kids, and to this day, I still don't know them. Blake's been around for a few weeks, and she already knows?

Then again, I'm really not surprised. With a face and scent that sweet, she could commit serious crimes and we'd all praise her for how smart she is to not get caught.

I tune back in to a sheepish Kas. "Ummm… not *that* long?"

She rolls her eyes. "You're not dying on my watch because I literally wouldn't survive it. Sixty seconds *MAX* underwater from now on, got it?" If I thought my Angel wasn't scary, I was wrong. This version of Blake is a little terrifying. Clearly, he thinks so too, since he readily agrees with her.

"Yup, you got it, Princess. Totally understand. No more than a minute. I swear it on my own grave," he rambles, kissing her forehead.

She stares at him, horrified, and my heart breaks when understanding hits.

"It's just an expression, Angel. When you want to make a really serious promise, sometimes people will say they swear on a grave to show how serious they are." My explanation is barely louder than a whisper. I deliver it gently because I know she's sensitive about things she should've learned during her childhood.

She smiles at me with gratitude plain to see on her face before staring at her other Alpha seriously. "I love you all, and the thought of not having you around terrifies me. Please be careful, for me," she pleads.

Walking over to my sweet girl, I gently kiss her lips and then her forehead. Kas comes up the stairs and scoops her up, kissing her cheeks as she giggles.

"You have our word, Princess."

And then the fucker picks her up and throws her in the pool.

I shove him in after her, baring my teeth and growling at

him. "What the fuck is wrong with you, asshole? You know her swimming isn't great yet," I grit out between my teeth.

If he hurt one hair on her perfect head, Kai is going to be an only child before morning.

Blake comes up gasping and sputtering, but she's also laughing. A giant gust of air rushes out of my nose as I sigh in relief and anger.

Splashing a small wave of water at Kas, she's still giggling when she speaks. "Of all the ways I thought tonight might go, being tossed into the pool like a floaty by my Alpha was not one of them."

He prowls toward her, and even though the chemicals in the pool block most of her scent, I can tell she's perfuming by the way her cheeks flush and her pupils dilate.

"Did you come out here hoping for a little attention from your Alphas, Princess?" he growls into her neck. I think I would be nervous about where this is heading if it wasn't so damned hot. Plus, I trust my pack with my life. Now that just includes my sex life, too.

Blake whines, wrapping her arms around his neck and her legs around his waist. "Kas… please touch me," she whimpers.

I've been hard as steel since the minute she came out here in my shirt, so I slip my boxer briefs off and slip into the pool behind her, cupping her ass in my palms.

Leaning down so my face is next to hers, I grab her earlobe with my teeth and gently bite down, earning a breathy moan from her. "You want your Alphas to make you feel good, Angel?" I ask her.

She nods excitedly, turning her head at an awkward angle to lathe sweet little kitten licks up my neck. Knowing she wants us as much as we want her makes me shiver.

I bring my eyes up to Kas', seeing his are full of molten heat.

"Set her on the ledge, Kaspian. I think we're gonna need to

work together to make our Omega scream." I grin at him mischievously, hoping he'll get my silent meaning.

He nods once, his eyes darkening even further as he gently sets her down on the edge of the pool at the shallow end. I can feel her confusion down the bond, so I don't give her a second to worry. Instead, I duck my head down and lightly pull her swollen clit between my teeth as Kas leans down to lap up the slick leaking out of her in a steady drip.

He's directly in front and below me, so I feel more than hear his low rumbling growl. "Gods, B. You taste fucking incredible. It's a miracle we're ever able to do anything but keep our faces buried in your delicious cunt." He lifts his head up to look back at me. "Think we could quit our jobs?"

Blake rolls her eyes. "No quitting your jobs, you weirdo. Now keep going. That feels really, *really* good." Her words trail off when Kas dives back in with renewed determination, licking up her soaked slit in long, leisurely strokes.

Now that she's out of the pool, her scent is so much stronger and if I don't get my hands on her right now, I might combust. Hopping up onto the concrete behind her head, I lean down and kiss her deeply, thrusting my tongue into her mouth as Kas works her pussy.

"Daddy," she murmurs against my lips when we come up for air. "Wanna taste you."

Leaning back, I brush some of her wet hair behind her ears. "You sure, Angel? You don't have to do this if you don't want to."

Instead of answering me, she reaches up and grips my bobbing erection in her hand, her fingers nowhere close to touching as she gently strokes me.

"Holy shit, Blake. That feels so—" My words are replaced with a ragged groan when she licks up the precum that's been gathering on my tip before taking me halfway down her throat in one go.

Suddenly, she gasps, her mouth popping off my swollen cock as her hand gently circles my nipple, making me shiver again as pleasure skates up my spine. "When did you get *those?*" she whispers in awe. "And how the heck have I not noticed them until now?"

A smirk plays on my lips. "These old things?" I ask, referring to the black barbels pierced horizontally through my nipples. "I usually have clear ones in, but one of them broke, so I had to put these in."

Her eyes are wide and she's silent long enough that I'm starting to get nervous when she moans again, and her perfume *explodes* out of her in a dizzying wave.

"That's so freaking hot," she murmurs, lightly tugging on one. My erection jerks, tapping her open mouth.

"Shit," I hiss. "Sorry, Angel. They're really sensitive."

A naughty gleam shines in her eyes as she silently tips her chin and takes me back in her mouth, bobbing a few times before taking me down to the root and swallowing.

"*FUCK!* Goddamn, Sweetheart." My breath speeds up as she repeats the process several times over, moaning and writhing around me as Kas eats her out.

"You ready for my knot, B? I need to get inside you. You taste so fucking good. Just licking your sweet cunt is enough to send me over the edge before I'm ready," he growls out.

She nods and swallows around me again, and I have to pull out before my knot swells anymore as Kas thrusts into her tight heat. When she lets out a keening whine, I bend down and devour her mouth to swallow the sound, licking over her tongue and getting some of her sweet strawberry taste. Doesn't matter where I kiss her, she's the best fucking dessert I've ever had.

"Don't wanna knot your mouth, Angel." She pouts at my words, writhing and panting from the intensity of Kas' thrusts. Chuckling darkly, I move my mouth slightly to the side and whisper in her ear, the words tinged with a seductive growl. "I could come down your throat, but I think I'd rather come all over those pretty little tits. What do you think, Baby Doll? Want Daddy to cover you in his come?"

Crying out, she grips my length again and starts stroking me, *hard*. It takes no time at all for her to bring me to the edge, my knot swelling painfully and throbbing every time her hand brushes it.

"Fuck, Baby Doll. Blake, I'm gonna come. Grab my knot and squeeze as tight as you can," I instruct her through gritted teeth. "I'm gonna paint your pretty skin and mark you with my seed while your other Alpha fills you with his. There won't be a single person who doesn't know you're *ours*," I growl out.

"Jesus, fuck, Rook. Get ready for my knot, Princess," Kas says as he gives two more hard thrusts and shoves his knot into her.

The sight is enough to set me off as Blake squeezes hard, overcome by her own orgasm.

My breath stutters as I find my release alongside them, thick ropes of come splattering over her perky tits and stomach. The sight is enough to have me stiffening again almost immediately, and I reach down to rub myself into her skin, marking her as she shudders.

"Ohhhhh god," she moans breathlessly.

In a move that shocks the hell out of me and turns me way the fuck on, Kas leans down and laps up a small puddle of my cum. He winks at me before pulling Blake into a filthy kiss, using his tongue to shove my cum into her mouth. My jaw is practically on the floor. An unfamiliar dark, possessive need rises up inside of me, watching my pack mate feed my cum to our Omega.

His knot must have deflated during their exchange because whatever he sees in my eyes has his widening as he takes a cautious step back. He gets a wicked smirk on his face and keeps his eyes on me as he speaks to Blake.

"Princess, you up for some more fun?" he asks. "Something darker and maybe a little scary?"

Her eyes widen, but from the way her scent intensifies, I can tell she's interested. The little nod she gives solidifies it. Tilting her head back, her pupils dilate when our eyes meet. I don't know what's happening, but I feel *powerful*. It reminds me of being on the edge of feral without losing control. It's intoxicating, and I know exactly what game I want to play with my girl right now.

"You want to play, *Omega?*" My voice is no smoother than gravel, as lust and primal need courses through my veins.

"Y-yes, Daddy," she stutters out. Her scent is drowning me, and her pupils are so blown I can't see the green anymore.

I smirk, letting the power I feel show in my expression as I use my Alpha bark for the first time ever.

"Run."

CHAPTER 26

BLAKE

"*Run.*"

Rook's Alpha bark washes over me like molasses, dark and slow. My feet are moving before my brain catches up through the cloud of lust fogging my brain. Turning away from my Alphas, I barely hear Kas shout, "Have fun!" behind me before I make it to the back stairwell.

I'm still shaking from their teamwork in the pool, but I'm nowhere near satisfied after seeing the change that came over Rook. For the first time since I met him, he looked *dangerous*. And this Omega desperately wants to find out how far my Alpha will take this.

Running up the stairs, I make my way across the wide landing at the top that leads to the master bedroom. The guys offered up the room as my space to get away from them, so they only come in if I ask. I haven't used it yet, which makes it the perfect place to go. Hearing footsteps pounding behind me, my heart rate picks up speed in time with my feet as I sprint for the large room.

At the last second, I dart to the other side of the landing

and into a small alcove, crouching to make myself as small as possible.

I hear his footsteps slow once he reaches the landing, and his dark chuckle sends a healthy dose of lust and anticipation straight to my senses.

"It's cute that you think you can hide from me, Omega," he growls. "But you should know better than to keep me from what's *mine*."

Slick is pouring out of me as my perfume floods out of the alcove and into the hallway. I know it's only a matter of seconds before Rook finds me. Peeking into the hallway, I don't see him anywhere so I run as quietly as I can towards the bedroom.

I'm just flinging one half of the double doors open when large hands wrap around my waist and pull me back into a solid chest. His hand wraps around my mouth to stifle my yelp of surprise as he slams the door shut with his foot, releasing my waist to lock it.

"Caught you, Angel," he growls into my ear.

Releasing his hold on me, he pushes us further into the room. His hands are still gentle, even though his actions aren't.

"*On the bed*," he barks. "Present for your Alpha."

Scrambling to do as he says, I drop to my knees on the edge of the bed, arching my back so that my face is pressed against the soft throw blanket they bought me.

I never thought someone chasing me and barking orders at me would be something I liked, but my heart is racing. My perfume is exploding, and slick is soaking my thighs at an embarrassing rate.

"Look at you," he purrs. "My dirty little Omega presenting for her Alpha." He trails a finger up the inside of my thigh, dragging it through the river of slick before shoving two fingers inside me.

"Ah!" I jolt forward, not expecting the simultaneous rush of pleasure and embarrassment at how wet I am.

"Hmm. I think I'll find out how you and Kai taste together," he whispers, kissing the back of my thigh before licking me from clit to ass. His feral snarl vibrates against my clit, sending a fresh wave of slick into his waiting mouth.

"Fuck, Angel. You really are my dirty fucking girl, aren't you? You like it when I taste your Alpha's cum out of your soaked cunt?" My answering moan has him chuckling. "Yeah, I thought so. *On your back*," he barks again.

I roll onto my back, eager to please him. I'm loving this new side of my Alpha. It's different from the stoic facade he held when I first met him, and especially different from my normal doting Daddy. This Rook is unhinged and dark and commanding.

"This is gonna be hard and fast, Baby Doll. I'm gonna fill your sweet pussy full of my cum and see how we taste together. Wrap your arms around my neck and hold on tight," he growls out lowly.

I do, and he picks me up, wrapping my thighs around his hips. He only walks a few short steps before slamming me back into the wall next to the bed. Removing a hand from one of my thighs, he wraps it lightly around my throat, his eyes clearing for just a second as he tugs on our bond. When I send back nothing but pure lust and excitement, his hand tightens. He restricts my air supply just enough to heighten the sensations running through my body.

I gasp lightly and he gives me a devilish smirk before thrusting into me hard. Right there against the wall he takes me harder than he ever has, pulling moans from me even as the lack of oxygen brings tears to the corners of my eyes. After a few minutes, he pulls out of me before dropping my leg and letting go of my neck.

"Turn around and put your hands on the wall, Omega. *Now.*"

I do, and he pulls my hips back a few inches before thrusting into me from behind. With his hands now free, he wraps one around my throat again, squeezing with slightly more pressure than before. His other hand drops to my clit and rubs it in circles as he growls and grunts with each hard thrust, his huge dick bottoming out inside me with each thrust. At this angle, the deep penetration is riding the knife's edge of pleasure and pain, and *I love it.*

He releases my neck and bites down over his bond mark as he spanks me, *hard.* Clenching around him, I cry out and claw at the wall.

"That's it Dirty Girl, come for Daddy. Come all over my cock while I fill you up."

His words aren't a bark, but they have the same effect as one, setting off my orgasm as I pulse around him. Groaning, he picks up his pace, releasing my throat to place a bruising grip on my hips.

"Fuck, Blake. Baby Doll, I'm gonna come, gonna knot you so hard you'll feel me for days. Fuuuuck!" he roars out as his knot slips into me, hot cum immediately filling me and flooding out around the base of his knot. "Jesus Christ, Angel," he pants after several minutes spent silently recovering. "Are you okay?" He turns my head to the side so he can see my eyes. "I didn't hurt you, did I?"

My eyes are heavy with exhaustion, but I lean up and kiss him, anyway. "You were perfect, Rook. We should do that more often." I sigh softly.

He chuckles, picking me up and walking us to the massive walk-in shower in the bathroom. It's so pretty in here. Everything is done in shades of sky blue and white, a total contrast to the rest of the house.

Starting the water, he angles me away from the spray until

it warms up, only turning me back once the water is warm and his knot slips free. The next several minutes I spend trying to keep myself from melting into a puddle as Rook carefully washes every inch of my sore body. He pays extra close attention to my hips and my throat.

"Tilt your head back, Angel. Let me wash your hair for you," he murmurs.

Tears are pricking my eyes as he massages my scalp with the shampoo. He rinses carefully, avoiding my eyes before taking the time to condition and comb everything through for me. I told him weeks ago how difficult my thick hair is to manage without conditioning properly and the fact that he remembered makes me love him even more.

Shutting off the water after quickly washing himself, he wraps a warm towel around each of us and leads me back into the room. Moonlight shining down on us through the large windows.

He clears his throat, looking uncomfortable. "I'm sure you miss the guys, but do you think we can stay in here tonight, just us?"

My heart hurts hearing the insecurity in his voice. "Of course we can, Daddy. I love sleeping with you." My tone is gentle as I wrap my arms around his waist.

His sigh of relief is audible when he hugs me back. "Thank you, Blake. My instincts are riding me hard right now and I don't think I could let you go if I tried," he mumbles sheepishly. "I actually... umm." He clears his throat again. "I was wondering if we could try something tonight?"

His cheeks are pink, and I think it might be the cutest thing I've ever seen. "Anything you want, Rook. You know that."

Taking a deep breath, he murmurs something so low I have to ask him to repeat himself. He sighs a little and hugs me tighter. "I was wondering if maybe I could try sleeping...

inside of you." It takes me a minute, but the emphasis on *inside* finally clicks and my cheeks flush bright red even as my scent intensifies.

"Oh... um... will that be... comfortable for you?" I ask gently.

His face lights up, and that expression will get him absolutely anything he wants. "I'm sure it will!" he says animatedly, picking me up and laying me on the bed facing him, one of my legs over his.

"I was reading about it the other day when I started researching things that might be comforting for an Omega during times of big life changes. You've been through so much your whole life, but recently your life has flipped upside down and inside out. It's my job as your Alpha to see you through it and make you as comfortable and happy as possible. The website called it cock-warming, but we can call it whatever you want. Doing it with all of us might actually help keep your nightmares away, too."

Stick a fork in me because I. Am. Done.

"Rook... *Daddy.* You are the most incredible person I've ever known," I start, gasping softly as he slips himself inside me. Clearing my throat, I continue. "I love you so much. Thank you for being mine, and for caring so much about my wellbeing without asking for anything in return."

His smile is so bright it practically lights up the room and he kisses me softly before pulling me into his chest tightly. "I love you so damned much, Blake Wilder Beaumont. Having you as our Omega is truly the most precious gift I could have ever been given, and I plan on taking care of you for the rest of our lives."

Kissing the top of my head, I squirm a bit at the new sensations before getting lost in his sweet orange creamsicle scent. I drift off to sleep in my giant Alpha's arms, knowing he means every word.

CHAPTER 27

HADES

*A*fter Blake and Rook's new little nighttime soothing technique was discovered when Kas snuck in to sleep with them, we decided we all needed to take turns *helping* Blake with her nightmares. I thought it would be weird, but after only one night I'm kind of fucking obsessed. It's my night again tonight, a week since our pack movie night, and I'm eager to get my hands on my girl.

Blake's been a little stressed all day, snapping at us and then crying because she feels bad, and making little nests all over the house. I panicked, thinking she might be going into pre-heat, but her scent is… off. I think she's anxious, and I'm determined to find out why by showing her what we have built for her on every house we own.

Walking into the living room, I look around in confusion when I don't see Shortcake. It takes me a full minute to recognize the lump of blankets on the couch as our Omega, and even then, it's only because she moved and let out a tiny growl.

God, even when she's upset, she's still so fucking cute.

I don't want to startle her, so my steps are loud as I walk

up to the couch, dropping to my knees next to it. Gently lifting the edge of her blanket up, I stick my head underneath and find myself nose to nose with my precious girl.

The anxiety she's feeling must be intense. Her normal sugary sweet strawberry shortcake scent has devolved into a sour, almost rotten smell. It's a fight not to wrinkle my nose, but I refuse to make her feel bad about it.

I brush her hair gently back from her face so I can see her shadowed eyes and keep my tone as soft as possible. "Hey Shortcake. Not feeling very happy today, huh?"

Her eyes may not be very visible, but I can still see the tear that drips down her freckled cheek when I ask that question. Sniffling, she shakes her head. "No." Her voice is barely a whisper.

"Sweet girl," I murmur. "Does the world feel too big right now?" She nods, breathing out a quiet, hiccuped sob. Gently running my finger down her nose like I did when we were kids and she got scared, I kiss her forehead, my lips moving against her skin as I speak. "Will you come with me? I have something I think might help."

My darling, temperamental Omega grumbles as she extricates herself from all but one blanket. She wraps the lone survivor around her shoulders and gives me a tiny, resolute nod. Holding back my laugh at her antics, I lead her up the stairs. I forgot how cute she is when she's like this, all pissed off and looking like a disgruntled kitten.

I fucking love it.

When we make it to the top of the stairs, I grab her hand and bring her to the master bedroom she's been sleeping in. There are enormous picture windows all along one wall that give you an incredible view of the mountains and forest. The other wall opposite the bathroom is windowless, at first glance. In the very corner of the room there's a small hidden switch and when I flip it, a panel on the wall slides open, revealing a door.

Blake turns, gaping at me. "Where does that go?"

Smirking at her, I tug on the tiny hand I'm still holding tightly in mine. "Let's go find out."

"You built this... *for me?*"

We've been sitting on the custom-built flat expanse of roof for the last hour while I told her stories of our pack and all the things we did, hoping we would find her someday. The most important of which are these roof additions we've had built onto every property we own. This particular one is only accessible through the master bedroom and is meant to be a hideout spot for Blake when she needs it.

Smiling at her, I drop kisses on her cheeks and nose. "Of course we did, Shortcake. Have you not realized you are literally our entire world? After you were taken the first time, I had nightmares for months. Nothing I did eased the guilt I felt leaving you behind or the anxiety I had being away from you. I was sneaking up onto the roof of the Beaumont's house almost every single night until one night Amy caught me."

The memory of that night is a mix of emotions, but most of them revolve around the relief I felt at not having to fight alone anymore.

"I was so heartbroken, Blake. I had lost my best friend in the world and failed in my promise to protect you. Amy sat with me and held me as I cried, finally admitting I thought you were taken because of me and how I didn't think I could live with myself," I whisper. Blake gently climbs onto my lap, throwing her arms around my neck and hugging me tightly. Burying my face in her hair, I let out a grateful sigh and continue.

"Mama recognized the signs of depression and anxiety in me and the very next day she took me to see a therapist and that helped a lot. The therapist told me I didn't have to stop looking for you, but I couldn't keep letting myself feel guilty for something that wasn't my fault." I stop as I feel myself getting choked up.

Pulling back the slightest bit to cup her face in my hands, I lay my forehead against hers. As I stare into her incredible green eyes, I take a second to revel in her sweet strawberry shortcake scent mixing with my rich caramel apple. You wouldn't think they would work together, but God, just the slightest hint of our scents together relaxes me and turns my dick to steel all at the same time.

"You need to know the other guys were with me from day one, Shortcake. They were there for every breakdown, every fruitless trip to another part of the country to find you. Every night I got blackout drunk because I couldn't handle the pain. I mean, fuck. Achilles sat with me in the bathroom every single time I got too drunk or had a panic attack and would throw up. I loved you first, but they loved you before they knew you." My voice is passionate with appreciation for my pack.

She's crying freely, not bothering to wipe away the tears, and the complete adoration shining in her eyes takes my breath away.

"I love you, D. I loved you then, and I love you now. I love our pack. You guys never stopped looking for me and for that, I will never be able to thank you. And look at us now," she murmurs, leaning in to kiss my lips.

Smiling softly, I pick up her hand and kiss her bond mark, biting down on it gently. "Look at us now, Baby."

My sweet girl leans in to kiss me again and I quickly shift us, so she's straddling my hips as I lay flat on the roof. The quick movement pulls bright giggles out of her and after how miserable she's been all day, that sound is music to my fucking ears.

"D, what are you doing?" She wriggles on top of me, sending my already heightened scent into overdrive and surrounding both of us in a cloud of rich caramel. I see the moment lust takes over her expression and a feral edge comes over me as she whines and grinds her already wet heat over my throbbing cock.

"Shortcake," I growl out. "You know, I still have a terrible sweet tooth. And I'm absolutely *starving*."

Her brow quirks. "You want me to go get—"

"I want you to take your panties off and sit on my face," I interrupt her with the blunt statement, loving it when her mouth opens in shock.

"You want me to *what?*" she squeaks.

"You heard me, Blake. Stand up and strip, then come sit on my face." She just blinks at me. "You like it when we eat your sweet pussy, don't you?" She nods. "Okay, so this is just another position we can do that in. You're gonna love it. Trust me, Shortcake. Let me make you feel good." I'm practically pleading now, my desperation for her growing with each swivel of her hips.

Silently, she stands up and starts to take off her clothes slowly. I push down my sweats, taking my cock in my hand and giving it a few long, languid strokes as I watch her. When she's fully naked, I take a second to just appreciate her beautiful body in the moonlight. We're all constantly trying to feed her, so she's put on some weight in the last few weeks and looks healthy and so happy.

"Come here, Baby." I guide her down so she's kneeling over my face, inhaling her intoxicating scent. Her breath is coming out in quick little pants, but she doesn't move. "I didn't say hover Shortcake, I said *sit*." I bark, pulling hard on her hips. And then my mouth is full of strawberries, cream, and sweet, buttery cake.

We let out twin groans of satisfaction as I devour her, circling her clit with my tongue as she writhes on my face. Her slick is so intense I feel like I could drown in it as it runs down my chin.

But what a way to fucking go.

After only a couple of minutes, Blake lets go and finally grinds into my face. "That's it, Baby. Use me, take what you need and come all over your Alpha's face," I growl out. Moving one of my hands from her hip back to my cock, I rub my thumb over the head, gathering the precum dripping off the tip. Using it as lube to stroke myself, I let my instincts take over as I please my mate.

Her moans get louder when I leave her clit to thrust my tongue into her tight hole, mimicking what I hope to do to her after I wring an orgasm from her sexy body. I stroke myself faster, running my tongue up her slit in long licks. I focus back in on her clit, sucking it into my mouth and gently biting down as she falls apart around me.

I lick her through her orgasm, and the gush of slick that covers my chin is enough to set off my own. Hot ropes of cum splash against my abs and her ass, the sensation pulling a whimper from her. I can't stop myself from massaging my release into her skin, soothing the primal need inside of me to mark her with my scent.

When she finally comes down, I lift her off and gently lower her body down so she's laying on my chest, her head resting over my racing heart.

We bask in the afterglow for several long minutes, neither of us saying a word. I startle and almost knock Blake off my chest when the sound of crickets chirping is suddenly interrupted by rustling in the trees directly in front of the roof.

Sitting up, I hand Blake her clothes and we both quickly

get dressed. I can feel her worry through the bond, so I try my best to reassure her despite my own rising anxiety. There shouldn't be anything big enough in those woods to make a noise that loud.

"It's probably nothing, Shortcake. There's a ton of wildlife around here, and anything that would come this close is harmless."

There's a quiet whistling sound to our right and a sudden sharp pain in my neck that sends me stumbling to my knees. I hear Blake cry out and feel her drop to the roof beside me before everything goes hazy as I try to reach out for her.

I don't make it.

CHAPTER 28

BLAKE

Freezing cold and feeling like death warmed over was not how I expected to spend the morning after my night with Hades. My head hurts so bad I'm afraid to open my eyes and the roof feels... different than it did last night. My stomach rolling dangerously distracts me from my scattered thoughts and I have to focus hard on not throwing up on myself.

After a few minutes, my stomach settles enough that I can open my eyes the slightest bit, only to slam them back shut immediately with a groan. Everything is blurry, and the light sends a throbbing pain to my temples that brings the nausea back full force.

Taking a few minutes to reorient myself, I notice a familiar sound and shoot up to a sitting position, banging my already aching head on what feels like metal bars. Steeling myself, I slowly peel my eyes open, rubbing them to dispel the blurriness. When my vision finally clears, my heart races.

I'm back in Phil's basement and I'm locked in a cage.

The familiar noise I heard when I first woke up is the TV droning on upstairs, but I tune it out as much as I can, breathing deeply. I'm desperately trying to recreate the feeling of being on the roof with my Alpha, so I don't have a panic attack and leave myself vulnerable.

Cataloguing my surroundings, I see that since my escape, Phil has added bars to the window and completely trashed the basement. There are fist sized holes in all four walls, proving his temper is still alive and well.

My books are torn apart, the pages scattered throughout the room, and the mattress I used to sleep on is sliced down the middle. There are springs sticking out and a knife handle barely visible through the fabric.

My heart beats faster when I see the knife is just out of reach. If I can just scoot the cage a little closer to the bed, I should be able to grab it. Gripping either side of what I think is a dog crate, I shift my bodyweight to the left, successfully moving myself closer to the mattress. Reaching my arm through the bars, an errant thought about how Ace would probably tell me I look like a T-Rex with my short arms brings tears to my eyes.

I just found my pack; I can't lose them now.

With renewed determination, I tighten my grip on the bars. Only this time, when I shift my weight, the crate makes an awful screeching sound without moving. I freeze, holding my breath and praying to all the gods I can the sound wasn't loud enough to be heard upstairs.

Less than a minute later, I realize my prayers are going unanswered once again as heavy footsteps sound on the stairs, the unsteady gait as familiar as the sound of my own breathing.

Tapping my fingers together, I almost smile at the memory from two weeks ago when Hades taught me the calming trick for my anxiety.

I've been sitting in the attic window seat for at least an hour now, hoping the proximity to the roof will allow me to calm my racing heart. So far, it's not working.

On nights like this, the panic is almost impossible to ignore, and since we arrived at the guys' house this morning, my mind has been spinning. I'm on the verge of a panic attack. Thoughts of how meeting my family and all the things that are going to change driving me into a spiral of terror.

Right when the panic really takes hold, there are footsteps to my right and then Hades is in front of me. His eyes are soft and sad as he takes in my curled-up position and the way I'm chewing on my cheeks. Brushing his hands through my hair, he lifts me up and tucks me into his chest.

"Shortcake, are you having a panic attack?" he asks quietly. He learned the signs when we were kids and I guess I haven't changed much since then.

Sniffling, I nod my head. "I'm really close to a bad one and I don't...I can't... I need help." I choked my words out on a sob as I break down in my Alpha's lap.

"Oh, Honey. It's okay, I'm right here. I knew this was going to get to you at some point. I'm just glad we're home now that it has. I know so many things have changed in such a short time, and even though you're happy to be free, you've had some massive emotional stressors. Add in to all of that you're seeing your long-lost family tomorrow? Anybody would be panicking," he whispers, still stroking through my hair.

"I just..." I clear my throat. "It's all so good and so happy. I don't want to ever make you feel like I regret meeting you or learning what we have. One of my biggest fears going into tomorrow is breaking down and seeming ungrateful or unhappy. You know how many times I wished for a family when we were kids, and now that I have that, it's daunting. What if they don't like who I am now?" My words come out on a gasping breath, the terror taking over once again.

"Blake, look at me. Watch my fingers, and do what I do." His voice is just shy of an Alpha bark.

Holding me tighter with one arm, he brings the other around in front of my face. Slowly, he taps his forefinger against his thumb three times, and then repeats it with the other three fingers. Repeating the odd actions one more time, just a little faster, he brings my hand up to replace his.

"Try it with both hands, Shortcake. If it doesn't help, you can stop."

I copy his actions three times before I realize my breathing is slowing. My racing heart calms the longer I do it, and after a dozen more finger taps, I feel more in control of myself.

Turning my head to look at D, my mouth parts in shock. "What was that, and why did it help?"

He chuckles quietly. "It's nothing magical. When I was younger and first started going to therapy, I couldn't regulate my own anxiety and they didn't want to put me on medication right away. I was having anxiety attacks so often; my therapist showed me this and called it a Stim. She said it would help temporarily focus my mind on something else and give my brain a chance to reset the Amygdala. That's the part of your brain that controls things like anxiety and fear."

I nod, fascinated by the thought that something so simple could help stop a panic attack. Reaching up, I hug him tightly before kissing his prickly cheek.

"Thank you, D."

Smiling gently, he kisses my nose. "Anything for you, Shortcake."

Until now I've only needed to use the tapping once or twice when the world got too loud, but I need the calm now more than ever as Phil rips open the basement door. His face is set in a mean scowl before he sees me, and then he lights up with the same sadistic glee I've seen countless times before, usually right before a lot of pain.

The one thing that has changed? The wiry man that

follows him into the room, his large nostrils flaring to catch my scent that I'm sure is acrid with fear.

Grinning salaciously, Phil crouches down in front of the cage and rattles the bars, startling me enough that I back into the corner of the small space.

"Well, well, well. Look who didn't make it out after all," he sneers at me. "You owe me, you dumb bitch. I didn't bribe that stupid social worker to place you with us and keep you alive for seven miserable years just for you to act like an ungrateful cunt and RUN AWAY!" He slams his hand against the cage, and I roll my lips inwards to hold back the whimper that wants to escape.

The man in the back speaks up then, not even sparing me a glance as he glares at my ex foster father. "You're lucky you found her when you did, or you'd have been dead weeks ago." His voice is somehow both raspy and high pitched, the sound grating on my ears.

He smiles, but it's not a friendly smile. No, this is something so cold it makes me shiver, his dead eyes raking over the Beta on the floor. "Instead, you'll die today."

The stranger raises a gun and shoots Phil directly in front of me.

CHAPTER 29

ACHILLES

Blake's been gone for two days and every single member of this pack is losing it except for me. I can't afford to lose it when I'm the only one keeping their shit together right now. I don't think a single one of us has slept in the forty-eight hours since Rook found Hades unconscious on the roof, alone.

We're holed up at the Beaumonts with every single member of all four packs and Detective Benson working around the clock to try to locate our girl. The bond spiked with her fear yesterday but has been pretty silent since then, leading us to believe she might be unconscious as well.

Rook is in the backyard yelling into his phone, trying to get answers from the higher ups at the Designation Intelligence Agency. When we realized Blake was likely taken by the same people who took her before, he started trying to contact his uncle Roman with no luck. Every call, voicemail, and message has gone unread and unanswered.

"God FUCKING DAMNIT." A crash follows the yell and I rush out to the backyard to see he's thrown a flowerpot

against the side of the house in his anger. Making my way over to him, I ignore his protests and throw my arms around the giant Alpha, holding him as tightly as I can.

"Just give in, big guy. You need this as much as I do right now," I mumble into his solid chest.

He finally relents, hugging me back. "I can't fucking do this, Lee. I need her," he says, his deep voice breaking on the last word.

Looking up and seeing tears running down his cheeks, my own eyes water in response. I've always been sensitive to the emotions of others as a Beta, but I feel my pack's as if they're my own. I'm incredibly grateful for that in times like these.

"We have to do this, Rook. Blake is out there alone, and she needs us to pull it together for her and send her as much love and calm through the bonds as possible. We're a fully bonded pack but right now we're acting like a bunch of rogue feral idiots who don't know how to trust other people to help us. We need to be leaning on each other. It's the only way we'll find her. And *we need to find her.*"

"He's right man," Hades croaks out behind us. I jump, my cheeks flushing slightly when I realize how close I am to Rook. I turn my head just as his arms circle us both and squeeze tight.

"I love you guys. We were a pack before we found Blake and we'll always be a pack no matter what, but she makes us better in so many ways. So, let's grab the others, hug it out, then buckle down and find our girl," he says passionately before yelling for Kas and Kai.

They come out of the house with somber looks on their faces until they see us. Kai's lips quirk to the side, but Kas' cheeks are sucked in like he's chewing on them. He and Blake share that anxious habit and thankfully it's easy to spot.

"Come on, y'all. Mandatory pack hug."

Kairo grins like a maniac at D's statement, wrestling his twin into a headlock when he groans in protest. Within seconds they're in on the hug and I'm being crushed by four enormous Alphas.

Tapping Rook and Hades' arms, I let out a dramatic gasping breath. "Y'all... can't... breathe... slowly... suffocating."

Their laughs are exactly what I wanted to hear, and I feel so much more centered than I did twenty minutes ago. These men are my family and feeling their heartbreak on top of my own is miserable.

"Alright," Kai claps his hands together loudly. "Let's find our girl."

THREE DAYS LATER, we finally have a lead. It's a pretty safe assumption her pig of a foster father kidnapped her, so we're back in Asheville at their house with a group of agents from the DIA.

"Listen up!" The agent in charge, Reid, shouts. "Team Alpha will be our tactical team. Team Bravo is the Beaumont pack accompanied by Detective Benson. Team Charlie is myself and the victim coordinators. This mission is arrest and recovery. We get in, look for the girl, and handcuff anybody in the house not wearing our gear. Got it?"

The mood is serious as everybody nods and I'm blown away by the amount of people that volunteered to be here to help us find Blake. Checking my bulletproof vest one more time, I take a deep breath when we're given the go-ahead to breach the shack behind the main house.

I can hear Dianne kicking up a fuss when the warrant is served, but honestly, I don't fucking care. That woman knew *something* all these years and chose to support her piece of shit husband.

The door is already open when we get there, and I exchange an uneasy look with the guys. There's a terrible smell in the air and the place is a disaster. There are open takeout containers and beer cans fucking *everywhere,* but that's not what the smell is. The closer we get to what's obviously the basement door, the worse the smell gets.

Gagging, Kas leads us down the stairs slowly. "Oh, holy fuck!" I hear him shout. Rushing the rest of the way down the stairs, I'm assaulted with a smell so bad I have to plug my nose and fight off a gag each time I breathe through my mouth. There, on the floor, is Phil. He's been shot point blank through the center of his head and this time, I do gag.

"If you're going to vomit, boys, do it outside. Don't destroy my crime scene."

Turning watering eyes to the doorway, I see Reid standing with his arms crossed, a slight tilt to his lips that wasn't there earlier.

Rook growls before lunging at the agent, gripping his jacket and shoving him into the wall. D and Kai pull him back, but they don't look much better off.

"Why the fuck are you smiling right now when our Omega is still missing and the fucker that took her is dead? We just lost our only viable lead!" he shouts, the orange in his scent going so bitter it's nearly caustic.

Reid looks a little more serious now, but not like he's angry. "We are going to do everything in our power to find your girl, Rook. I need you to trust me. Any joy on my face was completely due to the fact that there is now one less sick fucker in the world to do this to other girls. We have his cell, we have all of his bank records, we'll find the bastard that has your girl, okay?"

I find myself nodding, pulling their attention my way. I

shrink slightly under their glares but push on anyway. "He's right, guys. Hades, one of the reasons for your nightmares is gone, and the proof is lying cold in front of you. If anybody in this fucked up world can find out who has our girl, it's us. Get outside, take a deep breath, and let's get this shit done. We have an Omega to find."

CHAPTER 30

BLAKE

Numb. It's the only thing I can get myself to feel for however long I've been in this cage. Phil was a truly awful human being, but seeing him murdered right in front of me, feeling his *blood* hit my face. That broke something inside of me I didn't even know could break. The only way I know how to cope is to just… not feel it.

So, I sit in my cage. Cold, hungry, and silent. The stranger who shot Phil had men with him that loaded my tiny prison into the back of a large SUV before they plunged another needle into my neck, granting me the temporary bliss of total darkness.

I woke up here sometime later to screams echoing around the large concrete room, my hands instinctively flying up to cover my ears. I was glad to be seemingly alone when I winced and whimpered, the familiar feeling of bruised ribs and cut lips breaking into my post-drug induced fog.

"You'll get used to it fast," a small voice whispers from beside me. Crying out, I whip my head to the side. I can't make out more than a shadow since it's so dark, but a hand brushes my leg where I'm leaning against the metal bars.

Flinching away, the same voice whispers again. "Sorry, sorry. My name is Cove. They brought you down here a few days after they got me."

Relaxing slightly, I lean against the cage again. "My name is Blake," I whisper back. "Do you know where we are? Or how long we've been down here?"

Her hand brushes mine again, and I subconsciously grip it, desperate for the small amount of comfort it brings. She smells like s'mores and I find myself relaxing further into her sweet Omega scent. Gripping my hand back, she clears her throat.

"We're in the basement of an auction house. I saw it on our way in when I was pretending to be passed out. As for how long we've been down here, my guess is three days based on the number of times they've brought me food. There was another girl down here, but they took her away yesterday."

I shiver as I think about the screams that have since stopped. Something Cove said catches my attention, and I turn to where I've been hearing her voice. "What do you mean, an auction house? Like antiques? People auction those off, don't they?" I ask.

She snorts. "No, a human auction house. Specifically, Omegas." At my gasp, she grips my hand harder. "Blake, how old are you?" she asks incredulously.

Even in a situation like this, I can feel my face flushing with shame at the things I don't know. The things I never had a chance to learn living in the basement.

"Eighteen," I whisper. "But until a month ago, I was locked up most of my life. I was kidnapped at five and my kidnappers kept me locked in an attic room and homeschooled me, and then when I was ten, their house burned down, and I was thrown into foster care. My first set of foster parents had me for a year before the father kidnapped me and kept me locked in a basement, leaving me to educate myself." I grimace, not wanting to face her judgement, even if she is a stranger.

I ramble on, unable to keep my mouth shut in the face of her silence. "I just… there are so many things I still don't know. I escaped a month ago and found my scent matched pack the same day. One of them is actually my foster brother from way back when, and that's a whole other story. But whenever they say something they think is common knowledge, I get so embarrassed. I know I don't know you, but I don't want you to think I'm dumb because I'm really not, I promise! I even graduated high school at fifteen without any teachers or help! There are just things I didn't…"

"Blake?" The sound of Cove's voice stops my nervous babble. "Please stop apologizing for things that were out of your control," she says fiercely. "It's hard enough to be a woman in this country, let alone an *Omega woman*. The way people trade us like we're fucking commodities is sickening. The fact that you survived all that bullshit *and* found your pack is incredible. So what if you're a little behind the curve with life experience? You're gonna get out of this and find your pack and learn *everything*."

"What about you?" I whisper. "Can we both get out of this?" I may not know Cove, but there's something about her that makes my instincts trust her. If I'm going to find a way out of this, it's going to be because she helps me.

"Aww, don't you worry about me, Shortcake," she jokes, but I choke on a sob. Desperately trying to hold back the tears, I cover my mouth.

"What?" Her voice is panicked. "What just happened?"

"I'm sorry," I cry. "My… my Alpha has been calling me Shortcake since I was ten. I just… what if we don't make it out?" I'm fully sobbing now, tapping my fingers frantically to ward off the building panic.

"Hey…HEY!" Cove's voice is nothing more than a stage

whisper as footsteps sound upstairs. "None of that, Blake. If you're going to make it out of here and back to your Alpha, I need you to take a deep breath and *stay calm*. No matter what you see, what you hear, you keep it together and don't let them see your fear. You've survived worse."

Taking several deep breaths, her burnt marshmallow scent alerts me to her stress, and I know I can't make this harder for her by breaking down.

"I'm good. Sorry, Cove."

She starts to respond when a door opens, shining light into the large space. I'm terrified of whoever is coming down those stairs, but I'm thankful for my first look at Cove. She's sitting down, but obviously taller than me. She has long, thick black hair and defined features that are contrasted by the sharpness of her dark eyes. She's absolutely stunning.

Her eyes widen when they land on me just as a pair of heavy boots comes into view on the stairs. An incredibly large man appears a second later, curling his lip at us on the floor.

"*Get up,*" he barks at us with a thick accent. I bang my head on the top of the cage and wince at the pain when my body responds to the Alpha bark. Smirking, he walks over to open the cage and slaps a thick metal cuff on my wrist. "Stupid girl," he sneers. "All you Omegas the same, do anything for an Alpha knot and always listen to bark." His accent is thick and not one I've heard before, and it's hard to understand what he's saying.

Keeping my eyes lowered submissively, I let him drag me to a standing position next to Cove.

"You take showers now, da? Then put on robe. Look like pretty whores for new owners." His hungry gaze is a thousand times worse than the pizza delivery guy's was. The thought of taking off my clothes in front of him makes me physically ill.

Cove smiles up at the large man, and I was right in thinking she was taller than me. She's probably close to five foot eight. "Thanks, Nikolai," she murmurs with a sweet smile. My jaw is on the floor watching the interaction. "You wouldn't want to upset the bosses, would you? Let us shower alone. I promise we'll be ready when you come back."

He narrows his eyes at her suspiciously before nodding. "Da. Be back in minutes," he growls his words out like a warning.

The second he's up the stairs again, I whirl on Cove. "What the heck was that?" I hiss.

She looks mildly ashamed. "I learned quickly to stay on his good side by acting like a flirty little submissive Omega. It's the only reason I wasn't the one screaming when you woke up," she whispers, her voice cracking on the last few words.

"Cove?" I ask quietly. When she looks at me with tears brimming her lashes, I grab her hand and repeat her words from earlier. "Don't be ashamed of doing what you had to do to survive. You're strong, and I admire you for that."

Smiling at me softly, she lets one tear fall before visibly locking down her emotions and wiping the tear away. "Alright, enough of the sappy shit. If we're gonna escape, the auction will be our chance."

I raise one eyebrow in her direction. "Uhh... how is that gonna work?"

With a manic grin, she wiggles her brows. "We're gonna let somebody buy us."

CHAPTER 31

KASPIAN

n hour earlier

"Do y'all remember when we were kids and we would play cops and robbers and we'd constantly talk about being real cops one day?" Kai asks. We all nod at him, curious about where he's going with this.

"I don't think I could chase a robber in all this gear."

That earns a small chuckle out of most of us, but tensions have been high since we got word on Blake's location early this morning.

"Shut the fuck up, the phone is ringing," Hades snaps at us all as he answers.

Blake has been missing for five long days. We're all suffering without her here, but Hades is taking personal responsibility since he couldn't stop the kidnappers. We've tried to tell him countless times it wasn't his fault, but until we have her back, he's going to continue to spiral.

He's quiet, listening to whoever is on the phone until his jaw drops in shock at the same time he drops his phone.

"Get me a fucking laptop NOW!" he shouts, sprinting to the living room. I pick up his phone, intending to continue the call, but

the other person must have hung up because the only thing on the screen is a text with a link.

"Kas! Send that link to me now," he growls, his Alpha bark washing over me uncomfortably. Other Alphas can choose not to listen to an Alpha bark, but the compulsion still feels like needles under your skin. Normally I'd be a little annoyed if he tried to use his bark on me, but it's obviously urgent, so I'll let it slide. Sitting down next to him, I do as he asked, and he's clicking the link only seconds later.

When the screen loads, the air escapes from my lungs. "No. Jesus fucking christ. No, no, no! We promised her this would never happen again. God damnit!"

The room is silent around me as we watch the screen in horror. There, in high-definition night vision, Blake is curled up in a ball, passed out in a fucking dog crate in what looks like a fully concrete basement.

The camera is focused only on her, so we can't tell if there are other people in the room, but I'm willing to guess there are. She's shivering so hard the camera is able to pick it up, but she's still blank down the bond, so hopefully she's not awake.

Suddenly a large man appears on screen. He walks to Blake's cage, kicking it hard enough the whole thing shakes, but she doesn't move. When he opens it up and slaps her across the face, the room fills with menacing growls and death threats. This fucker won't be getting out alive if anyone in this room gets ahold of him before the police do.

"She's at a fucking human auction house," Rook spits out. We send confused looks his way. "Roman is on assignment and has been working on infiltrating this place for years," he grunts. "I recognize that bastard as one of the main enforcers. I need to call Ro's supervisor again and tell them what's going on. Lee, you get the jet on standby, everybody else? Pack up, we're headed back to Asheville."

All the men in the room hop up when we do, and Theo, one of the twins' dads, scoffs at us before smirking. "If you think we're letting y'all run off to save the day without us, you've got another thing coming. Slow your roll and accept the help so you can focus on your girl when we get there. We've got your backs."

So now we're waiting. We arrived in Asheville an hour ago and made the twenty-minute drive into the suburbs, where all five of us have been squished into a surveillance van ever since. Our fathers are in a trailer behind us, with Benson.

"*Ouch!* Can you keep your elbows to yourself, you dick? I swear I haven't been this close to you since we were in the womb," Kai whines from my right side.

I smile, growling playfully at my twin. "Nope," I say, popping the p obnoxiously. "Welcome back, womb-mate."

Rolling his eyes, Achilles looks back with a glare and smacks us both upside the head. "Will y'all shut the fuck up and *focus*? We're minutes away from getting our girl back and we have no idea what she's been through in the last week. We're all nervous, but let's put all that extra energy towards the staying safe, yeah?"

We both shoot contrite looks at our Beta and mumble simultaneous apologies.

"I swear, sometimes I wonder if all y'all lost all the good sense Mama Sparrow tried to grace you with," he grumbles.

Rook chuckles quietly. "You're preachin' to the choir, Ace."

The passenger door opening pulls me from my grumbling about our hard ass Beta as Detective Benson pokes his head in. "It's time to go," he says gruffly. As we follow him to the house, I set a reminder on my phone to ask Lee to open a college fund for Benson's kids. He's been helping us look for Blake at every turn for more than a decade, and we owe him big.

Walking up, the place looks strangely deserted. My gut tightens, and I know something isn't right. Grabbing Kai's arm, I pull him roughly to a stop. He's always been good at reading me, so while he looks concerned, he doesn't ask questions. As the guys get closer to the house, the feeling gets more intense.

"Guys!" I shout. They all go quiet and turn to look at me and that's when I hear it. A quiet ticking.

"*IT'S A TRAP! GET THE FUCK BACK! GET DOWN!*" I scream.

The world explodes around us.

Kairo and I are knocked back and I throw my hand out to protect his head from hitting the concrete, and it takes what feels like hours to reorient myself enough to check on the other guys.

Hades is lying still next to me, blood dripping down his temple. Lee and Rook were both thrown several feet away but are already getting up, looking relatively unharmed aside from some minor cuts and burns.

"Is everybody alright?" Benson shouts. I'm barely able to hear him over the ringing in my ears, but I nod anyway. "Good! We need to get y'all to the hospital right now! The tactical team lead on Roman's op just called me and some shit went down."

My head whips to the side and I immediately regret the move when my vision swims and nausea rises. Fuck, I think I might have a concussion.

"What do you mean, *shit went down?*" Rook rasps, staggering over to drop next to me before pulling me into a side hug.

"I mean, Blake was hurt, and we need to go *now*. I don't have any specifics, just that she was heading into surgery," he says urgently.

At that, we all crawl to our feet as quickly as possible. Which, admittedly, is about as fast as a snail crawling through molasses in winter. Eventually, we make it up and support each other into the car. Benson was the farthest from the explosion, so he drives while we call our dads.

Pulling up to the hospital twenty minutes later, we're no closer to figuring out what just happened.

How did we get the wrong address when everybody else got the right one?

Nurses rush us through the emergency room and into several bays to get checked out. Hades and I have minor concussions, but everybody else is fine, thankfully. Rook is absolutely losing it in the room next to mine, so as soon as the doctor gives me the go ahead, I rush in there to calm him down.

"Where the fuck is she?! Where's my goddamn Omega?" he shouts.

The nurse helping me down the hall whispers as she lets me into the room. "They're going to sedate him if he doesn't calm down. The last thing we need in here is a feral Alpha."

I don't bother acknowledging her as she leaves, I already know. "*ROOK*," I bark. He thrashes in the Alpha nurse's hold. "Rook, man, you gotta calm down. We need to get to Blake, and you can't be there if you're sedated for acting like a rabid raccoon on trash day."

His movements finally slow down as his eyes lose some of their feral gleam. Smiling, I gently grab his hands and pull him out of his arm-prison. He sighs and sends me a grateful look. "Thanks man. I needed that," he whispers, pulling me into a classic Rook bear hug.

I nod, enjoying the moment with one of my best friends.

"Let's go get our girl."

CHAPTER 32

Roman

t the same time across town
My phone has been ringing off the hook for hours, but I'm so deep into this op I can't risk answering for even a second. I'm just putting it away after silencing it when my partner looks at me suspiciously. "Problem?" he says in his thick Russian accent.

Schooling my expression, I send a bored look his way and scoff. "Of course not, Andrei. Let's just pick up this whiny brat and get her back to the boss so I can scope out the skin at the club tonight."

God, after this I'm gonna need a year long vacation and a fucking raise.

I've been undercover in this trafficking ring for more than two years. And I spent the five years before that begging the Bureau to let me form a team to infiltrate their ranks after I caught that tiny girl in Asheville and did a deep dive on her.

Truthfully, I didn't find much, which set off all kinds of red flags. I learned her name was Blake Connolly. She was ten years old, and she was now an orphan, being tossed into foster care after they presumed her parents were dead. They ruled the fire in their home as arson, but the girl was so small the police knew there was no way she had set it herself given the lock on the *outside* of the attic door.

The parents *conveniently* disappeared. I've seen enough trafficking cases in my career to know a fake backstory when I see one. And given the fact that Blake *also* disappeared a year later without a trace? Something didn't add up. I've spent any free time I had the last seven years looking for her, and I don't even really know why. Something about her reminded me of Rook and his friends, and my instincts were demanding I keep her safe after watching her make the three-story drop that day.

I haven't seen her since, but I also haven't been able to look in the two years since I started this assignment. As soon as it's over tonight, I plan on starting the search again. Based on my math, the girl should be eighteen, so maybe I'll catch a break and she'll resurface so I can bring her home and have mama help her out if she needs it.

I'm brought out of my daydreaming when we pull up to the auction house. I've been here several times in the past, but it still shocks me every time I see it. We're in an upscale residential neighborhood and the house is a white colonial style with dark blue shutters. There are kids playing in the street, and women are being fucking *sold* out of this three-story family house.

We get checked in and are informed that the auction will begin shortly, and that previews are available on the tablet sitting on our table. Andrei is drinking already and scoping out one of the waitresses, so I grab the tablet and start scrolling. There are only a few women being sold tonight, something about this being a "late batch" or some shit.

They present the women in what basically amounts to a

dating profile. Their height, weight, age, scent, and things like eye and hair color are listed, but there are also photos. I flip through, not really looking, since the raid will happen before they actually remove anyone from the premises. Suddenly, one specific picture catches my eye and I quickly flip back to look at the profile.

"Holy fucking shit," I whisper as the green eyes that haunt my dreams stare back at me through the screen.

"What? What is wrong?" Andrei asks me. I quickly shake my head.

"Nothing! I found the girl the boss will want, that's all." He grunts in response, and I let out a quiet sigh of relief.

You almost blew your cover, dumbass. Quit acting like a rookie.

There's no doubt in my mind this girl is Blake. The same hair and eyes, and the age is right.

How the hell did she end up in a goddamned auction house?

I put in our bid and start high. I'm getting her out of this place tonight, blown cover or not.

The lights flicker twice before going down like this is the fucking theatre and then the girls are led on stage in thick metal cuffs. Blake is nearly as small as I remember her, which scares the hell out of me.

What has she been through in the last seven years?

I know it must be hard to see the tables when the lights onstage are so fucking bright, but I swear when her eyes land on me, they widen in shock. Her lips curling in the corners before she fixes her expression into a timid one. My brows furrow as she starts to whisper frantically to the girl next to her.

As I take in the second girl, my own eyes widen. She's fucking *ethereal.* I don't think I've ever seen a more naturally beautiful woman in my life. Scrolling back through the tablet, I see her name is Cove, and she's twenty-two, which makes her ten years my junior. And she smells like my favorite dessert?

Good god, I need to meet her and get her the hell out of here.

They begin the auction with the highest bids, and we secure Blake quickly, but Vincenzo Vitali, the Capo of the Italian mob on the West Coast, manages to procure Cove. I'll need to keep an eye on the slick bastard, so he doesn't sneak out before the raid. They bring the girls down to us, and I see Blake shoot her friend a panicked look. When she looks back at me, I put my finger up to my lips as subtly as possible, and she gives me a minute nod.

The auction lasts another thirty minutes and then Andrei stalks off to handle payment. The second he's gone, I turn and grab her shoulders. "Blake?" My voice is clogged with emotion I can't afford to show here. Not yet.

She nods, tears in her eyes. "You really are Roman, aren't you?" she whispers. Her voice is hoarse, so I give her my water to sip on and she smiles at me gratefully.

"How did you get here? Why the hell are you at an *auction house*, Blake?" I growl low in my throat, not able to subdue the anger fast enough to keep it under the surface.

She rolls her eyes at me, giving me a droll look, and I chuckle. She's a little spitfire.

"It's a long story. Is Rook here? Are the guys?" she asks, and my jaw drops.

Before I have a chance to ask how she knows my nephews, Andrei comes back and announces it's time for us to leave. I hit the button concealed in my cufflink and count down from ten. As soon as I reach one, I grab Blake and pull her down to the ground, pushing the table forward to act as a shield as the room explodes in chaos.

Gunfire is everywhere, and more tactical agents than I knew we had flood the small house. "What the fuck?" I whisper as Blake whimpers. I shield her the best I can, but I can see her arm was grazed with a bullet, so I tear a piece of my jacket and tie it around her tiny arm. Without warning, she's ripped away from me. It shocks me enough that my reflexes are too slow to grab her.

"Blake!" I shout.

A massive man has his arm wrapped around her neck with a gun to her head, and she whimpers. Tears rapidly falling down her face.

"Nobody fucking move, or I shoot the girl," the man speaks with a heavy Italian accent, and I realize he's Vitali's right-hand man. Vitali must have wanted both girls and decided to just take Blake when we won the bid.

I put my hands up and stand slowly. "Alright, Marco. Your time's up. Let the Omega go, and I'll help you make it out of here alive."

I can't blow my cover now. Not when Vitali has Cove.

He's shaking his head manically before I even finish speaking. "*No!*" he barks. He may be enormous, but he's still a Beta, so his bark has no effect on any of us. "Vitali wants the girl, so he gets the girl. She comes with me, or she dies. Simple as that."

There's a commotion at the entrance to the room, and the shouting distracts Marco enough that I can dive forward and yank Blake to the ground with me. Several gunshots go off and Marco drops to the ground as Blake slumps in my arms. Looking down to check on her, I panic when I notice blood welling rapidly on her chest.

"Oh god, no," I whisper. "*I NEED A MEDIC!*" I scream desperately.

Laying her down flat, I rip off my jacket and use it to apply pressure on the general area near her shoulder since there's too much blood to see the wound itself. Reid Whitlock, lead for the local tactical units, leads a team of paramedics into the room where they load her onto a stretcher and check her over. It's several tense minutes later before the lead medic nods and says she's stable enough to transport. That she'll need urgent surgery to make sure the bullet doesn't travel in her chest.

Turning to me, she gives me a sympathetic smile when she sees my shirt that's now covered in Blake's blood. "Is there any family we can call?" she asks gently.

I shake my head. "Honestly, I don't know. But I'd like to ride with her until we find out if that's okay."

She nods and we're quickly led out the back door to the waiting ambulance. Just as the doors are closing, I could swear I catch sight of my brother and Ben O'Connor. That doesn't make any sense, so I shake it off, assuming it's the stress catching up with me. We arrive at the hospital less than five minutes later and she's immediately taken back to the operating room while I'm led to a family-only waiting room.

It's not even twenty minutes later when a doctor comes out with a huge smile on his face. "You're Agent Beaumont, I presume?" he asks, coming over to shake my hand when I nod.

"Miss Connolly is asking to see you. Your quick thinking and solid pressure pushed the bullet further into her muscle, which saved her from major surgery. When the bullet first hit her, it was an inch away from the subclavian artery. From what we can tell, your pressure combined with her movements had sort of a drilling effect, lodging the bullet into the muscle over her scapula. All in all, it was the best possible outcome."

I breathe out a sigh of relief, hardly believing her luck. Nobody gets shot in the torso and is just *fine*. The fact that it missed several major arteries borders on a miracle.

"Can I see her now? Is she on any pain medication?" I ask.

His face drops into a grimace. "Well... you see, Miss Connolly vehemently refused any IV medication after using a local anesthetic to remove the bullet shortly after she regained consciousness. I have never seen someone so young handle pain so effortlessly," he says suspiciously.

Nodding at him, my words are somber. "I noticed that too, and I intend to find out why that is."

He gives me a small smile and leads me back to Blake's room.

"Hey kiddo, how ya feeling?" I ask gently. She gives me a small smile and starts to speak before perking up suddenly and glancing over my shoulder. Her eyes light up even as she gasps, covering her mouth. I'm beyond confused until an enormous form I'd recognize anywhere fills the doorframe. Four others shadowing him closely.

"Holy shit," I whisper. Each of the five boys is covered head to toe in smoke residue, cuts, road rash, and burns. "What happened to y'all?"

My jaw is still hanging slack when Rook's wide eyes lift at the sound of my voice and find mine.

"Uncle Ro?" he chokes out. "What the fuck?"

"I could say the same to you, Rookie! How the hell do you know Blake? And what the hell happened?" I shake my head in exasperation. Clearly, I missed a metric fuck-ton while I was dark for what was supposed to be the end of this assignment.

"Oh, this pretty little one?" he smirks. "Roman Beaumont, meet my *bonded* Omega, Blake Connolly. Or, as you may remember her, *Blakely O'Connor*."

I choke on nothing. "You're fucking kidding me," I say, slowly connecting the dots. "*I* found Blakely all those years ago and didn't know?" Turning surprisingly misty eyes to Blake as her pack crowds in around us, I grab her arm lightly. "Blake, I am *so sorry* I didn't realize that was you all those years ago. My hands were tied at the time, but that's really no excuse. If I had known, I would've ignored the bureaucratic bullshit and taken you back that day without question. I'm sorry I couldn't save you from all of this," I choke out.

I'm not expecting her hug, so it startles me when the tiny arm not in a sling circles my neck and hugs me tightly.

"Thank you for saving my life so I could meet my pack," she whispers.

I squeeze her very gently back. "We always take care of family, Blake."

CHAPTER 33

The two weeks following my failed auction are long and painful. Between endless interviews with the police and Designation Intelligence Agency and the meds I'm forced to take to keep the pain at bay, I'm snapping at everyone by the time we finally get back home to Lockwood.

"Come on, Angel," Rook says sweetly. "Take your last dose of pain meds for Daddy and I promise we'll go to Mama's and get you some delicious food."

Tempted with the promise of more of Mama Beaumont's home cooking, I grudgingly take the pills and let Hades swoop in to carry me next door. The next several hours are spent laughing and bonding with my new family and eating some... mostly delicious southern food. Let's just say collard greens are not my thing.

I'm sitting in the center of my pack wiping tears from my eyes as Beck and Gray act out scenes from the Pirates franchise. Currently, they're using couch cushions to enact the scene where Jack and Will use a small boat as their air pocket to travel underwater. I'm laughing so hard I can barely breathe.

There's a knock on the sliding glass door that interrupts our fun and from my semi-hidden perch behind my mountain of an Alpha, I see Victoria. Tensing, Rook turns his body so I'm completely hidden by his large frame as she comes in without waiting.

"Hey y'all," her voice is technically somber, but something about it rings insincere. "I just wanted to bring this by and tell you boys that I am *so sorry* for your loss."

The parents stay silent, watching my men giving each other confused looks before Kai clears his throat. "Umm… our loss?"

She looks equally confused now but slaps a sickly sweet smile on her pretty face, the momentary crack in her mask. "I mean, yeah. I've heard that the death of a bonded partner can be devastating. Since you just lost Blair, I just wanted to let y'all know I'm here if you ever need anything. A hot meal, a shoulder to cry on, some comfort." She shrugs a dainty shoulder. "I'm here to help. Especially after that nasty explosion."

Her voice is practically a purr as she moves closer, and Rook growls low in his throat.

"Hey Vicky?" Hades asks.

Turning a blinding smile on him, she lightly touches his shoulder. "Yes, Alpha?" I start to move when I hear that, but Rook holds me back, sending patience through the bond.

"How did you know Blake was missing?" D asks casually. "And about the explosion? Neither of those things were on the news, and our parents haven't told anyone. So, how'd you know?"

Her face flushes bright red, but she still manages to giggle coyly. "Oh, that. Well, I saw the whole almost kidnapping thing when y'all were in town a few weeks ago. Then I ran into this guy who told me he's her foster father and he needed to talk to her. He wanted to make sure y'all knew the kidnapping was a misunderstanding, so I told him how to find your cabin. I ended up giving him my number, and he called me maybe a week ago to let me know she died in an explosion and that all of you were hurt," she says lightly.

There's not a drop of sadness or remorse in her voice as she details her role in my capture. Her words are met with snarls around the room, and she jumps back, her tan face draining to a ghostly white. "What?" she squeaks out.

"You know damned well *what*, missy." Mama stands up with her hands on her hips. "I've heard your parents tell you time and time again not to give strangers personal information about yourself and others. And yet the second some man shows up pretending to know Blake, you not only give out the address to the boys' *hidden* cabin, but you also give him play-by-play information about my daughter?" she shouts.

Turning her back to Icky Vicky, she looks at Dads. "Call the Cromwells. It's time we settled this nonsense," she says, casting a caustic look at the awful Omega on the other side of the room.

Achilles turns to me with a smile. "Do you need anything, ma jolie fraise?"

I shake my head no, cheeks flushing at being called out. Leaning out from behind Rook just slightly, I send a snarky little wave in Victoria's direction. Maybe it makes me a bad person, but the way her jaw drops, and sheer terror takes over her features brings me a small amount of joy.

A deep, booming voice that sounds through the house interrupts her screech of outrage. *"VICTORIA MARJORY CROMWELL!"* the voice shouts. Three Alphas and an Omega barge into the living room, the man in front breathing heavily. The Omega crosses to my mother, giving her a hug and a light kiss on the cheek.

"Natalie, darling." Her voice is smooth like honey as she speaks, and though she looks like her daughter, her eyes are kind, and her demeanor is gentle. "I'm so sorry I haven't been by to congratulate you on finding your daughter. There's no excuse. I was just swamped at work. The hospital is short staffed again."

Turning my way, her pretty blue eyes light up as they land on me. "You must be Blake," she extends her hand my way, and I flinch, curling back into Kaspian's chest. I feel awful when her face falls, but knowing what her daughter did, I can't blindly trust her. Her eyes shine with understanding as she turns to Victoria, crossing her arms.

"What did you do to this poor girl, Vicky?" she hisses.

Large tears immediately fill her eyes. "N-nothing, mother," she stammers out.

A scoff comes from one of her fathers. "Really?" he snarls out. "Because it sounds like you nearly had a fellow Omega sold into a trafficking ring because you were jealous. We didn't raise a spoiled, vindictive brat, Victoria. I don't even have the words to express how disappointed we are in you."

Her other father steps up beside the first. "As of right now, you're cut off. You'll be given a job at the hospital or my firm, but we will no longer be paying for your apartment, car, or credit card bills. I think moving back home may be the best thing for you right now," he says gruffly.

Victoria throws an epic tantrum as her parents escort her out of the house, all four of them apologizing profusely for their daughter on the way out. The entire room is silent for several seconds before erupting in laughter. The guys still look really angry, but even they can't help chuckling at the outcome of the situation.

Mama rolls her eyes and comes over to hug me. "Well, now that that mess is over, what's next?" she asks happily.

Tossing her arms around both of us, Amy smiles mischievously. "Now… we plan a wedding!"

I wasn't ready for marriage in London, but after everything that's happened, I'm ready to feel as close as possible to my pack. Looking around, I see love shining in the eyes of every single person here, and my heart feels like it's going to burst.

For better or worse, I'm finally home.

Smiling at my pack, I don't take my eyes off of them as I respond to Amy. "Let's plan a wedding."

CHAPTER 34

HADES

Six months later

I feel like I'm going to throw up because of how hard my heart is beating in my chest. The feelings through our pack bond are a mix of nerves, excitement, and an overwhelming amount of joy as we wait for the ceremony to start.

The last six months since we got our Omega back have been blissfully uneventful. Blake's shoulder healed well after an infection put her back in the hospital for a few days, about a month after we got home.

The moms went crazy wedding planning and other than making decisions on colors, songs, and food, we didn't have to lift a finger. Blake went wedding dress shopping with all of the parents, since we weren't comfortable sending her out without a trained Alpha escort yet. To say that we've been protective would be a gross understatement.

"I don't think I've ever been this excited about something in my entire life," Achilles whispers from my left. I don't bother telling him I can feel it through our bond, but I do chuckle because he's practically vibrating with it.

Tossing my arm around his shoulder, I pull him in tight to my side and look around at the rest of our packmates. "I love y'all." I keep my voice low so our guests can't hear. "I know our pack wasn't super happy before, but thank you for never giving up on me. For never giving up on *Blake*. I can't imagine our life without her, and I'm so fucking ready for her to be our wife."

Kas sniffles dramatically. "Aww, D. We love you too, ya big softy." He's clearly trying to make a joke, but the tears lining his lashes make it clear he's feeling the emotions just as much as I am.

We all straighten up when "I Guess I'm In Love" by Clinton Kane starts playing softly across the yard. We decided to have a small backyard ceremony with only our closest family and Detective Benson.

Blake wanted to invite the Omega she met at the auction house, Cove, but she disappeared. We asked Blake's brothers to keep an eye on the situation for us and let us know if they find her.

We see Blake's dads, Ben and Bas, come out first. They walk a few steps forward before breaking off to join their sons on the other side of the aisle across from us. As they get into position, I turn back when I hear a whispered, "Oh my god."

And I lose all coherent thought.

Blake is *breathtaking* and so fucking sexy I'm struggling not to get an erection in front of our entire family.

Her dress is a bright white slinky material that clings to her small curves from her chest all the way to the floor. Her shoulders are completely bare. The dress is strapless save for the small straps draped over her upper arms that look more decorative than anything.

There are several intakes of breath from the men around

me, and the wave of lust coming through the bond nearly causes my knees to buckle. Taking a second to appreciate her beauty, I'm blown away, knowing I get to spend the rest of my life with this incredible woman.

Her bright red hair lays in soft waves down her back and pinned up on one side with Achilles' mom's hair clip. Blake cried when she gave it to her last week for her "something old". And she's not wearing much makeup at all, but her cheeks are *really* flushed.

Turning to glance at Rook, I see his nostrils flaring and his eyes get that feral glint that precedes a rut. Turning back to Blake, I inhale deeply, trying to figure out what the fuck is setting him off, and that's when I smell it.

Syrupy sweet strawberries, rich cake, and vanilla whipped cream swirl around us, and three low growls sound out behind me. Clearly, I'm the only one keeping their shit together at the moment. So, I rush down the aisle and scoop up my Omega, tossing her over my shoulder in what I quickly realize is a terrible move. She giggles and squirms on my shoulder.

I'm smacked in the face with a heavy dose of her scent as she moves, and all thoughts flee my head that aren't *mount, rut, breed.*

Achilles rushes forward, ushering the other three toward us and pushing us further down the aisle to the confused laughter and murmurs of our guests. "Sorry, y'all!" he yells. "We're gonna need to cut this shindig a little short on account of a very unexpected heat." His statement is met by hoots and hollers from every single person in the room, and several exaggerated gags from our siblings.

My sisters give us all thumbs ups, and I smirk back at them. "I could say I'm sorry… but I'm not. See y'all in two weeks!"

Achilles

Wranglinɢ four feral Alphas is kind of like trying to herd cats. Blake's pheromones are so strong we barely make it back to the house before D is gently stripping her out of her dress and carrying her up to the newly finished nest on the third floor. I stand still and watch them for a second, seeing a bright red handprint show up on her cute little ass after Rook smacks it.

We've all gotten pretty adventurous since we got her back six months ago. Blake said she realized life is too short not to try everything, and so we've been slowly working our way through all of our bucket lists. The only thing we've told her no to was skydiving. Rook threatened to take her over his knee if she argued about it and I'm not even going to lie seeing him go all "Daddy" on her is hot.

I run to the kitchen and grab a few last-minute things for my girl before sprinting up the stairs. Thankfully, I had the forethought to stock the little kitchenette just outside the nest with snacks and drinks for us. I knew Blake's first heat would likely be coming up soon, but the timing is pretty funny.

I'm so thankful we finished her nest in time for this. The thought of designing her nest really overwhelmed her when she'd never had one before, so we took over and designed it as a pack.

The room is large and circular, with a separate bathroom and kitchenette that are light and open to contrast the darkness of her nest. The floor is covered in the softest mattress we could find, with only small ledges around the outside of the room to hold drinks and snacks.

Everything on the floor from the mattress to the bedding is black, with silver accents interspersed throughout. The walls are a gradient, starting from a deep blue into a hazy purple in the center, back to the same deep blue from the bottom. We made the room to mimic the night sky, so there are stars on every wall, and along the back there are "constellations" that spell out the names of every member of our pack.

Stripping down outside the door, I walk in to our Omega frantically placing things around her nest. She's muttering to herself about how everything needs to be just right for her first heat. This goes on for several more minutes until she finally spins around and grins proudly at us, putting her hands on her hips and drawing my attention there.

My gaze lingers on her breasts for a minute before slowly moving down her incredible body, gasping when my eyes catch on her left hip. Rushing forward, I drop to my knees in front of her and trace the small lemon freshly inked into her skin. I look up at my perfect girl through glassy eyes, my heart racing, knowing she did this for *me*.

"Pretty Girl," I whisper reverently. "When did you get this?"

She smiles wide, a blush covering her pretty cheeks. She looks at the twins before locking her eyes on mine. "You remember a week ago when the twins and I had a date day and said we were going to check things off of our bucket list?" I nod. I had assumed it was sexual based on the looks the twins shot us when they got back.

Her smile gets even wider. "Well, this is what we did! I've been really sad that I couldn't have a bond mark from you, so instead we can have bond tattoos!"

My jaw is practically on the floor the more she talks and between the gesture and her scent, I can't hold back. I dive onto the mattress, pulling her down with me in a heap of giggles and smooth, hot skin.

Stroking her hair back from her face, I take her lips in a deep, possessive kiss. "I know you'll need a knot soon - I can feel the fever under your skin — but for now you're *mine*," I breathe out harshly against her lips.

She whines, grinding her slick core against my thigh. "I'm yours, Ace. Touch me, please."

Her scent has me hard as a rock and desperate to taste her again, so I grab her hips and pull her so she's hovering over my face as the guys surround us. Yanking her down, I dive in, licking and sucking her clit until she's drenching me in her sweet slick as Kas and Kai each take one of her nipples in their mouths.

"Ooooh god," she moans loudly.

Grinding herself even harder onto my face, I move so I can thrust my tongue into her tight hole. I get a potent hit of her incredible flavor straight from the source. My nose bumps her clit each time she moves her hips. Within seconds, she's crying out and coming all over my face as she grabs the twins' heads and holds them to her chest.

Breathing heavily, her eyes are glazed over as she beams and backs up so she can lean down to kiss me. My dick jumps, knowing she's tasting herself on my lips right now.

"You ready for more, ma jolie fraise?"

She nods and slides down my body. I jump when I feel a hand on my dick that's definitely *not* hers. Leaning to look around her, I see D guiding her back with one hand and holding me in place with the other. He winks at me, lining my shaft up with Blake's center before lowering her slowly onto me. Letting go of her, he straddles my legs so he can play with her tits while Rook pulls her in for a dirty kiss.

She tightens around me, and I let out a loud moan. "Fuck, Pretty Girl. I'm not gonna last if you keep doing that," I pant out. The little tease gives me a wicked smirk before lifting almost all the way off my cock and dropping back down as slowly as she can. "Fuuuuck, baby."

"That's it, Shortcake, ride your Beta. Show Lee who owns him," D whispers into her ear.

"Hell yes. Listen to your Alpha, Pretty Girl. I'm yours."

Kairo

BLAKE IS RIDING Achilles like she can't get enough and *holy fuck,* I never knew watching would be this hot.

I'm sitting back against the wall listening to her moan and I can't help but give a few hard tugs on my cock to get some relief. When Rook stops kissing her and steps back, he gestures to Kas and me; I hop up. Like hell am I gonna ignore an invitation like that, knowing how much our girl enjoys taking my twin and me at the same time.

The guys may think the only thing we checked off our lists last week was Blake's tattoo. But my sweet baby Switch also made all my fucking dreams come true when she asked to dominate me *and* Kas. Turns out my twin is as much of a kinky fucker as I am, because he loved it.

Holding out a hand to help him up, we walk over to stand on either side of our Omega. Wrapping my hand in her hair so it forms a ponytail, I yank her head back, so she's looking at me with blissed out gorgeous green eyes. "You ready to show the rest of your pack what you can do with two cocks, Sugar?" I growl against her lips.

She nods, her eyes lighting up until Kas kisses her and she shudders. "Oh god... yes, just like that!" she shouts, eyes closed, and mouth parted just enough so we can see her pink tongue.

I look down to see Lee circling her clit with his thumb and, based on the sweat beading on his forehead, I'd say he's close. Kas grips her jaw with his thumb and forefinger and pulls her mouth open, licking along her lips to wet them before he smirks at her and spits in her mouth. She goes off like a fucking bomb, coming all over Lee and taking him over the edge into his own orgasm while the rest of us watch on in awe.

As soon as he pulls out of her, she's presenting, her instincts riding her as hard as ours are riding us. "Please, I need a knot," she begs. "I'm so hot and it *aches*."

"Hush, Angel. You take care of your Alphas and I'll take care of you like I always do, okay? Hard and fast, Baby Doll. Brace yourself," Rook grinds out, his voice low and gravelly.

Stepping closer, I check in with her one more time before gripping my dick and bringing the head to her puffy pink lips. Opening her mouth wide, she flicks her tongue over it, licking up the precum beading on the tip before taking me to the knot in one go.

"Holy fuuuuck, Sugar. I will never get over how good you are at that," I say, a purr rattling in my chest as she works me over. Rook pounds into her from behind, unintentionally guiding her mouth onto my shaft with each thrust.

Her moans are vibrating my cock in the best way, and I know I'm only seconds away from coming, so I pull out of her mouth and turn her face to Kas.

"You are so fucking good at that, Blake, but I think Kas needs some attention now."

Kaspian

Smirking at me, my dirty little Princess doesn't hesitate to wrap her lips around my aching cock. She pulls a deep moan from my lips while Kai gets down on his knees and laps at her clit, making her cry out loudly. Watching her take my identical twin down her throat is like looking in a mirror and it turns me on so much I know I won't last long.

"That's it, Princess. You gonna let Daddy Rook fill your pretty pussy while I fill your pretty mouth?" I growl down at her. He's fucking her so hard now I hit the back of her throat each time he bottoms out and the second she swallows around the head of my cock, I'm a goner.

"Goddamnit, B. You're too fucking good at that. You ready to swallow, Princess?" She nods. "Good girl," I moan. "Fuck, yes!" I grip the back of her head and thrust into her throat two more times. Then I'm holding her head far enough back that she'll be able to taste my come on her tongue before she swallows.

The second I pull back, Rook snarls and yanks her up against his chest, rutting into her *hard* as she whimpers. Her moans bordering on sobs the longer she goes without a knot. Kai finally sits back on his heels and begins to stroke his cock, his eyes locked on Blake's bouncing tits. Rook's wild eyes shoot toward my brother briefly before he leans down and licks over his bond mark possessively.

Rook

"YOU'RE SO FUCKING SEXY, Angel. Look at what you do to your Alpha," I whisper in her ear. Gripping her chin, I turn her head so she's looking straight at Kai, who's stroking his cock faster now that her eyes are on him. "You want him to come all over your gorgeous tits, Baby Doll? Cover you in his scent better than any t-shirt ever could?"

"Yes," she sobs out. Clenching around me so hard I'm a little worried my knot won't slip past her entrance.

Locking eyes with Kai, I bark at him. "Kiss her, Kairo. Show her who she belongs to."

As soon as he kisses her, she relaxes. "That's it, such a good girl for your Alphas. You ready for my knot, Omega?" I growl into her ear.

My hand goes around her throat, squeezing tight, and when she nods, I thrust hard one final time, my knot locking into her as she comes with a choked scream. Kai grunts out his release, spraying ropes of come across her chest. A feral growl of satisfaction rumbling through his chest as he rubs his release into her skin.

Hades slides in front of our needy girl as soon as Kai moves to the side. He strokes his hand down her face and leans in to press his forehead to hers. "Last but not least, Shortcake. Can you handle one more?"

She nods, whimpering. "Please, Alpha."

He looks at me. "Lay her down on her side for me?" I do as he asks, bringing her down with me so she's facing Hades.

"Okay, Baby. How about you hold those pretty tits together for me and stick your tongue out?"

My jaw drops and he shoots me a wink as he lays down on his side and spreads Kai's come up the center of her chest before lining himself up and thrusting his cock through her gorgeous tits. "Oh holy fuck," he groans loudly. "That's even better than I imagined. Stick your tongue out just a little further, Blake. I'm close."

A few short minutes later he comes with a grunt before pulling our girl in for a filthy kiss.

Exhausted, we collapse onto the soft floor of the nest in a pile of sweaty limbs and satisfied sighs. Pulling Blake back into my chest, the position moves my knot inside her, forcing moans out of both of us as I shudder at the intense sensitivity.

Burying my nose in her messy hair, I breathe deeply. "We love you so much, Angel. Thank you for being ours," I whisper softly into her ear.

I see her cheeks bunch with a smile as D snuggles close in front of her with Lee close behind him and the twins by her feet. "I never thought my life would be safe or happy until the day I met you guys. I can't wait to spend the rest of our lives together just like this." She sighs contentedly, wiggling just the slightest bit against my chest.

Her scent has settled a bit now that we sated the first wave of her heat, but I know it will spike again soon.

I can't fucking wait.

"Angel?"

Rook's question startles me back to reality, and I spin around in my chair with a sheepish smile. Shortly after my first heat three years ago, I finally went to college with the support of my pack. I entered an accelerated program to get dual degrees in crisis management and adolescent psychology. I submitted my final paper half an hour ago and have been zoning out since, almost unable to process that I really did it. My smile widens as his eyes catch on the laptop screen, still frozen on the submission page.

"Baby Doll," he breathes out. "You finished?" I nod. His answering grin is *blinding*. "Y'all get in here!" he shouts before picking me up and squeezing me as tight as he possibly can, whispering how proud he is in my ear.

"What? What's wrong?" Hades' eyes are wide and wild as he skids into the room, nearly crashing into the desk as his socks slip on the dark wood floors.

Rook and I laugh, and when he sets me down, I hold out my arms for my insanely overprotective Alpha. Breathing out a huge sigh of relief, he picks me up and spins us until he can plop down in the chair I just vacated, setting me on his lap just as the others join us.

"We have a lot to celebrate today," Rook says. "Our girl is officially ready to come work with us at OHP!" The room erupts into cheers and laughter at that as all five of my guys shower me with kisses and praise.

"Wait…" I look at him, confused. "What else is there to celebrate?"

His breath hitches as he holds up his phone, eyes sparkling with unshed tears.

I gasp, tears flooding my own eyes. "No…" I whisper.

The guys' eyes volley between us, confusion evident on their faces for several seconds until Kai catches on. "Holy shit!" he yells, startling us all.

Kas looks annoyed now that he's not in the loop, so I grab his and Ace's hands, tugging them to me in an awkward hug.

"We got the call," I whisper to them.

They meet my statement with gasps as all eyes in the room turn to our lead Alpha.

Nodding, he rakes his hand through his hair, showcasing his nerves. "There's a ten-year-old little boy who was rescued from an auction house." He pauses at my sharp intake of breath, shooting a concerned glance my way before continuing.

"His story is a lot like yours, Angel, only his didn't have a happy beginning. He was born to drug addict parents who sold him at a year old and he's been bounced around the country ever since. He's tiny and scared and he's already showing signs of an Omega presentation. I think we need to make sure he has a safe place to land before he gets his happy ending."

Tears are running freely down my cheeks, and I see a similar level of emotion echoed around the room and through the bond. Sucking in a shaky breath, I wipe my cheeks and move to get off Hades' lap, only to be immediately pulled into Kas' arms.

"When can we see him?" I ask quietly.

"HE'S INCREDIBLY skittish around men right now," the social worker's voice is barely more than a whisper. "I think it's best if Mrs. Beaumont speaks to him alone first." Soft growls meet her statement, and she quickly works to reassure us. "He's not dangerous at all. He's just a scared kid who won't even tell us his name. And I think Blake will make him feel safe."

I nod, knowing she's right. "I'll be fine, guys. He needs somebody in his corner, and that somebody is going to be me." My voice is firm and steady as I look at my pack.

Ace is the first to nod, and Hades quickly follows, their bond ensuring they almost always vote the same way. D may be the most overprotective of any of them, but he has a soft spot for hurt kids, just like I do.

Turning to the most stubborn of the five men, I face down Rook and the twins. Kai is the first to concede, giving me a peck on the cheek before moving to stand behind me, pulling me into his arms for a brief hug. "It's so sexy when you stand up to us," he whispers before nipping my earlobe.

My face is flushed when I look up, but Kas and Rook have identical scowls on their faces. I roll my eyes at them, walking up and giving them each a peck on the lips.

"Trust me?" I whisper.

Their faces soften immediately and when they glance at each other, I feel in the bonds the second their minds change.

"Of course we do, Princess. Be careful," Kas whispers, gently kissing my cheek.

Rook pulls me into a deep hug. "You're going over my knee later for your defiance, Angel," he growls. I shudder before pulling out of his hold and turning back to the social worker and nodding. "I'm ready."

I don't feel anything but calm walking into the small room. I know in my gut this is exactly where I need to be. A shuffling sound pulls my attention to the corner where a tiny boy is curled up in a ball underneath a table.

"Hello," my voice is as soft as possible when I speak. "My name is Blake." I drop quietly to my knees and shuffle over slowly, encouraged when he doesn't move away. Stopping maybe a foot from where he's lying, I mirror his position. "What's your name?"

His eyes are wide and terrified, his nostrils flaring as he takes me in. His body visibly relaxes when he catches my scent, and he scoots the smallest bit closer.

"My name is Oliver," he whispers. He's dirty and has cuts and bruises all over his body, but he has the most brilliant blue eyes and shaggy, dark hair. "Do I have to go back there?"

My eyes water as my heart breaks for this precious boy. "Oh honey, no. Absolutely not. You will *never* have to go back to a place like that again," I say gently. "Can I hold your hand, Oliver?"

He thinks about it for a few minutes before silently reaching his tiny hand out and gripping mine tightly.

"Do you know how I got this scar?" I ask, moving my neckline to show him my shoulder. He shakes his head, tracing a finger over it lightly and shuddering before tracing a scar of his own on his arm. "I was like you." His eyes dart up to meet mine and I smile softly. "When I was your age, somebody took me and locked me up in a cage for a really long time. And I didn't get out until my pack saved me a few years ago."

"Did they hurt you?" he asks quietly.

Nodding, I tell him a bit about the things I went through, and by the end, we're both crying.

"But you're okay now?"

I smile and squeeze his hand gently, feeling the cuts on his palm. "I am now," I say. "Because of my pack."

He nods like he expected that answer. "They hurt me too," he whispers. "And I want to be okay."

"Oliver? Would you like to meet my pack?" He looks terrified, so I keep talking in the same quiet tone. "They look a little scary at first, but I promise you, Oliver. They're the good guys." Nodding slowly, I catch the smallest glimmer of hope in his eyes. "If you meet them and like them, would you like to come live with us?"

His eyes go wide as saucers, and he launches himself at me, wrapping his arms around my neck and squeezing as tight as he possibly can. I hug him back, noting how skinny he truly is. This boy and I are one and the same and I know without a doubt he's meant for us.

ACKNOWLEDGMENTS

This book wouldn't have been possible without so many people, but most importantly Sarah, for keeping me sane and talking me through this wild process of self-publishing and introducing me to some amazing people along the way.

My family and my in-laws, for not balking when I said I was going to write a romance book, and being my personal cheerleaders. Please never speak to me about what you just read.

My PS family, for being endlessly supportive in person and on social media.

My incredible team of Alpha and Beta readers, Kayla, Ashley, Abigail, and Amber.

And finally, you. Thank you for taking a chance on a new author and sharing my love for spicy books and *literal* Alpha males.

ABOUT THE AUTHOR

Hallie Grace writes sweet why-choose romances with a kick and lives in small-town Washington with her toddler and dog. When Hallie's not writing, she works for a romance book merch company and reads way too much.

Her favorite things are a toss up between apple flavored/scented anything, her perfume collection, and music.

instagram.com/authorhalliegrace
facebook.com/halliegracereadergroup
tiktok.com/authorhalliegrace

ALSO BY HALLIE GRACE

<u>The Lost Series</u>

Forget Me Knot

<u>Packed Up at Harbor U</u>

An Omega's Guide to Falling in Love

An Alpha's Guide to Finding the One (Summer 2026)

Book 3 (TBA)